THE COURTSHIP
CALCULATION
LAWS OF ATTRACTION
BOOK I

LAURA TRENTHAM

Damien Northcutt is a gambler, a rake, a bastard, and... bored. Madeline Barnes is a botanist, a lady, an innocent, and... curious.

When Damien accidentally plays knight-errant and rescues Madeline from the clutches of her scheming relatives, he discovers she might be the key to getting what he's always wanted—revenge.

Even though Damien has warned her repeatedly he is no gentleman, Madeline is sure deep down underneath his rakish demeanor he is a hero. Why else would he secret her out of a ball to safety?

Damien's plan includes seduction but not marriage. What he doesn't expect is being seduced himself by Madeline's smiles and laughter and passion. But she is meant for Damien's half brother, and enacting his revenge means ruining the match... and breaking her heart.

ALSO BY LAURA TRENTHAM

Historical Romance
Spies and Lovers
An Indecent Invitation, Book 1
A Brazen Bargain, Book 2
A Reckless Redemption, Book 3
A Sinful Surrender, Book 4
A Wicked Wedding, Book 5
A Daring Deception, Book 6
A Scandalous Secret, Book 7
Spies and Lovers Boxset

LAWS OF ATTRACTION
The Courtship Calculation, Book 1
The Marriage Experiment, Book 2
The Passion Project, Book 3

FIELDSTONES ADVENTURE NOVELLAS BY LEAH TRENT
An Impetuous Interlude, Fieldstones Adventure Book 1
A Naughty Notion, Fieldstones Adventure Book 2

A Mysterious Masquerade, Fieldstones Adventure Book 3
A Dangerous Desire, Fieldstones Adventure Book 4
The Fieldstones Adventures Boxset

CONTEMPORARY ROMANCE
Sweet Home Alabama Novels
Slow and Steady Rush, Book 1
Caught Up in the Touch, Book 2
Melting Into You, Book 3
The Sweet Home Alabama Collection

COTTONBLOOM NOVELS
Kiss Me That Way, Book 1
Then He Kissed Me, Book 2
Till I Kissed You, Book 3

CHRISTMAS IN THE COP CAR, BOOK 4
Light Up the Night, Book 5
Nobody's Hero, Book 6

LEAVE THE NIGHT ON, BOOK 7
When the Stars Come Out, Book 8
Set the Night on Fire, Book 9

HIGHLAND, GEORGIA NOVELS
A Highlander Walks Into a Bar, Book 1
A Highlander in a Pickup, Book 2
A Highlander is Coming to Town, Book 3

. . .

HEART OF A HERO NOVELS
The Military Wife
An Everyday Hero

I love to hear from readers! Come find me:
Laura@LauraTrentham.com
www.LauraTrentham.com
Sign up for Laura's Newsletter
Join Laura's Facebook Squad

Are you interested in receiving a FREE book?!
Join my newsletter! There will be links in your Welcome Email for TWO free books!

Sign up for Laura's Newsletter

⚜ I ⚜

Damien Northcutt leaned into the shadows of a column on the garden balustrade and took a deep breath of the late-spring air, nursing his ennui and a cheroot. The fire crept up the leaf wrapping as if it were his soul being consumed by the ton. He took a long draw and blew the smoke out in rings, caught between disgust and amusement at his overly melodramatic thoughts.

After all, the ton wasn't evil, merely shallow and tedious. It had also provided him with a very comfortable living. He could afford a town house within walking distance of Hyde Park, a carriage and fine horseflesh, and a wardrobe crafted by the finest tailors in London. He had risen so far above the privations of his childhood to be the stuff of dreams.

Or nightmares.

He had chosen to sell his soul but only now wondered if it had been worth it. Would he have been happier as a tradesman with a bosomy wife to welcome him home each evening? Or as a barrister or accountant or banker? Maybe. Probably. A life that had once seemed boring and unsatisfying was an unattainable fantasy.

Another season was upon him, and while he couldn't

complain about the crop of reckless bucks fresh from school with more money than sense, he no longer felt a thrill when he revealed a winning hand. Fleecing them to support himself and his endeavors was necessary but had grown tiresome and, frankly, depressing.

Establishing himself on the fringes of polite society as a high-flying gambler had been a way to make coin, yes, but also to thumb his nose at his father. The early days had been heady. His charm, connections, and the accident of his birth had garnered him invitations to exclusive events.

Once upon a time, it had been uniquely satisfying to meet his father's gaze across an expanse of Italian marble, knowing there was nothing the man could do to rid himself of Damien. If his father had given Damien the cut direct, he was as good as admitting the rumors of Damien's parentage were true. Although no one spoke of their kinship in polite conversation, it was as obvious as the nose on Damien's face. Quite literally. Not to mention his black hair, stubborn chin, and dark, devilish eyes.

As the years passed, however, Damien's presence no longer seemed to needle his father, and his gambling didn't offer even a hint of revenge, only dread at quite possibly ruining the prospects of a young man who might mature into someone honorable and worth knowing. After all, several of Damien's classmates from Eton had transformed from idiotic skirt chasers into sober pillars of society.

One only had to look at his friend Simon, the Duke of Bellingham, for proof. He had been an absolute bounder until the influence of Lord Drummond came to bear upon him. Now his friend spent inordinate amounts of time at home, probably in bed with his new bride instead of at his club or in gaming hells. It was unfathomable.

Could Damien possibly be... developing a conscience? He shuddered to think of acquiring the condition so late in life. It might prove a mortal disease. Although, at thirty-one, the stone around his heart was already tomb-like. The maudlin thought made him roll his eyes at himself for a second time.

Anyway, he couldn't afford to develop anything as inconvenient as a conscience in case an opportunity to bring dishonor to his father came calling. He must be ready to heed the knock.

His cheroot burned close to his fingers. The smell incited vague memories of falling asleep wrapped in the scent of his uncle's pipe in the days after his rescue from the slums of London. Nostalgic memories were rare and lovely, which meant he hoarded the few he possessed.

More pertinent to his current situation, smoking had offered an excuse to beat an exit after his most recent win to cut off the pleas of the vanquished. He stubbed out his cheroot on the stone pillar and mentally prepared himself to return to the gaming table, hating himself just a bit. Voices turned his attention outward. A garish pink feather bobbed over a lady's coiffure. The Duchess of Ralston. Damien had noted her attendance earlier while he had skirted the edge of the dance floor.

A man in a peacock-blue velvet frock coat spoke in low, urgent tones with the duchess. It was her son, Damien's half brother, the Marquess of Thornbury. Unfortunately, he took after his mother and not the duke. The sloping, narrow shoulders that looked elegant on the duchess only emphasized Thornbury's long neck and weak chin. With the feather from the duchess's headdress bobbing over his shoulder, Thornbury took on the mien of a crane.

Damien slipped closer to eavesdrop. It wasn't gentlemanly, but then again, he had never claimed the title. He was more likely to be called a scoundrel or a scamp in tones either disparaging or affectionate depending on who was speaking.

"She disappeared after the waltz but did not retreat to the ladies' retiring room. I would not be surprised if she snuck into the gardens to pursue her interests." The disapproval in the duchess's voice sparked Damien's curiosity.

Only one activity took place in darkened gardens at a ball, and it was not for the innocent.

The duchess gave her son a shove in the arm. "Go find her. We can't have her caught by a fortune hunter. Already there are whispers."

What sort and why hadn't he heard them? His curiosity was piqued even as frustration rose. He had become lax in reaching out to his informants and lost his edge.

"But Mother dearest—"

Thornbury's wheedling tone was cut off by an icy expletive from the duchess that raised Damien's eyebrows higher. "You of all people should understand how important this is. She is too rich to be wandering the gardens at a ball alone. It could spell disaster."

Grim satisfaction flooded Damien. While he had not caught the whispers of a possible match between Thornbury and the unknown heiress, rumors of the dukedom's financial difficulties had sifted to him like an ephemeral fog. Until this moment, he hadn't known if they were true or merely a product of jealousy or malice.

Damien's only regret was that the family's current difficulties were not due to him, although not for lack of trying. He had never been able to tempt Thornbury into a game. Gambling was not his vice. Actresses were, but even if Thornbury's current mistress had expectations, she alone could not bring about the downfall of one of the oldest duchies in England.

"But, Mother, she is so odd. I would rather not marry her."

"What you want does not matter. If this is about Mrs. Fields, then understand I can end things between you like—" Her snap fell as heavy as a hammer. "You can fuck your little actress privately, but you will no longer flaunt your relationship. Is that clear?"

"Yes, Mother," Thornbury said between clenched teeth. He might be unhappy with the edict, but he wasn't man enough to refuse his mother's wishes.

She pointed into the darkness of the garden. "Your charm does not seem to be making an impression on the chit so far. If you cannot woo her, then you must ruin her."

"You don't mean... You can't mean... *Tonight?*" Disbelief sailed Thornbury's voice high.

"It appears as if the opportunity has presented itself through her recklessness, but we must ensure there is a witness to force her hand. I will bring one of the other dowagers out for air. Be ready." A winter's breeze in spring cooled her tone. "This is for her own good. She doesn't understand how society works and has proven to be surprisingly intractable on the subject of marriage."

Thornbury trotted down the steps, hesitating at the edge of the gardens to glance over his shoulder. The duchess made a shooing motion as one might to a stray hound. Thornbury set off with a hesitant, mincing walk. The duchess watched him disappear before whirling around to reenter the ballroom.

Thornbury would inherit a dukedom. He was young and eligible and prized by the debutantes and their mamas. A marriage to him would be considered a triumph. It sounded like the *intractable chit* in question did not long to be a duchess. Damien was intrigued.

While he was certainly no knight to rush to a lady's rescue, neither could he allow Thornbury to acquire what he needed—a wealthy wife. The current situation trumped his plans to fleece yet another young dandy. Even though Damien and Thornbury grew up in different worlds, Damien had a very childlike desire to steal his half brother's toys away.

Plunging into the garden after Thornbury, Damien veered onto a narrower path under a bower of yellow flowers on his left. As he entered the heart of the garden, he slowed, stepping lightly and listening.

Footsteps clomped and Damien ducked into the shadows between two sculpted evergreens. Scowling, Thornbury stalked by, sans lady. He made enough noise to send a pair of roosting birds out of their nest. Damien's start rustled the fronds. Thornbury halted and peered toward Damien's hiding place.

With a stealth he'd learned escaping titled bullies at Eton, Damien melted farther into the shelter of the evergreens until he was on the other side of the makeshift wall, crouching slightly. Thornbury moved down the path and out of sight.

"Is Thornbury attempting to woo you too?" Warm breath tickled his ear.

Damien couldn't quite stifle an unmanly yelp. An ungloved, feminine hand slapped over his mouth. The fresh tang of greenery was on her fingers. It was pleasant compared to the overly perfumed ladies in the ballroom, yet her touch was shocking in its intimacy.

He rose to his full height, pulled her hand away by her wrist, and turned. The lady before him—and based on the exquisite cut of her frock and the baubles glittering at her throat and ears, she was most certainly a lady—was a pretty, doe-eyed innocent.

An innocent who had experienced something terrible. Her golden hair, which had once been arranged in artful curls, now hung askew with twigs taking the place of pins. A loamy streak of dirt marred the light pink fabric of her bodice, and a piece of lace had come unstitched at the edge of one cap sleeve.

He had not been quick enough to save her. The story of his life. The failure cracked into the stone around his heart.

Yet Thornbury had a decidedly thwarted air about him. Another gentleman—the word made his lip curl—must have accosted her just as the duchess had feared. While he was not above using the power of seduction to acquire his goals, he would never take advantage of any woman by virtue of his superior strength.

"Are you injured, my lady? Is there some way I may assist you?" His voice was rough with a variety of emotions. Anger at himself. Fury at whoever had hurt her. Despair at the world in which he was forced to operate. Perhaps there were honorable men steps away in the ballroom, but the evidence was rather thin on the ground.

The woman pressed her hands together and held them to her chin, gazing up at him as if he were her savior. "I would be most grateful for your assistance, my lord."

He made a habit of preying upon the foolish and naive at the gaming tables, yet he detested seeing the truly vulnerable, those without a choice in their future, used and discarded like refuse. It reminded him painfully of his mother. He might be a bastard, but he still had the fortune of being born a man, which afforded him infinitely more opportunities and freedoms than the woman before him no matter her station.

He laid a hand over his heart. "Anything within my power."

She pointed into the branches of the tree offering them shelter. His gaze instead fell to a scratch along the pale skin of her wrist and extending up her forearm. Taking her by the elbow, he twisted her arm toward the moonlight. "You're injured."

"Oh dear. I was in a bit of a rush to hide, you understand. I spotted Thornbury heading in my direction. It was a near thing. Of course, if I were wearing my tramping clothes, this would never have happened." She let out a put-upon sigh. "But who would have guessed I would have come across exactly what I was looking for at a ball?"

Questions crowded his mind, adding to his confusion. He looked her over once more from head to toe, his gaze finally meeting hers.

He had been grossly mistaken.

This was no doe-eyed innocent. Her lips curved into a half smile that could only be described as mischievous. With her blond hair, snub nose, and petite frame, she might very well have stepped out of Queen Mab's court to torment him. He had thought he was playing Ivanhoe, but had he instead stepped into *Twelfth Night*?

"Are you implying you were in a tree?" He attempted to make logical sense of her admission, glancing up into the leaves. The bottom branches would be difficult for her to reach, much less climb.

"I wasn't implying it."

"I didn't think so."

"No, I was most definitely in the tree." She shrugged. "I have no wish to encounter my cousin in a dark garden."

"Cousin. Thornbury is your relation?" The twists and turns of the evening would strain even Shakespeare's credulity. "My condolences."

"A cousin removed several branches down my family tree. My father and the duchess are related. Unfortunately, one can't choose their lineage. A pine cone will never yield a chestnut tree." She made a chuffing sound of amusement. "However, I do appreciate a good pruning."

"How exactly is your father related to the duchess?"

"I suppose they, too, are cousins of a sort. My father is a third son of a poor offshoot of the family. He emigrated to America, married my mother, and made a fortune." Her accent landed somewhere between a genteel English rose and a hardy American oak.

"You are being sponsored by the Duchess of Ralston then?"

She gave him a distracted nod and hum, still examining the boughs of the tree.

"When did you arrive in England?" How had Damien not heard of the household addition? He would need to recultivate his sources among the duke's staff immediately.

"A fortnight ago. According to the duchess, I arrived without a suitable wardrobe. Or manners. I had to wait for my new dresses before being presented. This is my first ball. I was specifically told not to get into any trouble, and now look what's happened." She shook out her skirts, and leaf litter drifted to the ground. Her expression turned speculative. "Since I've made a hash of this evening, perhaps the duchess will give up and leave me to my own devices."

"That's a bet I wouldn't take. The duchess is aiming for a

match between you and Thornbury." A warning crept into his tone.

"Indeed." Her brows drew together, and the lightness he'd sensed in her vanished. "My parents are encouraging the match as well."

"And what of you?"

"What of me?" She appeared taken aback.

"Do you wish to wed Thornbury?"

Her eyes widened. "No one has asked me what I want."

"I'm asking now."

"I'm not sure it matters."

"Of course it matters."

The pause she took was long and thoughtful, her head tilting slightly as she stared at him. He wasn't sure if she was considering his question or him. Finally she shrugged, the torn lace at her sleeve fluttering. "Thornbury isn't an ogre. He has all his teeth and most of his hair. He's polite. I could do worse."

"That's not an answer."

"No, I suppose it's not." She dropped her gaze, and he missed the forthrightness of it. "Considering I risked a broken neck to avoid the man, you can safely assume I'm not keen on marrying Thornbury. Or any man for that matter."

"You mean having one's teeth isn't enough to ensure a blissful union of souls?"

He was rewarded when she raised her face and shot him a smile. It knocked him back a step. The women he pursued were jaded and cynical, their smiles cool and calculating. He understood them because he was just as cynical and calculating. This woman smiled with the openness and warmth of the noonday sun against a blue sky, and he wanted to bask.

"In my two and twenty years, I've seen little evidence any marriage is blissful." Her smile twisted, and he was relieved. Derision he was intimately familiar with.

"Shockingly, I know of one or two happy unions." Damien

thought of Simon, Lord Drummond, and Sir Gray Masterson and their love matches. "But it is rare."

"I don't wish to marry, but if I must, I'd rather it not be to a pompous ass."

Damien barked a laugh. A *laugh*. Only when the sound registered did he realize how deeply his lingering moroseness had festered. "Thornbury is indeed a pompous ass."

"You are well acquainted with him then?"

"Somewhat." Damien didn't believe in luck, which meant their paths crossing must be fate at work. How should he play the hand that had been dealt? He wasn't sure yet, but he would keep his cards close.

She sighed heavily, set her hands on her hips, and stared upward once more.

"Have you misplaced something in the tree? Your gloves perhaps?" While Damien made it a habit to avoid gloves as a signal to any debutante who got it into her head to pursue him he was an unsuitable partner in every way, a lady wasn't seen without a pair at such events as a ball.

"Entirely impossible to climb a tree in satin gloves. Nearly impossible to do it in a dress." She brushed at the streak of dirt on her bodice. "No, I need to retrieve the berries from that clump of green in the vee of the branch. I almost had them when Thornbury made an appearance. I got flustered and slipped."

Damien peered into the branches. Although the moon was full and high, the shadows were deep under the protection of the leaves. "Is that mistletoe?"

The lady clapped her hands together. "Oh, well done, my lord. Indeed it is."

He couldn't stem a shot of schoolboy-like satisfaction puffing out his chest.

"I need as many berries as you can gather," she said.

His gaze fell to hers. "You want me to haul myself into the tree for mistletoe berries?"

"You did offer to help me in any way that was in your power."

Her gaze took him in from head to toe much the way he had sized her up earlier, inciting an odd tingling in his nerves. Not arousal exactly, but awareness. Her gaze returned to his, and her lashes quickened into a cajoling flutter. Her voice, however, held a tease that fired his blood. "And my request seems to be quite within your power, my lord."

The result was another spontaneous smile from him. Schooling his features into a semblance of his usual sardonic glower, he said, "I am not a lord."

"Even better. I must say after being forced to dance with several peers this evening, I have come away unimpressed with the feudal institution." Her expression turned serious once more. "If you have a fear of heights or other impairments, you could merely give me a leg up. Without an overly amorous gentleman to distract me, I'm sure I can accomplish the task forthwith."

"How do you know I'm not an overly amorous gentleman bent on seduction?"

"Most rakes don't engage in conversation before pressing their suit."

"And how do you know that?"

"I am quite well read," she said with a misplaced authority on the behavior of men that affirmed her basic innocence.

"I didn't realize a how-to guide existed for rakes," he said dryly.

"Along with all the novels I have read, I also have three brothers. They provided enough examples." Her indulgent smile took any sting from the insult.

"You find rakes charming?"

"My brothers certainly are. They are great fun too. Or at least they used to be when I was young." Her expression darkened.

"What happened?"

"The older I grew, the more protective they became. It was all well and good for them to carouse and have fun, but I wasn't even to be left alone with a man. In their estimation, as my bosom grew bigger, my brain shrank in equal measure." She gestured to her torso, and he couldn't help but glance down.

While the cut of her gown was modest as befitting a young lady entering the marriage mart, the pale curves on display were lush and tempting. He'd never heard a lady talk with such freedom unless they were in the bedroom. He should be shocked. Instead, he was fascinated. And a tiny bit aroused.

He had a sudden image of stripping away the pink gown to study the way her flesh filled his hands and to map the contours with his tongue and mouth.

He had to steer them back into safer waters or his pledge to not seduce her—this evening at least—would not last the hour. "I have no impairments to prevent me from retrieving the berries. May I ask why you want them? Are they considered a delicacy in America?"

Her laugh was unexpectedly throaty and sensuous. It was a laugh that wasn't measured or suppressed to fit into the narrow expectations of ladies of her station. And no matter her lack of gloves and title, she was a lady.

"I do not recommend eating them. They are, in fact, quite poisonous."

"Would you recommend using them in order to rid myself of enemies?" He raised a brow.

In a manner devoid of any amusement, she shook her head sharply. "They would only make a man miserable. No, if you want to rid yourself of an enemy, I would recommend angel's trumpet. It offers a relatively painless death. If you prefer your enemy to suffer, then use ground castor beans."

He swallowed. "How do you know that?"

"I'm a botanist. My specialty is medicinal and poisonous plants, which are often one and the same. Although I enjoy a field of blooming wildflowers as much as the next botanist." Everything about her seemed to tense, and he realized she waited for his judgment.

He could imagine she faced scorn on a regular basis with such a pronouncement, but he only felt admiration. Botany must be the unladylike interest the duchess had referred to. If she married Thornbury, or any other gentleman of the ton for that matter, her scholarly pursuits would be limited to giving the gardeners their orders.

"I was rubbish with the natural sciences at school," he said.

Her shoulders retreated to a more relaxed stance. "What were your talents?"

"Getting into scrapes." It wasn't a lie. But he'd also been a gifted mathematician, which he put to good use at the gaming table. Most men didn't understand winning or losing had nothing to do with luck and everything to do with probabilities.

Damien reached for the lowest limb and pulled himself up until he could swing a leg over and shimmy toward the mistletoe nestled in the vee at the trunk. His valet was going to ring a peel over his head at the state of his trousers and coat when he got home. After gathering a palmful of berries, he hopped to the ground.

"This is most appreciated. I will call on my friend tomorrow and help her cultivate them."

"Does your friend want the plant in order to lure gentlemen in for a kiss at Yuletide?" He dropped the berries into the reticule she held open for him, spying her wadded-up satin gloves inside.

"No, nothing of the sort. She has a special gentleman she hopes to marry." She drew her reticule closed and tilted her head slightly. "Perhaps you know her? Miss Adriana Coffey?"

"I haven't had the pleasure." He didn't add that if she was a young eligible miss, he had gone out of his way to not make her acquaintance.

"She and I have conversed through letters for the past three years. Coming to London and finally meeting her has been worth all the trouble with Thornbury."

It wasn't often anything left him nonplussed, but the interaction he was engaged in was beyond the pale. He was enjoying every second of it.

"Is she a botanist as well?"

"No, she is a lepidopterist specializing in moths, and there is a particular species that overwinters in mistletoe. In an attempt to attract it, she needs to cultivate mistletoe in her garden. I believe her true gift lies in her artistry at capturing the beauty of the natural world. If you saw one of her drawings, you would swear the moth was ready to take flight."

"How fascinating." And it was.

She smoothed her dress and smiled up at him. "You have been a great help, Mister...?"

"Northcutt."

"Mr. Northcutt, I must repair my appearance and slip back into the ballroom before I'm missed. Thank you for all your help. I hope to see you again."

She turned to duck between the evergreens. He grabbed her hand and tugged her back toward him. "Will you grant me your name?"

Although her smile had turned quizzical, she did not look scared or alarmed in the least. "Madeline Barnes."

"Miss Barnes, I'm afraid I can't allow you to return."

2

Maddie's heart picked up speed, and heat flushed her body. She was unable to quantify her physical reaction to the man before her. In the countless novels she'd read, the heroines perpetually seemed inflicted with weak knees and trembles when confronted by an attractive man. The descriptions had made her roll her eyes even as she continued to devour the stories.

She should have paid more attention to the particulars. Her knees were undeniably wobbly, and while she might not be trembling, gooseflesh ran up her arm from his touch. His hand was large and his grip warm and firm. Although gloves were de rigueur for young ladies at balls, Maddie found them uncomfortable—her hands ended up a damp mess—and dangerous. A lemonade glass had gone sliding through her satin-covered fingers to stain the hem of a lady's gown earlier. The glare she'd received from the lady had left her feeling singed.

She forced herself to focus on Mr. Northcutt. The moment had turned precarious. Something about him niggled at her memories. He was vaguely familiar, and yet she was sure she had never seen him before. He was too handsome to forget.

"You must allow me to return, sir." Her tone was more

breathless than she would have liked. How many dances had she missed? Although who would notice except the duchess? Few even knew her name.

"Must I?" His lips quirked.

The first word that came to mind was *scoundrel*. *Charming* was a close second. With all their talk of rakes, she was certain he wasn't one. He could have taken advantage of her a dozen ways yet hadn't touched her inappropriately. His bare hand on hers notwithstanding. Nor had he attempted to call for a witness to their solitude in order to force her hand. It was difficult to remember her dowry made her a target of more than just Thornbury.

"Yes?" She cleared her throat to stamp out the lilting uncertainty. "Of course you must. What else would you do with me?"

His eyes flared and danced with amusement. The shadows suited his dark good looks. His face was one of classic handsomeness with chiseled features under wavy black hair a bit too long for current fashion. What would his hair feel like under her fingers? She slapped her overactive curiosity down. It seemed to rear its head at the most inappropriate times.

"There are many things I can imagine doing with you, Miss Barnes."

Oh dear, the heat in her cheeks had turned from a cozy warmth into an inferno. Hopefully the night threw her into a similar relief of grays and he wouldn't notice her banter was born of bravado.

Although she wasn't a green girl straight from the schoolroom, New York society wasn't as polished or formal as London's famed ton. Even so, she knew how to drink tea properly—even though she preferred coffee—was an enthusiastic dancer, could bang out a passable tune on the pianoforte, and was a decent artist. What she was not was an accomplished flirt.

Lectures about the vagaries and untrustworthiness of men, especially English gentleman, had been a staple of Maddie's life.

Pointing out that her mother had married one herself had resulted in stony-faced silence.

Perhaps she should have taken the lectures to heart, because in one evening, her mother's fears had come to fruition. Her cousin, Thornbury, had set his sights on winning her hand through whatever means necessary, and she was in a dark garden with a man who flirted like a rake. Her gaze fell to their still-joined hands. The natural ease between them was as equally disconcerting.

Pulling free, she crossed her arms and said briskly, "Don't be ridiculous, Mr. Northcutt. Speak plainly of your intentions. Are you planning to ravish me?"

He blinked and looked taken aback. It was not the first time she'd seen such an expression on a man's face. Usually it was unintentional on her part, but sometimes she enjoyed setting a man back on his heels. It was always telling how the man reacted. Most could not keep their hackles from rising.

"Not at the moment, but you cannot possibly return to the ballroom looking as you do without stirring talk." His voice bordered on bland, but underneath was a surprising rumble of amusement.

She stole a glance at her gown. He might have a point. "I can repair myself in the retiring room."

"How will you navigate to the ladies' retiring room with no one seeing you? And how will you avoid questions once there? It's doubtful you will be allowed privacy."

She touched the streak of dirt across the front of her dress. It could be sponged clean, and the lace along her sleeve could be stitched by the attending maid. Patting her hair, she smothered a curse her eldest brother used on a regular basis that had no place at a London ball.

Her hair was a problem she couldn't solve on her own. The English lady's maid the duchess provided had spent over an hour with heating tongs and pins to tame her mass of unruly waves into sleek sausage curls and a gravity-defying swirling mass at her crown.

She huffed, tilted her head, and looked speculatively at Mr. Northcutt. "I don't suppose you possess any skill with women's hair?"

He coughed into his fist, but his lips were curled upward. "Ah, no. However, I am rather talented at making escapes."

Yes, she could imagine him pitching himself out of women's bedroom windows to avoid outraged husbands on a regular basis. "What are you suggesting?"

"I am suggesting you allow me to whisk you away."

Now she was the one nonplussed. "I'm not... You shouldn't..."

He held up his hands. "I promise you my intentions aren't nefarious. I will return you to Thorn House none the worse for wear."

Her mind zipped around possibilities. New York society had already spit her out for being... *unsuitable* was a nice way of putting it. Eccentric, scandalous, and dangerous were other labels bandied about.

In a mere fortnight in London, she was already on the edge of being beyond the pale for entirely different reasons. This was supposed to be her fresh start, and she was mucking it up already.

In her mother's lengthy list of causes of a lady's ruin, running off with a man at a ball had been near the top. "I'll be ruined, won't I?"

"Only if we're caught." His sleek eyebrows rose fractionally as he cast her a look from under his lashes that could only be termed reckless. "I can assure you that you will be ruined if you return to the party in such a state. The duchess will have you married to Thornbury by morning to quell the talk."

Maddie tapped her lips, casting about for another option. One that didn't carry with it the risk of ruination or debauchery or, even worse, marriage. "How can I possibly trust you, Mr. Northcutt?"

Instead of the glib answer she expected, his face took on a serious cast. "You can't, nor should you. I'm ruthless and have no qualms about fleecing a man at the gaming tables. Lucky for you, there is no love lost between me and the Ralston family. Helping you escape will thwart the duchess's plans for you and Thornbury. That is reason enough for me to help extricate you."

She was not privy to ton gossip or the details of the history between Mr. Northcutt and her English relatives. If she pressed him, she guessed he would merely evade answering directly, but she could discover the source of hostility through simple gossip on the morrow. *If* she made it through the night with her person and reputation unscathed.

Keeping her voice light, she said, "In short, you are not a knight riding to my rescue but a villain seeking revenge."

"We are all the heroes of our own stories, Miss Barnes." His insouciant shrug almost masked his raging antipathy. *Almost.* "But you are correct. No lady should mistake me for a knight-errant."

She narrowed her eyes and studied him. He truly believed what he said was true, yet he was wrong. A villain would leave her to face the wrath of society. Her humiliation would bring even greater censure to the Ralston name. No, his heart might be tarnished, but it was made of sturdy stuff and merely needed a bit of polishing.

"I will accept your help, sir. How do you propose we escape without being seen?"

"Over the garden wall and into the mews." At her frown, one corner of his mouth tipped up. "You've proved adept at climbing trees. Surely you can handle a stone wall?"

She couldn't argue his logic and didn't want to when his hand encased hers once more, warm and slightly rough. The sensation drove all rational thought from her head. The next time she picked up a novel, she would be much more sympathetic to the plight of the ninny-headed, overly swoony heroines.

They crept along, winding their way through arbors and

around shrubbery to avoid others seeking the darkness for their own reasons. She tucked the information away for further study.

Just as she was beginning to think she would escape with her reputation intact, female giggles from only a few feet away froze them both.

"Stop it, Frederick. You are a bounder." Her tone was full of tease.

"You wound me, my love." The man's voice was moving closer. "You must know I only have eyes for you."

At the sound of their voices, Maddie and Mr. Northcutt paused next to a stone bench tucked into an arbor. It was private and romantic and perfectly situated for a liaison, which made it the most likely destination of Frederick and his lady love.

She tugged on Mr. Northcutt's sleeve and pointed to the bench. He grimaced but hesitated. The rustle of leaves sprang Maddie into action. She let go of his hand, grabbed the lapels of his jacket, and swung him in front of her.

His height blocked her from sight, but the last thing either of them needed was to engage in conversation with the amorous pair. Therefore, their mouths needed to be otherwise occupied. Her solution was common sense and had nothing to do with her raging curiosity.

She slipped a hand around Mr. Northcutt's nape, beneath his stock and collar, and tugged his mouth to hers. Their lips collided with no finesse. His were warm and firm and slightly parted as if he had been ready to give voice to an objection. The press of their mouths was pleasant enough but not something to inspire centuries of poetry. A smidgeon of disappointment rose.

The man, Frederick, guffawed a not-so-subtle laugh. "I say, isn't that Northcutt? Who has he lured to debauchery?"

Mr. Northcutt tensed for a blink. She knew because her eyes were still open, staring blurrily at his face. He wrapped his arms around her and curled his body around hers as if protecting her from an attack. He shuffled her backward into the deeper shadows until the leaves of the bushes brushed her shoulders.

The woman giggled, but it sounded farther off now. Was that because the couple had moved away, or had Maddie's pounding heart muffled the sound?

Something extraordinary was occurring. His mouth was no longer still on hers. The friction incited shivers all over her scalp as if her very hair was standing on end. His lips caressed hers as if prodding her for a response. The act felt like an extension of their verbal banter. She parted her lips and answered him as best she could considering this was her first kiss.

Her inexperience lay at her brothers' feet. Not that she had expected them to instruct her. Heavens, they might be American, but they weren't savages. No, her brothers were bruisers, every one, and the few young men who had ventured to court her had been scared off within a visit or two.

According to her brothers, no one was good enough for her. She'd attempted to convince them she wasn't interested in marrying any of the men; she merely wanted to broaden her experience. It had been the wrong argument to make.

While her current situation might be less than ideal, the surroundings exceeded all expectations. The arbor filtered the moonlight around them. The sharp scent of the evergreens with overtones of spring flowers tickled her heightened senses.

She tightened her grip on his nape and raised on tiptoe to meet his lips more firmly. If this was her opportunity, she refused to let it pass without taking full advantage. His lips softened under hers, and he cupped her cheek. He tasted of smoke and whiskey and experience. Did the tang of the lemonade she'd drunk in the crush of the ball reach his tongue?

His body was composed of intriguing angles and ridges. He was muscular yet lean in the way of a big cat on the hunt. He lifted both her hands to wind around his neck and pulled her tight against him. Her breasts mashed against his chest in a way that made them ache.

Slanting his mouth over hers, he touched her lips with his tongue. Her eyes popped open at the sensation, but his remained closed. She processed the new information. Kissing was more complex and interesting than she had imagined. It was a dance, and besides concocting a new medicine from her plants, there was little Maddie enjoyed more than an energetic twirl around the room.

Reclosing her eyes, she let her body meld against his and darted the tip of her tongue against his lower lip. Her touch acted as an invitation, and his tongue made a bold foray into her mouth. He held her more firmly when she might have jerked away in surprise.

The invasion was unbearably intimate. She squirmed, not sure if she wanted closer or to pull away even as her tongue twined with his. His chesty growl sent a shiver up her spine. The sound was altogether foreign and animalistic. It was a warning. Before she could do the wise thing and heed it, power surged through her. This sophisticated, urbane, experienced man was on the edge of his control.

Because of her.

His hand shifted from her waist to her bottom, cupping and squeezing. A pulse between her legs made her wonder if her heart had relocated. Somehow he fit their bodies even closer together, his leg notching between hers, frustratingly hampered by her skirts. A hard ridge pressed along her hipbone. She was hot and uncomfortable in the confinement of her clothes and wanted to rip them off. Surely he felt the same.

She slid a hand beneath his frock coat to clutch at the muscle of his shoulder. The fine lawn of his shirt was the only thing separating her from his bare skin. He tore his mouth away.

"What's wrong?" she whispered as out of breath as if she'd run up a dozen flights of stairs.

"Nothing." He swallowed hard. "Everything. This was..."

"Invigorating?"

"Madness," he said at the same time.

"Oh." She considered his assessment. "It was reckless and

perhaps unwise, but I don't believe either of us are ready for Bedlam, Mr. Northcutt."

He stared at her blank-faced before letting out a sighing laugh and touching his forehead to hers. "You are in shock, no doubt. I promised not to ravish you, and yet I came damnably close. Come and let us make good our escape before we are caught."

Did a kiss amount to a ravishing? She had been the one who smashed their lips together, so did that make her the ravisher or the ravishee? Granted, she wouldn't have known what to do next, but she had been willing. More than willing, she was enthusiastic to remedy her lack of experience.

"I assumed fewer clothes would be involved in a ravishment," she said thoughtfully as he tugged her alongside him.

He stopped next to the garden wall and looked down on her. "You are the most unusual lady I have ever encountered."

She wasn't sure if he intended the statement to be an insult or a compliment, but it was her nature to be optimistic. Smiling, she murmured, "Thank you. That is a kind thing to say."

He looked bemused. "You're welcome."

She faced the wall and set her hands on her hips. It was six feet high and pocked with cracks and divots. If it weren't for her dratted skirts, she could be up and over in seconds. She gestured him closer with a hand while she gathered her skirts higher in the other, raising them almost to her knees.

"Do you suppose you can actually climb the wall?" He looked at her and then the top of the wall.

"I don't suppose it, I know it. With a bit of help anyway. Come on and give me a leg up." When his only answer was a smile that was both infuriating and charming, she narrowed her eyes. "Is this where you leave me to face my ruin?"

"Miss Barnes, you wound me. I am not without honor even if it might be a bit tattered." He gestured toward a sickly rosebush in the corner hiding an old-fashioned wooden door. "As lovely as

I find your limbs, I believe we can keep your feet planted firmly on the ground."

His gaze lingered on her exposed ankles. She let go of her skirts with a swish of the delicate layered fabrics. "A gentleman wouldn't look."

"We've established the fact I'm not a gentleman." His expression could only be classified as wicked, yet something bitter projected from the tightness around his eyes and the firm set of his jaw.

He turned to the weathered wood of the door. It took the application of his shoulder to heave the little used door open with a screech of hinges. With a sympathetic glance to the browning rosebush, she followed him. "The gardeners couldn't have picked a worse location for a rosebush. It will never thrive in the damp shadows, poor thing."

"When did you become interested in botany?" Mr. Northcutt asked in a low voice as they exited in the middle of a dark alley running between the town houses and leading to the mews. It smelled not unpleasantly like a barn.

"I find plants to be less judgmental than people." The truth was more complicated, of course. When his eyebrows lifted to frame the questions she could see plainly on his face, she looked away. "What happens now? Do we scamper through the alleys and over the rooftops?"

He pulled out a fine silver pocket watch and tilted it toward the meager light before snapping it shut. "I planned my escape earlier in the evening, although I expected to leave from the front door. My carriage should be waiting. Let me signal my man, and I'll have him pull up as close as possible to the curb."

She remained in the shadows at the mouth of the alleyway while he disappeared to fetch his carriage. Out of the scope of his magnetism, her wits made a grudging reappearance. Was she actually going to climb into a stranger's carriage? What if the entire evening had been orchestrated in order to lure her into a forced elopement? A hefty dowry was her father's way of ridding himself of a liability.

For the first time since leaving home, she missed her over-protective brothers. They had no respect for titles and would lay out any man who tried to hurt her. Maddie had little experience or respect for titles either, but unlike them, she did not have the freedom naturally bestowed on them because of their sex. They were able to pursue their dreams without asking anyone for permission.

It was not so easy for a woman. The British Isles were rife with medicinal plants she wanted to collect and study. Once she married, she would be hampered by the strictures of society to bear children and play hostess. Her dreams felt so out of reach to be laughable.

She would have settled for a string of afternoons exploring the Chelsea Physic Garden. It was full of plants specifically culti-vated for the healing arts, her particular interest. Unfortunately, she discovered the Physic Garden did not allow women. She'd been too flabbergasted to argue with the attendant, not that it would have done any good. He obviously believed her brain too tiny to comprehend the reasons behind the rules.

The rattle of wheels focused her whirling thoughts. A shiny black carriage without a crest or any other adornment pulled by a pair of matching black horses rolled to a stop at the entrance of the alley. The door opened, and Mr. Northcutt looked up and down the pavement before gesturing her toward him. He made the perfect picture of a villain luring her to her ruination.

While their kiss might not qualify as madness, leaving the ball unchaperoned in the company of a not-gentleman edged alarmingly close. The coachman might as well drop her at the nearest asylum.

With a glance over her shoulder, she considered a retreat, but there would be no safety at the ball. She darted to the carriage, taking the hand he offered. Before she could do more than gasp, he had hauled her inside and onto the backward-facing squab. They set off with a jerk that jostled her forward.

Her hand landed on his knee. Even once her balance was restored, she didn't immediately straighten. She glanced up at him through her lashes. Although small oil lamps were mounted, they were not lit. The only light sifted in through the windows. The moon was high and full and for once not concealed by clouds. Tension rose like floodwaters ready to drown her.

A shallow breath restored her sense of emotional equilibrium, and she removed her hand. Pressing back against the plush cushion, she linked her hands in her lap. "I'm sorry, I shouldn't have—"

"No, it's I who owe you an apology." The regret in his voice was heavy in the darkness.

Fear swamped her. Had she made a dire error in judgment after all?

3

Damien's tongue stumbled to a halt. Had he ever apologized to a woman before? Women usually thanked him for seducing them before he was tempted to offer a mea culpa. He swallowed hard and studied the woman sitting across from him, swathed in shadow and swaying with the motion of the carriage.

Miss Barnes wasn't the kind of woman to turn heads on her entrance to a ballroom, but she was lovely in the wholesome, healthy way of a country milkmaid. If Thornbury didn't manage to snare her, she might even garner an offer from a second or third son, especially if she possessed an ample dowry.

Yet, she was wholly arresting to him in a way he couldn't quantify. It had nothing to do with her dowry or her connection to Ralston.

Was it the sparkle in her eyes when she had looked up at him in the garden? Perhaps her brash bravado when faced with the unexpected? Or was it the open, mischievous smile she had tossed him like it had cost nothing but felt priceless?

Ladies greeted him with a variety of smiles. Fake ones dripping with disdain were expected among the matrons. Fear-tinged smiles with a spark of interest were frequently bestowed by the eligible young misses trolling the ballrooms for a suitably bred mate. And then there were the smiles that were invitations from the experienced ladies of the ton. He had accepted more than his share of such come-hither smiles.

Miss Barnes's smile was a different species altogether. Was the thrill zipping through him like lightning what an explorer felt discovering a new land?

At the moment, however, her mouth was tight with disapproval and her eyes wary. "An apology for what you have done or what you plan to do?"

Her blunt question held an accusation that set off an instinct to squirm. His stillness was forced and tense. The answer to her question was both.

The Duke of Ralston had destroyed Damien's mother. If it was the last thing he did, Damien would return the favor. Miss Barnes might not be the queen to put the duke in check, but she might be a valuable pawn Damien could use to wound his father before the man could sacrifice her to Thornbury for his own gain. It was a start.

With his mind refocused on revenge and not how soft and pliable and welcoming she had felt in his arms, he forced a smooth charm into his voice when inside his emotions were jagged. "I apologize for our indiscretion in the garden. I must have been overcome with moonlight and madness."

Miss Barnes braced her palms on the edge of the squab and leaned forward. Her gaze scoured his face. It was an uncomfortable feeling, but if he looked away, she would never trust him, and for his still-burgeoning plan to work, he needed her trust.

After a long moment, she relaxed into the velvet cushion to look out the window. Shadows flashed over her face. The street wasn't empty, but it wasn't as busy as it would be as the evening's festivities ended.

"There is no need to apologize for what happened in the garden. After all, I am the one who kissed you." A discordant note in her voice made him wonder at her emotions. Was she disappointed or hurt or angry?

He opened his mouth and then closed it, not sure how to respond. For a man who prided himself on his ability to read women, he felt unusually ignorant. "Any number of gentlemen would be more than happy to debauch you in the gardens. Including the heir to a dukedom this very evening."

"While you are very sweet, I am well aware Thornbury does not want me; he wants my dowry. There is no need to soothe my ego. I am not fragile." The look she sent him made him wonder where his brains had scuttled off to. Why was he attempting to convince a well-born innocent of her ability to lure gentlemen into indiscretions?

Sweet? Had he ever been called sweet? Not that he could remember. He should feel insulted. Instead, a gooey, warm feeling made him wonder about his health.

Miss Barnes was wrong, of course. Damien wasn't sweet. He was ruthless and heartless and too many lesses than he could list. What he wasn't was a liar. He never offered false flattery or promises he never planned to keep. Believing such flattery and promises had proved his mother's doom.

"You may have instigated our kiss, but I thoroughly enjoyed it. If you couldn't tell." He paused to gauge her understanding of his meaning, but her face gave nothing away. "Not only are you lovely, but you are something even rarer."

"What's that?" The lilt in her question gave him satisfaction. He'd done well to turn the conversation.

"You are interesting."

Her dry laugh was full of irony. "Yes, that I have heard before."

How often had the term been applied by well-meaning or maybe not so well-meaning people? She didn't realize how high a compliment it was in his estimation. "There are worse things to be than interesting."

"Like what?"

"Boring. Simpering. Dull. Stupid."

"You have aptly described a majority of the ton." The corners of her mouth quirked. "Present company excluded, of course. I find you interesting as well."

He leaned forward as if he were filings to her strangely magnetic pull. "However misplaced, I am honored at your good opinion."

Her harrumph did a poor job covering her amusement. "My good opinion counts for little."

He glanced to the window to check the carriage's progress but also to break eye contact. His cheeks grew warm and tight. It was only then that he realized he was smiling, wide and true.

He schooled his features into bland banality, yet was unable to do the same with his curiosity. "Why are you here?"

Her arched brows lifted. "I was under the assumption I'm here for a ride back to Thorn House in Grosvenor Square. Have you decided to abscond with me instead?"

"If you suspect such a nefarious plot, shouldn't you be more frightened?" Actually, why wasn't she more afraid of him? His reputation might not be black, but it was definitely gray. He couldn't afford to live as black-and-white a life as his friend Simon, the Duke of Bellingham. Although even that fine upstanding gentleman had traipsed along the edge of morality's cliff to win his lady love.

"I have three brothers," she said simply.

"Are you implying they would sail the ocean to avenge you?"

"Well, yes, that too, I suppose, but my eldest brother also taught me how to handle myself in such situations as a possible abduction."

He was wrong. She wasn't interesting; she was fascinating. "And what would you do to escape my clutches?"

"If I told you, then I would lose the element of surprise, which was lesson number one." She narrowed her eyes at him, the picture of seriousness.

Was she bluffing? Maybe. Probably. But he had a feeling she

was often underestimated. Thornbury and the duchess had certainly fallen into that trap. Miss Barnes wasn't a woman who would be easily manipulated.

She leaned over to glance out the window. "Unless I am mistaken, we aren't on the north road headed to Scotland but almost to Grosvenor Square."

There were more dire possibilities than a trip to Gretna Green for a vulnerable woman. His mother's fate had taught him that much. "I promised to return you home safe and sound."

"I knew you would keep your promise." Her satisfied smile made his internal organs career into one another in a most disconcerting way.

"Do not mistake me for a gentleman. I have not earned the title through birth or deeds." It was the second warning he'd issued. He had done his due diligence.

"Like any good scientist, I can only draw conclusions based on my observations, and if it walks like a duck and quacks like a duck, then..." She shrugged.

Was she likening him to a *duck*? No, he was a predator. A panther or wolf at the very least. Before he could argue his point, the carriage turned onto the wide lane leading to Thorn House.

She brushed at her filthy dress. "Oh bother. The duchess will have my head if I've ruined another frock."

Another frock? How many had she ruined and through what circumstances? Another smile threatened, but he quashed it. Along with the curiosity about her frocks and her brothers and her life. She would be a pawn and nothing more.

"What will your maid say?" Gossip could spread from house to house through the servants with the speed of a fire.

"Probably something like 'You didn't climb another tree, did you?' while shaking her head and giving me the evil eye."

"The duchess will have questions."

"Yes, she will."

"You don't sound concerned."

"She's not my mother." Defiance clipped her words.

"No. She's someone infinitely more powerful and influential." While Ralston could be ruthless, if the whispers could be believed, his duchess was diabolical.

"I can manage the duchess."

Damien kept his doubts to himself. "What of Thornbury?"

"Thornbury is attached to his mama by apron strings. I'm not afraid of him."

Damien shook his head. He couldn't allow Miss Barnes to be maneuvered into a marriage with Thornbury before Damien could enact his as-yet-unformed plan. That was the only reason worry squeezed his chest. After all, he was a self-serving scoundrel.

The carriage rolled to a stop at the grand entrance to Thorn House, Ralston's London home. The house was large and stood proudly on the corner. It was grand, austere, cold and, while handsome, inspired a great amount of antipathy in Damien. Much like its owner.

"Since you have no fear, do you plan to march to the front and ring for the butler to let you in?" If that was her plan, he wouldn't allow it.

"Of course not. I am in possession of my wits, thank you very much." The disgruntled look she sent him was only slightly reassuring. "If you'll have your driver pull around, I will make my way through the gardens and into the house by the stillroom. From there I should be able to take the servant's stairs directly to my room."

It made sense Miss Barnes would be familiar with the room used to dry herbs and make medicines from the garden's plants. At this point, there was little Damien could do to protect her. She must navigate the web the duchess weaved and try her best not to get stuck in a marriage to Thornbury.

Had the duke instigated the machinations to secure Miss Barnes's dowry? It was up to Damien to discover just how desperate the duke was and thwart him.

Damien gave instructions to his driver. She was silent as the carriage pulled around. A crinkle between her eyes made him wonder if she were more uneasy than she allowed him to see. "Thank you for your assistance this evening, sir. I don't want to imagine what would have happened without it."

"My pleasure, Miss Barnes. I would offer to escort you, but I fear that would do more harm."

She gave him a nod and opened the carriage door, glancing up and down the pavement before turning back to him. "When will I see you again?"

The question startled him. "The season is young. I have no doubt our paths will cross once more." He would make sure of it.

"You could call on me one afternoon." Her head tilted as she studied him.

"I am not what you believe me to be, Miss Barnes."

"Or perhaps you're not what *you* believe you to be, Mr. Northcutt." With that, she hopped to the ground, shut the door, and scampered out of sight behind the garden door.

He was still mulling her words as the carriage pulled to deposit him at the steps to his town house.

"What in the devil are you playing at, sir?" The question came from Damien's driver. The "sir" tacked on the end lacked the proper respect usually afforded a master.

"This is no game, as well you know, Alcott."

"Does she know that?" He thumbed over his shoulder in the general direction of Grosvenor Square.

"She doesn't want to wed Thornbury."

"I doubt she wants to be ruined by you either."

"I don't pay you for your opinion."

"No, I offer it for free." Alcott spit a stream of tobacco from his perch on the carriage. He adjusted his cap and cocked his head. "You going to sack me for it?"

Alcott knew Damien would do no such thing. "Put the carriage away."

Alcott harrumphed and slapped the reins. The horses stepped forward as if knowing oats and a rubdown awaited.

Alcott had been with Damien since the beginning. He was an ugly cuss—pockmarked with a squashed nose and beady eyes—but he was trustworthy and brave and a good man despite his checkered past.

The door of the town house opened as he crested the steps, but it wasn't his butler waiting to greet him.

Damien ruffled the already messy hair of the young boy in a nightshirt grinning up at him. A gap where his two front teeth were missing gave him an impish air.

"Shouldn't you be in bed? Where is Costa?" Damien threw the locks on the door. Young Timothy was too short to reach the uppermost one.

"Sick, sir."

His butler had a weakness for blue ruin that had cost him his previous employment without a reference. Damien tolerated the occasional bout of drunkenness because Costa could coax gossip from the most uptight servants in the ton. His ebony skin, ready smile, and lilting West Indies accent made him a favorite among the female servants, and his ability to tell a bawdy joke ingratiated him to his male counterparts. His service was priceless.

Timothy yawned with the enthusiasm of a tiger.

"Let's get you back to bed, young man. Hop on." Damien squatted.

Timothy giggled and threw his arms around Damien's neck. The boy would soon be too big for piggyback rides. He would become a man and learn hard truths of the world. But tonight was not that night. Tonight he was an eight-year-old boy who smelled of lavender soap and milk and rested his head on Damien's shoulder with the trust of the innocent.

Mrs. Henshaw popped her head out of the butler's room as Damien and Timothy made their way down the narrow servant's hall. Her eyes grew large seeing her son on Damien's back like a wild monkey.

"I'm terribly sorry, sir. He's *supposed* to be in bed." Her voice veered from apologetic to admonishing as her narrowed gaze settled on her son.

Timothy's response was another huge yawn, his breath warm and moist in Damien's ear.

"He's no trouble. In fact, he greeted me at the door. I think he might be after Costa's position. How is your patient?"

Mrs. Henshaw adjusted her mobcap and shook her head. "As usual after one of his bouts. The poor man has spent the evening fighting his demons, but he's beginning to settle."

If past incidents were any predictor, Costa would be contrite and tender his resignation by early afternoon. Damien would rip it up and insist he remain in his post. Costa would get teary-eyed and look like he might hug Damien, and then their lives would resume uninterrupted for weeks, sometimes months before the pattern repeated itself.

"You tend to Costa. I'll tuck young Timothy back in bed."

Mrs. Henshaw looked as if she might argue, but Damien merely reached out, patted her arm, and walked on to the end of the corridor to the housekeeper's quarters. Two single beds were set on opposite sides of the room. One bed was neatly made, and the other was a mass of rumpled sheets, a dented pillow, and a stuffed dog made from calico fabric.

Damien sat on the edge of the bed. Timothy flopped backward and burrowed under the covers, his eyes already closed. Damien picked up the dog and smoothed a finger over one of its threadbare ears. It was ragged and well loved. He had never had the comfort of a stuffed toy. Even as grief pinched his heart, he smoothed a hand over Timothy's hair, grateful this boy wouldn't face a grim future.

Damien slipped out and met Mrs. Henshaw coming out of Costa's room. "He's asleep," she whispered.

"So is Timothy." Damien inclined his head with a smile, scooting around her to retreat to his study for a glass of spirits.

"Sir, I don't know how to thank you. I'm sure Costa would say the same."

Damien stopped and turned halfway around to favor Mrs. Henshaw with a glance from the corner of his eyes. It was obvious she was referring to more than putting Timothy to bed, but Damien didn't want to discuss the reasons behind who he hired. Like he told Miss Barnes, he wasn't a gentleman. He wasn't even a particularly good man. He hadn't broken all of God's commandments, but he'd shattered a fair number.

"Good night, Mrs. Henshaw." Damien left without a second glance.

He settled into his study with a glass of brandy. He had warned Miss Barnes repeatedly about his true nature, yet she seemed unwilling to see him as he was—a profligate gambler and unrepentant rake with an unhealthy obsession with revenge.

He quaffed the brandy and let the alcohol dull any guilt he felt over using the lovely, vivacious Miss Barnes in his dastardly plans. He had begun to despair he would ever attain his goal of destroying his father, but if Ralston was indeed short of coin, then Miss Barnes might prove to be more than a pawn. She might be the key to everything.

4

Maddie had slipped into her room without being seen, but it had been a close thing. Footfalls had caused her to freeze for what felt like forever in the hallway, exposed for anyone to catch, dirty and disheveled and alone. Her bravado in Mr. Northcutt's carriage seemed foolish now that she was confronted with a dark house and the possibility of being dragged in front of the duke or, even worse, the duchess.

It was just that Mr. Northcutt made her feel... She searched through a laundry list of words. Bold. Funny. Smart. Yes, all those were true, but even more, he made her feel balanced. She hadn't felt that way since her world had gone topsy-turvy in America. The more adamant he was about not being a gentleman only hardened her good opinion of him.

The door to her room creaked open, and Maddie whirled around. Was it Thornbury? The duchess? Why hadn't she locked it? Sally, the maid, entered, holding a candle in one hand and with a white bundle of cloth draped over the other. She let out a little scream when the circle of candlelight touched Maddie. "Miss! What are you doing home? Has the family returned?"

"They will arrive shortly." Maddie's heart was pounding like a blacksmith's hammer.

"Why did you not send for me?" Shock and fear, the same emotions afflicting Maddie, were uppermost in Sally's voice.

Her brain worked to formulate an excuse. It would be good practice for later when the duchess came asking questions.

"I was feeling unwell and retreated to the garden for some air. I'm afraid I've dirtied my frock." She presented her back to Sally. "I hope you'll be able to clean and mend it?"

The candlelight wavered closer. Sally placed the brass holder on a nearby table and fingered the torn lace at one shoulder. "What on earth did you get up to, miss?"

"A tree, actually."

Sally deftly stripped the dress off Maddie, and her brow crunched when she studied the bodice, whistling softly. "I'll try my best to repair the dress. I might need to ask Mrs. Galloway to help me."

"No!" Maddie cleared her throat. Mrs. Galloway was the duchess's lady's maid and the eyes and ears of the household. "Do your best, would you, Sally? I would rather the duchess not hear of how badly I treated the dress."

"I understand." A coolness edged Sally's answer. Would the young maid scurry straight to Mrs. Galloway or even the duchess herself and tattle on Maddie? "The water in the ewer is fresh but cold. Would you like me to heat you some more?"

"No, thank you. I'm exhausted as you must be. I can ready myself for bed."

With the dress draped over her arm, Sally hesitated in the doorway. "Miss?"

Maddie wanted nothing more than to be alone, but she forced a smile. "Yes, Sally?"

"Hockney wanted me to pass along his thanks for the salve and medicine. It has worked wonders for his cough."

"I'm glad. Happy to help if I can." Once she was alone, Maddie let her smile fall and locked the door.

She'd made it over the first hurdle. Hopefully the dress could be laundered, repaired, and slipped back into the wardrobe with none the wiser. If not, she would offer it to Sally to sell at the secondhand shops. Between the extra coin and the help Maddie was providing for the servants, she could surely earn Sally's loyalty.

Maddie had not fibbed. She *was* exhausted. With a headache blooming at her temples, she lay stiff as a board under the covers, attuned to any noise. Footsteps and the murmur of voices sounded on the main stairs. The voices stopped outside her door. Even though she was expecting it, the decisive knock made her heart accelerate at an alarming rate. What if she buried her head under the covers? Would they leave her alone?

The handle turned and the door rattled. "Madeline. Open the door."

The duchess had not made a request. Maddie's boasting about being able to manage the situation seemed naive now that she was faced with the prospect. Nevertheless, it would do no good to hide. It would only make her appear as if she had something to hide. Maddie slipped on her dressing gown, cinched it tightly, and unlocked the door.

The duchess pushed inside her room before Maddie could react, making her stumble backward. "Where did you go? How did you get home? Did anyone see you?"

The duchess held a candle toward Maddie's face. With narrowed eyes, the duchess studied her. Maddie didn't shy away from the older woman's gaze. The soft light was kind to the duchess, muting the wrinkles beginning to fan around her eyes and mouth. It was easy to picture the younger version of her capturing Ralston's attention so many years ago.

Another lesson learned from her brothers was to veer as close to the truth as possible when explaining any misdeed. "It was quite hot, and several dances on my card were unclaimed. I escaped to see the gardens I'd heard so much about. You know how much I love flora."

The candle flame wavered with a long sigh from the duchess.

Maddie had learned the sigh signaled frustration and anger when she'd run to catch a loose dog in Hyde Park her first week in London. Her actions were deemed unladylike even though the dowager Viscountess Linley had been most appreciative to have her furry companion returned unharmed.

"You wandered into a garden at a ball. Alone. Do you have any idea what could have happened to you?" The duchess didn't blink at the irony of her words, considering Thornbury had been hunting Maddie. It was this very fact that made Maddie think the duchess wouldn't interrogate her too closely.

"Nothing untoward happened." Maddie barely resisted the urge to look at her feet to escape the duchess's sharp gaze. "I ruined my hair trying to reach a pretty patch of violets and deemed it wise to return home instead of rejoining you in the ballroom. I trusted you to make the proper excuses."

The duchess harrumphed, which was better than another excruciatingly long sigh. "Who escorted you home?"

The truth would never do. Yet Maddie did not possess a close circle of acquaintances in London. There was only one possibility. "Miss Adriana Coffey and her family kindly escorted me."

The duchess's head tilted. "I do not recall seeing them at the ball."

Because they hadn't been in attendance. Adriana's father had recently inherited a barony—which, according to Maddie's peerage lessons, was a lesser title and beneath the duchess's notice. It seemed silly that an accident of birth determined where one landed on the hierarchy of invitations issued. The only thing that spoke louder was money. Although even money was ranked by how old or new it was and if it was inherited or made through trade.

"I'm sure you merely overlooked them." Wandering eyes were a dead giveaway of a lie, so she kept hers focused on the duchess.

"Perhaps." The duchess did not sound convinced. "Baron Coffey and his family aren't bad ton, but I would encourage you to form attachments to young ladies who might further your connections. Miss Coffey is... odd."

Was she odd? Maddie thought she was intelligent and interesting, which she supposed only bolstered the duchess's assessment. Maddie's introduction to Adriana had been fortuitous.

A pamphlet on native English plants had made its way to the circulating library. It hadn't been a gardening manual. It had been scientific and detailed and, even more shockingly, written by a lady. The moment had changed the trajectory of Maddie's world. Possibilities she had never considered littered her imagination.

She had sent a letter straightaway to the author, a Mrs. Vivian Walsh, who had since passed on. Mrs. Walsh had sent a warm reply, and it wasn't long before she had sent on the addresses of other ladies with like-minded interests. Maddie had been desperate to correspond with anyone who understood her passions. Some had replied, some had not. Only two, Adriana and Lady Geneva Dorn, had been equally as lonely and longing for friendship as Maddie. It seemed easier to share hardships through words on a page. Almost like a confession. It was a shame an interest in something other than marriage made one a pariah of society.

Maddie knew better than to put voice to such principles at the moment and pasted on what she hoped was a vacuous smile. "Yes, Your Grace. I will attempt to cultivate more fruitful connections."

"With my guidance, you are sure to be a success in spite of your"—the duchess glanced down to Maddie's toes and back up —"lack of polish. You are two and twenty, nearly on the shelf. It is past time for you to marry and have children."

Maddie's smile faltered. "I would rather not do either. There are things I still wish to see and do."

"Women don't get to do as they wish; they do what is

expected of them." The hint of bitterness in the duchess's voice took Maddie aback.

Had the duchess always been this fierce and cold, or had a choice been snatched away and turned her into the woman before her? Maddie wanted to ask but knew the duchess would never confide her secrets.

"You cannot travel unchaperoned if you remain unmarried. Marriage doesn't have to be a cage," the duchess said.

Was that true? Why then did Maddie feel a noose tightening around her neck at the increasing pressure to marry? "I plan to eventually return to America."

Even as she said it, she heard the uncertainty in her voice. What did she have to return to? A blackened reputation and parents who had washed their hands of her. This was her final chance to toe the line and become respectable. Her brothers loved her but would be of no help. They were all off forging their own paths. How she envied them. Who is to say what fate awaited her in America? It might be even worse than what she faced in England.

One of the duchess's brows arched higher. Maddie had tried to perfect the same supercilious gesture, but she had burst into laughter at her reflection. Maddie had looked silly, and now, faced with the duchess's pitying disdain, she felt silly.

"Your family expects you to make a worthy match while in London. An unmarried daughter is a burden." The duchess lightly touched the hair at Maddie's temple. It was all she could do not to jerk away as if the duchess were a walking poison garden. "My dear girl, you must allow me to guide you with my experience."

Would her parents approve of Thornbury as a potential husband? Would his title and connections override any objection Maddie could muster? Of course they would approve. They would celebrate. The match would be beyond what they could have imagined after the ignominy of her departure.

"Of course, Your Grace. I will rely on your wisdom to guide

me." The lie landed like a feather on Maddie's conscience. Her well-being wasn't a priority for the duchess; her dowry was.

"Call me Aunt Elizabeth. I insist." It was not the first time she'd insisted. At Maddie's nod, she continued, "Tomorrow after luncheon we will visit the modiste for the final fitting of the blue gown, and we will attend Lady Haversham's ball in the evening. I'll ensure your dance card is full, so there will be no need to retreat to the gardens. Justin will be your first partner and also take the dinner dance. His attentions will raise your stock in the eyes of the ton."

It would also signify his pursuit of her, possibly driving away any other suitors. Maddie murmured an agreement even as her heart organized a coup.

"We will not have a repeat of this evening. No gardens. Is that understood?" A hard edge entered the duchess's voice, and at the extended silence, Maddie realized the duchess required her acquiescence.

"I will not enter the gardens," Maddie vowed. Although faced with the wolfish challenge in Mr. Northcutt's dark eyes, she would probably follow him like a sacrificial lamb to be devoured. What would that experience be like? Her mind drifted to the possibilities.

The duchess took Maddie's chin in a firm hold, snapping her attention back. "Rest now. Tomorrow will be busy and the evening long."

"Yes, Your Grace."

"Aunt Elizabeth," the duchess said.

"Yes, Aunt Elizabeth." Maddie corrected herself, but the familiarity made her feel more uncomfortable, not less.

Once the duchess had departed, Maddie crawled under the covers, her head spinning with the revelations of the evening and her complicated path forward. She slept fitfully and woke earlier than she planned considering the long day and evening ahead. Lying in bed would only lead to more fretting, so she splashed cold water over her gritty eyes and rang for Sally to ready her for the day.

The peacock-blue morning gown was embroidered with multicolored flowers along the high color, cuffs, and hem. It was one of her favorites. Sally kept her hair simple and eschewed the clusters of curls for an elegant upsweep that was more flattering even if it was considered less fashionable.

The house was quiet, and she saw no one on her way to the morning room. Her brain was muddled from lack of sleep, and she couldn't imagine maintaining her lies if the duchess decided to question her further. Stopping at the edge of the door, she stole a glance around the jamb. The room was empty.

"His Grace has taken a tray in his study, and duchess and the marquess are still abed, miss." The butler stood behind her, his mouth pursed.

Maddie's heart pounded hard. Between the fright and the stab of anger over the butler's supercilious expression, she was definitely awake now. "Thank you. I would like hot, strong coffee this morning."

"Very good, miss." The butler nodded once and melted away.

A sigh of relief accompanied her solitude. Even worse than facing the duchess would have been spending time alone with Ralston. She wasn't sure what to make of the duke and avoided him when possible. He was darkly handsome but intimidating and solemn with troubles weighing him down. Was he unhappy? Whatever his torments, his coldness did not feel as biting as his wife's. Or perhaps she just didn't know him well enough yet to experience his brand of cruelty.

After the coffee had been delivered, Maddie breakfasted on toast and jam, slouching over the table, reading a novel and glorying in the solitude.

The butler returned bearing a silver salver with an envelope on top. "A letter arrived for you, miss."

"Thank you." With coffee buzzing through her, her sense of

goodwill had returned, and she sent the butler a genuine smile. His expression didn't alter on his crisp turn to leave.

He was forgotten when she recognized her mother's handwriting. She hastily slit the seal. She had been anticipating a letter. Given enough time, she was sure her parents' attitudes would soften. Had they reconsidered her banishment? Would they welcome her home? She scanned the contents.

Oh dear. It was not an invitation to return home but a warning. Miss Prudence Courtright was traveling to England with her aunt to visit family. While the Courtrights did not have the same social cache as the duke and duchess, their connections would ensure their welcome on the fringes of society. Miss Courtright seemed nice enough, but the elder Mrs. Courtright, her aunt and chaperone, was venomous and had been one of the loudest voices to condemn Maddie.

Once the shock wore off, Maddie attempted to study the situation as dispassionately as possible. The Courtrights did not know Maddie was in London. All they knew was she had been sent away. Considering her transgression, they might have assumed Maddie was tucked away in an asylum. How long until the Courtrights arrived in London? And how soon until their paths crossed? Perhaps they never would.

No, that was too optimistic a thought. Mrs. Courtright had a nose for scandal and would sniff Maddie out in short order. Maddie's father was known to have connections to English aristocrats. It was a logical conclusion that London was her destination, and news of an American being presented to society by a duke and duchess would make the gossip sheets.

She read the letter once more, slower this time. With anger and urgency leaping off the page in equal measure, her mother reiterated in no uncertain terms that Maddie must secure her future with a suitable gentleman before Mrs. Courtright could ruin her chances. There would be no support forthcoming except in the form of a dowry to meet the singular goal of a suitable marriage.

Failure was not an option. Neither was returning home. A shard of grief worked its way into her chest, but she would have to tend to her wounds later. Now she had to plan.

Women were ruined by whispers whether they were true or not. The ton seemed to take pleasure in tearing women down. She would be no different. In fact, as an American riding the coattails of a dukedom, her downfall would be all the sweeter.

Would her dowry override her reputation? Would she be forced to marry Thornbury because she had no other options? She would make a terrible duchess. Their marriage would be miserable. How could she avoid her looming fate?

Only one solution presented itself. She would have to marry someone else.

Her hands grew damp at the thought. Suitors were not exactly lined up on their doorstep, and she had not put forth any effort to cultivate one. Her experience in New York society had taught her the care and feeding of a man's ego was a necessity if they were to come up to scratch.

What she required was an unsuspecting man who wouldn't stifle her interests. Someone who might even appreciate them. Someone, dare she hope, interesting and attractive and chivalrous.

The perfect gentleman waltzed into her head. Actually, she wasn't sure Mr. Northcutt danced, but he did kiss. While she had nothing to compare it to, womanly intuition told her his kisses were unique. They had definitely been stimulating.

Was she seriously considering marriage to a man she had met only the night before? The thought was preposterous. Madness, much like their kiss.

No, she must consider her situation rationally. Her parents would never deem Mr. Northcutt a suitable husband and might even withhold her dowry. How long did she have before the Courtright ladies arrived? No long enough.

She needed help, and there was only one person in London she trusted.

MISS ADRIANA COFFEY SWEPT INTO THE DRAWING ROOM, HER smile warm, her movements elegant. The duchess would have approved. If only Adriana's connections rose higher than being the daughter of a mere baron.

Adriana was like the moths she so dearly loved to study. Her beauty was understated, but she was as captivating as the flashier butterflies who populated the ballrooms of London. She favored gowns in earthy rich browns or greens or deep golds over the white of the typical unmarried young lady. This morning she was in an evergreen frock with small cream-colored flowers. The cut was severe and without adornments, which suited her striking features and lithe frame.

"It's shockingly early to be making calls." Adriana took Maddie's hands and gave her a buss on each cheek.

"I knew you'd be available, and I'm rather desperate for advice." Maddie pulled off her kid gloves and rubbed at the headache she hadn't been able to shake with her poor sleep and morning letter.

"Did something happen at the ball?" Adriana gestured toward the sitting area.

"Only tangentially. By the way, if the duchess asks, your family escorted me home after I ruined my gown in the garden last night." Maddie plopped down on the settee.

Adriana lowered herself in a neighboring armchair with an enviable grace, her gaze never leaving Maddie's face. "Is your dress the only thing that was ruined?"

How did Adriana manage to cut straight to the heart of the matter? It must be her artist's eye, always searching past the camouflage of a smile or laugh. Usually Maddie admired her friend's abilities, but when that intensity was directed at her, it was disconcerting.

"If I had been caught, I would have been ruined."

"By whom? Thornbury?"

"Not Thornbury. Although that is a story in itself."

"I am agog." Adriana leaned forward. "Tell me everything."

Maddie scooted to the edge of the settee until they were only inches apart and whispered, "His name is Mr. Northcutt. Do you know him?"

With a sharp shake of her head, Adriana sat back and tapped her lips. "I'm not acquainted with him. Not that my ignorance signifies anything. We are consigned to the edges of society, much to my stepmama's chagrin."

Adriana's mother had been Italian and died soon after giving birth to her. Her father had been a country squire with land and wealth but no connections until a distant uncle had died and left him as heir to a barony. That had been four years ago. Three years and eight months ago, her father had married the widow of an impoverished viscount. In the way of lovesick men, the baron did not connect his newly acquired title with the advent of admiration from his now lady-wife.

Adriana had, of course, but her father had not heeded her concerns. Once they'd married, Adriana had put her suspicions aside and done her best to get along with her stepmother, Sarah, with some success. It was her stepbrother she detested.

Adriana's expression hardened. "Did this Northcutt fellow act in an ungentlemanly fashion?"

"No, he was a perfect gentleman." It was not a lie. After all, it had been Maddie who had kissed him. Even so, heat blazed up her neck and into her cheeks. Maddie cursed her fair skin.

Adriana's gaze narrowed. "You are being unusually reticent. What happened?"

Maddie picked at the fringe along a pillow and looked anywhere but at Adriana. "Nothing happened during the carriage ride. He acted an exemplary gentleman."

"Ah! So something happened outside the carriage? Mayhap in the garden under the moonlight?" Adriana's voice was laced with equal parts amusement and misgiving.

"We kissed. Or, rather, I kissed him because we were about

to be discovered. It was..." Too many inappropriate adjectives jumped to mind. Arousing, exciting, heated. She couldn't think about that now. "There's more."

"You did more than kiss?" Adriana's eyes widened with full-blown apprehension.

"No, nothing else of note happened." Why was she suddenly thinking about how his hand had felt squeezing her bottom? Maddie rose and paced in front of the settee to keep from squirming at the memory. "I received a letter this morning from my mother."

After Maddie summarized the news, she turned to Adriana. "Do you have any words of wisdom?"

"They stopped burning witches ages ago in England." Adriana's lips twitched slightly.

Maddie stamped her foot. "I'm not a witch! I'm a botanist. Ignorance is so frustrating."

"I'm sorry. I shouldn't make light. Are you worried your American friends will gossip?" Adriana pulled Maddie back down to sit and patted her hand.

"Even calling Miss Courtright an acquaintance is being generous. She is pretty and pleasant and admired. We have nothing in common." Maddie ignored the way Adriana's lips twitched at her pronouncement. "It is her aunt that is the worry. She is a harridan who does not hold me in great esteem. Her tongue is venomous, and she will do her damnedest to ruin me."

Adriana's brows knitted. "Women in England take pride in their gardens, and every house has a stillroom. There is nothing nefarious about your interest. I wouldn't worry."

Maddie bit the inside of her lip. Adriana was her dearest friend, even more so now they got to visit regularly, yet Maddie had kept secrets. One because it was not her secret to divulge and another because she was embarrassed. "I told you my parents sent me to England to gain polish, but that's not entirely true. I was banished."

"Banished?" Adriana's voice had turned wary.

"Yes. Banished. Shunned. Cut. There is no nice way to put it."

"Why?" At Maddie's pointed look, Adriana huffed in disbelief. "Surely they don't actually believe you're a witch. That's preposterous even for Americans."

Maddie ignored the urge to defend her countrymen and women. "No, not a witch, but I am considered dangerous. Haven't women been sent away to asylums for worse?"

"Yes, but—" Adriana made a scoffing sound. "Look at you. You are not dangerous. You are sweet and funny and smart. I realize your family views your studies as a mere hobby but—"

"I poisoned someone," Maddie blurted out. "On purpose."

Adriana covered her mouth with her fingertips. "Did they die?"

"No. I didn't dose him with enough buckthorn for that." Before she could stop herself, she added with some satisfaction, "He might have wished he'd died though. He soiled his trousers in front of the crème of New York society."

"You don't sound particularly remorseful."

"I'm not." This time Maddie's defiant gaze didn't waver from Adriana. "He deserved the humiliation and more for what he did to my friend Kathleen."

"What did he do?"

"He forced himself upon her. She is the daughter of the local apothecary. We became friends as I often brought her father tinctures and poultices to sell. Remus Younts is the son of a well-to-do banker. He had power. Kathleen had none." Tears born of grief and anger stung Maddie's eyes.

Adriana's silence was the kind that encouraged her to continue her tale at her own pace. Through the lump in her throat, Maddie said, "Kathleen came to me terrified she might be with child from the attack. I gave her something to make sure that did not happen."

Adriana's swift intake of a breath was audible, but all she said was, "Good."

"But she was not the same happy, carefree girl after everything that happened. Younts destroyed her spirit. She was sent away to live with her older sister and her family. I was so angry. It wasn't fair."

Adriana covered Maddie's hands and squeezed. "I would be angry too."

"I made him pay and watched him suffer his own humiliation. He guessed it was me, of course, and when he confronted me, I didn't deny it." Maddie should have been less brazen. It was her only regret. "He made it his mission to ruin me. Some of what he accused me of I couldn't even deny because it was true. I became a pariah. My parents had no choice but to send me to England."

"It's not right that women must suffer so." Adriana's gaze had settled on the hot coals in the fireplace, but Maddie wondered where her thoughts had gone. Perhaps to her own mother, who had died to bring Adriana into the world.

"Life is not fair." Maddie sat back into the corner of the settee, closed her eyes, and pinched the bridge of her nose. "I hoped I had left it behind, but Mrs. Courtright will spread her malicious gossip, and I will be tossed into the streets by the duchess. Or else married to Thornbury for my dowry and then sent to an asylum."

"Stop it right now. You don't know any of that will happen." The pert tone of Adriana's voice got Maddie's attention, and she cracked her eyes open. Adriana had left her memories behind to fix Maddie with a glare.

"What would you have me do?" Maddie asked.

"You are the smartest, most optimistic person I know. I would have you make a plan." Adriana sat up straighter like a soldier at attention. "And I will assist you as much as I am able."

Maddie had never had a friend like Adriana. Someone she

could be honest with and who didn't judge her solely based on her misdeeds. "My reputation is ruined at home and will soon be ruined here."

"It's not ruined yet. There is time, but you must make the most of it."

"Are you telling me I should I marry Thornbury?"

"Of course not! You detest him. Find someone you don't detest and marry him." Adriana's simple yet impossible declaration made Maddie shake her head.

"That sounds all well and good for you. Cyrus is pining for your hand and will come running whenever you snap your fingers."

Adriana brows drew in and her mouth tightened. "I don't know about that. He seems to be reveling in his Grand Tour, and his letters have grown infrequent of late. That is a problem for another day. At the moment, let's concentrate on you."

"No man is coming to save me, Adriana. I have no prospects except for Thornbury, who is being forced into this arrangement in order to claim my dowry."

"There are countless men in the ton who will also want you for your dowry. The trick is finding one you can control in order to live your own life."

"That is... cold-blooded." Maddie was torn between horror and admiration at the way Adriana delivered her idea.

Adriana gave a one-shouldered shrug. "It's an option. What about your Mr. Northcutt?"

"Firstly, he is not mine. Secondly, he is the opposite of weak-willed. I would be more likely to control a lion than him. Anyway, he stated more than once that he is not a gentleman. I was left in no doubt if we were caught, he would not have done the honorable thing and offered his hand."

"This is promising. You've already discussed marriage."

"Only insofar as the constant reminders of his ungentlemanly status." Maddie harrumphed. "Now that I consider it, I feel like

I should be insulted he felt the need to bring the fact up multiple times in an hour."

Adriana put on a mysterious smile. "A very busy hour."

Maddie could feel the heat rising in her cheeks and glanced toward the clock. It was getting late. The duchess was surely up by now. "Mr. Northcutt is not in contention as a possible match. Try to think of someone else. I must take my leave. The duchess is dragging me to the modiste. I don't suppose you are attending Haversham's ball tonight?"

"We are. Richard procured invitations." Her lips thinned.

Adriana's father and stepmother, Sarah, would prefer her to make a match with Richard Pace-Varney, her stepbrother. It would be a neat solution to the question of inheritance as Adriana was an only child. The few times Maddie had crossed paths with Mr. Pace-Varney had left her feeling like she had stepped in something slimy and foul-smelling.

"Cyrus will return soon to claim your hand," Maddie offered reassuringly.

"England must seem very far away for Cyrus. I fear I have become an afterthought. Or even worse, a millstone around his neck."

Maddie doubted that was true. Adriana might not be a typical London beauty, but she was arresting in a way that drew the eye. Her olive coloring was from her Italian mother. Her eyes were large and tipped up in the corners like an exotic cat. Her nose was worthy of a Roman statue, complementing her high cheekbones and was the perfect foil to her wide, full lips.

She was also twenty-two and in her second season. Her interests were varied and included science and the arts. She was quiet and introspective and more than a little shy. It had earned her a reputation of aloofness.

Not that she was trying to charm the gentlemen of the ton. The only man Adriana had eyes for was her childhood friend Lord Cyrus Shaw, but he was young (and in Maddie's estimation immature) and showed no signs of coming up to scratch.

"I shall look for you this evening then." Maddie gave Adriana's hand a squeeze. "Wish me luck."

"With the duchess or with Mr. Northcutt?"

"You must stop bringing him up. He is not an option. In fact, I will need to make a list of suitable candidates. Can you help me?"

"I will be happy to offer my opinion, but my circle of acquaintances is limited." Adriana walked Maddie to the front door of the modest town house the baron had rented for the season.

"Goodness, with all the excitement, I forgot to give you these." Maddie reached into her reticule for the handkerchief she had tied around the mistletoe berries.

"Thank you. How did you manage to procure them?" Adriana's smile was incandescent, and it made Maddie realize how shadowed her friend was with worries.

"Oh, it was actually Mr. N—" Maddie bit off the words.

"Yes, I must stop bringing Mr. Northcutt into the conversation." Adriana's dry humor was something Maddie would like to master but feared she would never do. "You take too many risks, but I thank you nonetheless. Hopefully they will last until we return home."

"And when will that be?"

The baron was miserable being away from his country estate and returned with regularity. Adriana usually accompanied him. "I have no idea. Sarah has a list of invitations she has already accepted on our behalf."

"Selfishly, I would like to see you stay in London."

"Perhaps you could accompany us home. You would love to explore the garden and the countryside." Adriana's voice sparked with hope.

Maddie felt the same spark for a moment, but it fizzled. "I doubt the duchess would allow such a thing in the middle of the season."

She didn't mention the duchess's opinion of Baron Coffey's

low standing in the ton. While Adriana's support was invaluable, it was Maddie's future that hung in the balance. The clear night and given way to a gray, misty day to go along with her current mood. With a deep breath, she turned to face an uncertain world. But face it she must.

5

The morning was gray, the misty breeze carrying the distant scent of the countryside. Or was that Damien's imagination? He had been born in a third-floor room of a leaning tenement infested with rats and roaches. It had been all his mother could afford. Women who found themselves unmarried and pregnant and dismissed without a reference couldn't expect anything more.

Thankfully, his memories of their first home were vague. When he was three, his mother had found work in a church-supported charity home at the edge of Clerkenwell and Seven Dials. His mother acted as cook and maid, and in return, they were given food and a pallet to share in a small, airless room that didn't leak sooty rainwater and lacked the rats and roaches.

He had learned to read and write and work his sums. Books had been the one thing not in scarcity. Looking back, it was idyllic compared to how some children scrabbled to survive. In fact, most children didn't survive. One step in the wrong direction would have sent them from poverty into abject squalor.

It wasn't until he was twelve that he saw a field of wavery grass and an expanse of a sky so blue it hurt his eyes. He had felt as unmoored as if he was in the middle of the ocean. Yet another experience to be unlocked later. Too much anger resided in the hollow place of his memory.

Damien took a deep breath and concentrated on the present. He pulled his hat lower and tucked his chin into the collar of his greatcoat, shifting to find a more comfortable position. Mist gathered in droplets along the brick wall next to where he was sheltering under an overhang. A quarter hour passed before a footman with a shock of red hair and broad shoulders ducked out the servants' entrance of Thorn House.

Damien slipped into the lane leading to the mews to rendezvous. The footman's quickened steps sounded on the pavement. Seamus's gaze darted, his nerves taut.

"Did you manage it?" Damien asked.

"Yes, but it wasn't an easy task. Her Grace has been dithering over the invitations, and she accepted far more than usual." The footman glanced over his shoulder and handed over a list scribbled on a torn piece of parchment. Inkblots emphasized the haste in which it had been copied.

"No one saw you?"

"No. Leastways I don't think so." He bit his lip and then shook his head, saying more definitely, "No. If she knew, I would be straight out on my ear."

Damien tucked the paper into an inside pocket of his coat before the mist could run the ink.

The coin Damien handed Seamus disappeared in a blink. "Thank you, sir."

"What else can you tell me about the goings-on in the house?" Normally, a footman would be hesitant to divulge gossip about his employers, but Damien was trusted to a certain extent because his uncle was the butler at the Drummond town house across the square. Damien straddled two worlds, truly belonging nowhere.

"His Grace spends his time either in his study or at his club. Mr. Cobb had to order more brandy than usual. Her Grace and his lordship have been in one another's pockets lately. We all figure it has something to do with the American relation who is visiting. Miss Barnes is her name."

"Is the duchess playing matchmaker between Miss Barnes and Thornbury?" Damien asked even though he knew the answer.

"With all the subtlety of a horse breeder."

"How is Miss Barnes handling the situation?"

"As far as I can tell, she is more interested in the gardens and the stillroom. The housekeeper was complaining about her just yesterday taking over. Miss Barnes called for a carriage early this morning to visit Miss Adriana Coffey with her maid as chaperone. The duchess is still abed."

Miss Coffey was the recipient of the mistletoe berries.

"Her maid said she has an appointment with the dressmaker for a final fitting of a gown for a ball they will attend this evening," Seamus said.

Damien retrieved the paper from his pocket and scanned it. The name Haversham was halfway down. If he wasn't mistaken, the Haversham's ball was scheduled for that evening, and he didn't have an invitation. An inconvenience he must remedy.

Damien hesitated over his next question, but his curiosity won. "What do they say about Miss Barnes belowstairs? Is she well liked?"

"Very well thought of. She has passed along remedies for coughs or aches to several servants." Seamus's cheeks turned redder still. "And she always has a smile for us. Visitors usually treat us like pieces of furniture but not her."

Damien rubbed his chest. Why did that news make his heart skip along faster? "If you catch wind of any interesting tidbits, send word to my uncle."

Seamus shifted on his feet. "If I'm found out..."

The young footman sent the extra coin he earned from Damien home to his parents and younger siblings. While Seamus had the name and coloring of an Irishman, his roots ran deep through the family farm in Devonshire.

LAURA TRENTHAM

Love was a fool's weakness. A weakness Damien exploited at the gaming tables and beyond. Whether it was a love for family or a woman or a place, the feeling could be manipulated.

"If that should come to pass, I will ensure you obtain another post," Damien said.

Seamus nodded, relief flooding his face. The boy was too trusting. It would be easy enough for Damien to turn his back on Seamus and any troubles he might incur by acting as Damien's informant. Yet Damien wasn't entirely heartless even if the organ was defective.

"I'll give you double next time you have useful information for me," Damien added.

Seamus's eyes widened, and the possibility wiped any fear from his face. "Yes, sir. I'll keep my eyes and ears open."

"See that you do. Now get back before you're missed."

Damien remained under the eaves until Seamus had disappeared into the duke's mansion. Damien closed his eyes and set his palms against the cool, damp bricks. If he had the strength, he would destroy the mansion brick by brick.

Instead, he would dismantle Ralston's life and watch it tumble into ruin. Like his mother's after Ralston tossed her to the streets with nothing but his babe in her belly. Because of the Ralston's callousness, she'd died penniless and pitiable in that dark airless room in the church.

He had to turn his thoughts from the past to the future. If he wanted to see Madeline Barnes again (and he very much did for reasons he didn't want to examine too closely), he must secure an invitation to Haversham's ball.

It was an unfashionably early time to call, but Lord Drummond kept country hours even while in the city. His visits to London were reluctantly made and only when required for parliamentary business or his wife's insistence. Damien's knock was answered by his uncle. The usually stoic mask, which seemed a requirement for all butlers, broke into a sunny smile.

"Ah, my boy. It's good to see you."

They grasped forearms, the intimacy of a hug in the entryway of the Drummond town house beyond the pale for a servant and guest. "You too, Uncle. How are you?"

"Busier now Lord and Lady Drummond and the little ones are in town. The house is fair to bursting."

"And the earl?" Earl Winder, Lord Drummond's father, had achieved legendary status during the early conflicts with France, but his health had been in decline in recent years.

His uncle's smile dimmed. "He's in Bath taking the waters with the countess." He put his dour half frown back into place. "Are you here to take tea with me or to see my lord?"

"Both, actually. If Drummond is up and about, I'll see him first."

"He's in his study. Let me ask if he's home to receive you." Northcutt led the way and scratched lightly, waiting for the man inside to acknowledge the interruption with his customary grunt.

Damien grinned. He enjoyed Rafe's lack of social artifice. His uncle cracked the door open enough for Damien to see one book-lined wall. "Pardon, my lord, but you have a visitor."

"Whoever it is, inform them I'm not home. I'm in no mood to make asinine chitchat with some fop wanting my vote or my money."

Damien tapped his uncle on the shoulder, gesturing him out of the way before pushing through the door. "It's a good thing I'm in need of neither. I am, however, here to beg a favor."

"Oh, it's you. Do you want tea?" Rafe made a gesture, but Damien waved him off.

"I'm taking tea with my uncle after we're finished."

"That will be all, Northcutt," Rafe said.

"Very good, my lord." Like any butler worth their salt, Northcutt melted away, the door latching softly in his wake. Damien sprawled in the armchair across from the desk.

"A favor, you say?" Rafe sat back and gave Damien his full attention.

"I'm in need of an invitation."

"To which event?"

"Haversham's ball."

"Why? There will be no gaming room and no alcohol. The countess doesn't approve. The only purpose of that ball is to—" Rafe's eyes widened as he leaned forward, pointing at Damien. "Are you in the market for a bride?"

"No! Absolutely not. You are being utterly ridiculous."

Rafe dropped his accusing finger, but his harrumph was full of suspicion. "Are you saying this doesn't involve a woman?"

"A woman?" Damien chuffed, but he felt his collar growing tight. "I mean, only in the most circumspect manner."

"Ah, so it does involve a woman. How interesting." Rafe stroked a finger down the long scar that marred his face from forehead to jaw. "Is she rich?"

Upon initial acquaintance, Rafe Drummond could prove intimidating to the extreme. However, those few not scared away by his brusque demeanor discovered a man who was intelligent, loyal, and fiercely protective of those he cared for. Damien was thankful to count himself among Rafe's small circle of friends.

The worst of Rafe's scars weren't visible. Neither were Damien's. The two understood one another, yet Rafe had a romantic streak that had only grown wider since his marriage while Damien possessed no such streak at all.

"This is not a courtship. This is revenge." Madeline's vibrant smile flashed through his head, leaving him surprisingly muddled, and he had to force his trademark insouciance into his tone.

Rafe narrowed his eyes. "This has to do with your father then."

Damien squelched the urge to squirm in his chair like a recalcitrant child. "You sound disappointed."

"I had hoped, after seeing Simon and Jessica, you might get the itch to obtain similar marital bliss."

"If I did get such an itch, I would visit the apothecary for a healing cream immediately," Damien said dryly. "Anyway, no decent lady would align herself with a bastard."

"Some lady might be desperate enough. You are the bastard of a duke and not terrible to look at after all. Your obsession for revenge will eventually ruin your life." The seriousness of the statement was in juxtaposition to the slight smile Rafe wore.

"Excuse me?"

"You heard me." Rafe leaned back in his chair and propped one booted foot onto the edge of his desk. Sod and dirt from a morning ride were embedded in the soles.

"My uncle will have a fit if you've tracked muck through his hallowed halls." Damien tsked.

"You are attempting to deflect. It doesn't work with me." Rafe was silent for a long moment before he said in a softer voice, "I know what it is to be eaten up with resentment and hatred. You think you are hurting your father, but you are only hurting yourself. The best revenge is your success and happiness."

"What will make me happy is to see the duke destroyed," Damien said coolly. "Can you procure me an invitation or not?"

"No, I can't." After an intense stare down, Rafe rolled his eyes. "But I'm sure Minerva can finagle one for you. She and Lady Haversham sit on a charitable committee together."

Damien rose. "Thank you."

Rafe swung his feet to the floor and grunted. "Perhaps Simon can talk some sense into you tonight."

"Is he actually leaving his bedchamber long enough to attend a social function?"

"That is his plan, but Jessica might end up changing his mind." Rafe's head was down, and he was already making notations in the margins of the ledger.

"I'll see myself out, shall I?"

"Think about what I said," Rafe called out before the door shut.

Damien slipped into the servant's hallway toward the kitchens. He found his uncle decanting brandy in the butler's pantry, half-moon glasses perched on his nose.

His uncle's thick, white hair was his one vanity, and he kept it trimmed and pomaded. Wrinkles cut deep grooves alongside his mouth and across his forehead. He was a tall man and still lean in spite of the years.

Damien wasn't sure if they were true memories or only distortions, but he thought his mother had possessed the same mouth and aquiline nose. She was the feminine version of her brother in Damien's mind, except she hadn't lived long enough for her hair to grow white.

A clog of emotion rose in his throat. What would his mother's life had been like had she not been saddled with Damien? Would she have risen to the role of housekeeper? Or would she have married a merchant or a pub owner? Any happy future he pictured for her didn't include him. A bastard son would not be welcomed in any household or by any husband.

His uncle finished with the brandy and turned to welcome Damien with a smile full of curiosity. "Was your meeting with Lord Drummond successful?"

"I need to acquire an invitation for me to attend a function out of my social reach. Rafe promises me Lady Drummond can make it happen." Lady Drummond was as formidable as her husband although with a much prettier veneer.

"What a lark to picture my nephew squiring young ladies at a ball." His uncle took a seat behind the small desk with its own ledger. In fact, the room had the air of a miniature version of Rafe's study.

"I do not squire young ladies. They give me hives." Damien gave an exaggerated shudder and took the only other seat. "I don't mean to take you away from your work."

His uncle waved him off. "I have time before the morning calls begin. Tell me why you need this invitation so badly."

Considering Rafe had just grilled him on the same subject,

Damien wasn't in the mood to defend himself again. Yet he could hardly lie to his uncle. Damien did live by certain rules, warped though they might be. "Ralston will be in attendance."

His uncle sighed, and once more, Damien felt the weight of disappointment. "Your mother would not wish you to waste your life."

"He deserves to pay for what he did to her. You of all people should be cheering me on."

"He paid for your schooling. Elevated you even if he doesn't acknowledge your birth. You are successful because of what he has done for you."

"A paltry sum to alleviate his guilt. If he had done his duty to my mother and not treated her like so much refuse to be cast out, she would be alive."

"How do you know the duke does not pay a penance every time he lays his head on a pillow to rest and can't?"

Damien's smile was shaded with dark bitterness. "I only pray Mother's spirit haunts him relentlessly. Now, tell me how everyone fares."

His uncle launched into the goings-on of the other servants. The people who worked by his side were his real family. He was the best of men, and Drummond and the household were lucky to have him.

The shame his mother had felt at her unfortunate situation—yet another reason Damien hated Ralston—had kept her from going to her only brother for help until it was too late. Richard Northcutt had only been a first footman then with little power to help his sister and her bastard child, but he'd done what he could to make her final weeks more comfortable. And then afterward, he had set into motion events Damien alternately loved and resented him for.

"Well now, I must get back to work and set a good example." His uncle stood and Damien followed suit. "Will you stop by for a visit one evening? Or we could meet at the Rose and Sword one Sunday for a bite and a glass of ale."

"Yes, let's do that." Damien hesitated before clapping his uncle on the back. His uncle pulled him in for a tight hug, and Damien felt himself relax into the embrace for a moment. Clearing his throat, Damien stepped back. "I'll send a note around."

"I look forward to it. Don't forget what I said, son." His uncle waved him out of the servant's entrance.

Back on the street, Damien strolled to where Alcott waited with the carriage.

"Nice visit with your uncle?" Alcott tossed aside whatever he'd been picking his teeth with.

"I got what I needed from Drummond. That was the point." Damien opened the carriage door himself.

Alcott grunted.

Damien knew that grunt. It was full of judgment, and Damien had had about as much judgment as he could handle for one day. He swiveled toward his coachman and narrowed his eyes. Alcott was the image of innocence.

"You obviously have something to say, so spit it out," Damien said.

"It wouldn't be seemly."

"When has that stopped you?"

Alcott cocked his head with a wry smile. "True enough. You are going down a road you will regret."

"You mean relish. The means to ruin Ralston might be within my grasp. Finally."

"I'm all for you destroying the duke—I enjoy the Shakespearean drama of it—but that girl is innocent. Like your mother was. You plan to use her, ruin her, and discard her. How is that any different than what your father did to your mother?"

"I'm not going to ruin her." After lectures from both Drummond and his uncle, Alcott's accusation was alcohol in a wound.

"Oh really? I saw the way you looked at her."

"The most beautiful women in society are more than willing to warm my bed." Damien gestured around them at the row of fine town houses. "Miss Barnes is a bluestocking who would rather climb trees than be seduced."

"Exactly." Alcott's tone was one of knowing wisdom. Wisdom that was out of reach for Damien.

"You are a cipher, and I tire of attempting to unravel your meaning. Take me back to the house." Damien pulled himself into the carriage and slammed the door after him.

They were all wrong—Drummond, his uncle, Alcott. They didn't understand. The universe would remain out of balance until the scales of justice were righted. Ralston must pay, and Damien must see it done. Miss Barnes was nothing like his mother. She would survive and probably even thank him for spoiling a match between her and Thornbury.

He would tell himself that as many times as he needed to until he believed it.

6

"Justin, you will claim the first waltz along with the dinner dance." The duchess's tone didn't invite dissent.

"Yes, Mother." Thornbury stared out the carriage window with the mien of a man who was considering how best to throw himself to the cobbled street.

Maddie rolled her eyes, propped her chin on her properly gloved hand, and looked out the opposite window. He could have at least tacked on an "it would be my pleasure" even if it wasn't true.

This was what marriage between them would look like. They would travel in the same direction but with completely different views. There would be no teasing or laughter or glances full of portent. They definitely wouldn't share kisses of passion. She shuddered to think of the cold abyss that would be their wedding bed.

How long did she have to find someone more malleable? Someone who would let her pursue her passions without trying to mold her into what was expected of a lady? Expectations she would never meet. After all, she was in England because she had bitterly disappointed her parents. A pang in her chest made her breath catch painfully.

Her natural optimism had taken a hit. Maybe even a mortal blow. Time was short, and she did not possess the feminine tools needed to mesmerize men. The only man who had shown even a passing interest in her was Mr. Northcutt. While he was attractive and fascinating, she must forget he existed. Which would be easier to do if he would stop making appearances in her dreams. Her nap that afternoon had ended with her waking flushed and frustrated, and she wasn't even sure why.

They joined the line of carriages waiting to discharge their occupants at the bottom of the stairs leading to the Havershams' grand house. Were their gardens large and diverse? She quashed the thought. Wandering into the gardens would not be in the cards for her this evening. She had work to do inside the ballroom to cultivate suitors.

After navigating the receiving line, Ralston had stopped to converse with a group of soberly dressed older gentlemen, leaving Thornbury to escort his mother into the ballroom. She followed like a docile lamb to slaughter. Already a crush was forming. A small orchestra provided music, and the dance floor was full.

The duchess turned with a smile too full of sharp teeth. "The waltz is next."

Thornbury held out his arm without a word, and Maddie laid her hand lightly on top, both of them doing their best to limit contact. They garnered looks along the short stroll to the dance floor. Some were curious, some envious. If only the gawkers knew how much antipathy existed between them.

An idea bounced into her head, and she rolled it around, searching for flaws. Why must she and Thornbury be cast as adversaries? After all, weren't their aims the same? Neither wanted to marry the other.

The strains of the waltz began, and Thornbury positioned them on the edge of the floor. He was tall, and she tilted her head back to attempt to catch his gaze, but it was fixed over her shoulder.

"What the devil is he doing here?" Thornbury muttered.

Maddie twisted to get a peek at the man who had inspired such vitriol, but before she could, Thornbury whisked her into the steps. She tried not to enjoy herself, but as usual, the dance swept her up into its energy. There was a reason children liked to twirl until they were dizzy. It was fun.

But she wasn't here to have fun. She was here to find a way out of a mess. "Do you wish to marry me, Thornbury?"

That got his attention. His gaze dropped to hers, and if the question wasn't so important, she might have laughed at the shock on his face.

"You are very impertinent, cousin."

"I know. It is only one of my many defects." When he didn't argue the point, she rolled her eyes and continued. "Another is stubbornness. I desire a truthful answer. Do you wish to marry me?"

"I will do what is expected of me." The bitterness pinching his mouth would have been offensive if she was actually interested in marriage.

"I'm going to assume that is a no. As it happens, I don't wish to marry you either," she said lightly.

Anger reminiscent of his mother flashed across his face. "I will be a duke. You would be lucky to be my duchess."

The blasted man should be relieved. It was a shame men's egos were so fragile.

"I would prefer to marry someone with similar interests to mine." She raised her brows, but it was clear he hadn't followed her train of thought. More leadingly, she added, "I thought perhaps you might know some suitable gentlemen to introduce me to?"

Two turns later, he whispered, "You are suggesting I play matchmaker for you?"

"Exactly so."

The dance ended, but instead of depositing her back into his mother's care as if she had the plague, he led her behind a pillar for a modicum of privacy. "My parents are insistent that we marry."

"Because of my dowry, yes, but you don't wish to marry me."

His jaw muscle ticked. "Mother won't approve of us thwarting her plans."

"Which is why neither of us needs to mention this little spot of subterfuge." She touched his arm to draw his gaze. It was troubled but sparked with hope as well. "In the guise of courting me yourself, you can squire me around and introduce me to suitable gentlemen of your acquaintance."

"What would you deem suitable?" he asked.

What were her requirements? An image of Mr. Northcutt popped into her head, but she shook it away. He was handsome and urbane with a wit and charm that was... well, charming. One thing he was not was malleable. "A man I will be able to control."

Thornbury gave her a hard look. "That's the extent of your wants in a husband?"

She wanted many things, none of which she would share with Thornbury. "It's the one quality that will allow me to achieve what I want above all else—freedom."

"You are a woman. You will never be truly free." He was already looking around the room for candidates and didn't see how his offhand remarks sent ice into her veins. "Are you ready to begin? I believe I've spotted a covey of suitable gentlemen for you to take aim at."

She darted a glance toward the doors leading to the gardens. The urge to run and hide under the branches of a tree that had stood for years, solid and stable, was overwhelming, but she was no longer a child. She was a woman who must face her future and wield as much control over her destiny as she could afford. It felt like a pittance, but how long did she have before the poison of rumors began to filter through the ton about her and any power she held was snatched away?

Thornbury cleared his throat, and she returned her attention to him. He stood with an offered arm and a furrowed brow. Squaring her shoulders, she took a deep breath and lightly set her hand on his forearm and a smile on her face. She should be pleased. The suggestion they work together had gone over without an argument.

Thornbury was as much a pawn as she was. He wished to be with his opera mistress, and Maddie assumed the mistress did not wish to lose her benefactor. There was no use in making three people miserable, most pertinently herself.

An ember of the optimism she had written off as dead sparked. She could do this as long as she kept her expectations low. Three young men stood in conversation but made room as they turned to greet Thornbury.

They were neither too young nor too old, which was heartening, although none were as handsome as Mr. Northcutt. Maddie gave herself a mental slap. Comparing every gentleman she met to Mr. Northcutt would offer nothing but heartache for what she could not have.

Thornbury performed introductions. Mr. Hamilton had graduated from Cambridge and fancied himself the next Sir Walter Scott. He was skinny and pockmarked and wore his disdain like armor. While he was suitably dim-witted, his overinflated opinion of himself might prove problematic. She did not relish being forced to praise bad poetry the rest of her life.

She turned her attention to the next man. Mr. Pomeroy was a bit older with a dingy collar and a limp cravat. His thick spectacles gave him an owl-like expression but happened to emphasize his best feature, which were his chocolaty-brown eyes. Unfortunately, his intense stare made her feel like a rare animal he wanted to put under glass. He bobbed his head and mumbled a greeting.

Lord Stratton was the final introduction and the most promising prospect. Not because he was a viscount but because he had an interest in ornithology and spent the majority of his time on his estate in the south of England along the coast. His plain features weren't unpleasant, but more attractive was his enthusiasm about the natural sciences. His eyes lit up when she shared her own scientific pursuits in the field of botany.

"My dream is to be invited into the Royal Society." Lord Stratton's smile revealed a set of crooked teeth.

That was her dream as well, but at least it was possible and even probable for Lord Stratton. The mere fact of her sex made it an impossible feat for her. Therefore, she had lowered her aim. "My dream is to visit the Chelsea Physic Garden."

"There are dangerous plants cultivated there."

"Yes, I know. Those are the plants I'm most interested in."

Lord Stratton made a little sound of distress. "Women aren't allowed inside the gates."

"Yes, I know." More than a hint of her frustration shortened her reply. "What is your opinion of the policy of exclusion?"

"Exposing the fairer sex to such dangers would be inappropriate and dangerous."

"Yes, a woman might swoon and fall into snakeroot or pocket hemlock to slip into her husband's tea."

Missing her sarcasm entirely, Lord Stratton smiled as if she were a child getting her sums correct. "Exactly so."

If this was the best Thornbury could conjure up, she was in trouble. Nevertheless, she penciled each gentleman onto her dance card.

"Mother is glaring at us from across the room. I'll escort you to her," Thornbury whispered close to her ear.

She turned to ascertain the duchess's displeasure for herself but locked gazes with none other than Mr. Northcutt as if she had somehow conjured him. He stood with his shoulder propped against one of the faux pillars, fiddling with an unlit cheroot. His hands were bare, his long fingers graceful. Had he been watching her? A tingle went up her neck.

Her heart raced along as she leaned closer to Thornbury.

"You are acquainted with the dark-haired man leaning on the pillar, are you not?"

Thornbury glanced over and his lip curled. "Unfortunately. A man of his vices should never have been invited. I'll be sure to have a word with Lady Haversham. I wouldn't put it past the man to have snuck in. He is a dishonorable devil and very bad ton. You are not to associate with him."

The imperiousness of Thornbury's dictates reminded her of the duchess. Would he be equally dictatorial as a husband? Maddie hoped to never find out. She stole another glance at Mr. Northcutt. The man might be devilish, but he was no devil. He'd shown her more kindness than any so-called gentleman of the ton.

The urge to defend him was strong, but she bit her tongue and merely nodded as if agreeing with Thornbury's command. No one except for Adriana knew about her moonlit meeting with Mr. Northcutt. She must keep it that way.

Thornbury led her away. It took considerable restraint to keep herself from looking over her shoulder, but she could almost feel the touch of his gaze as she walked away.

◈

"Who has you so mesmerized?" Simon asked.

Damien hadn't even been aware of his friend's approach. He had been focused on trying to read lips and failing miserably. Madeline looked awfully cozy with Thornbury, considering her recent disdain toward him.

What had changed? Had Thornbury located a well of charm Damien was unaware of and drowned Madeline in it? Had she decided the heir to a dukedom was an excellent catch after all? His burning sense of frustration was only because a burgeoning relationship between the American heiress and his half brother would botch Damien's plans. He had to keep her dowry out of Thornbury's, and by extension, Ralston's, hands.

The group of sops Thornbury had introduced her to was yet another puzzle. A woman as vivacious and intelligent as Madeline would surely never choose to burden herself with such a bland, boring husband, would she? Any of them would prove a disaster, but her acceptance of Thornbury's suit would be an outright tragedy.

"Damien? Are you well?" Simon sounded genuinely worried.

Damien pasted on his usual devil-may-care smirk, but it was brittle and fell into a glower. "I'm excellent. In fact, I've never been better."

"Why are you here?" Simon's bluntness was a relief after the past half hour of meaningless conversations.

"Whispers carry the news that Ralston is in financial straits."

"Because of your machinations?"

"Unfortunately not. However, the means to his salvation, like so many others before him, is to lure an heiress into marriage with Thornbury. That's where I enter."

"You plan to thwart a possible match?"

"Precisely."

"I assume the heiress in question is the American relation staying with the duke and duchess?"

Not surprised word of her entrance into society had reached Simon's ear, Damien nodded and searched the ballroom. She wasn't dancing this set, and there was no sign of her in the scrum of eligible ladies on the far side. Surely she hadn't wandered into the gardens again. He craned his neck but couldn't see beyond the lanterns set at the doors to the balustrade.

"Her name is Miss Barnes," he said absently. "Madeline."

"I assume that means you've already fired the first salvo and contrived to meet her. Did she fall under your spell?"

"Not exactly." A true smile snuck past his insouciance. "She is an unusual lady."

"In an interesting way or an odd one?"

"Definitely interesting." Considering what transpired during their garden meeting, he added, "But also odd."

"You are pursuing her for your own gains?" Simon's stuffy disapproval was unexpected. The man had hardly lived the life of a saint.

"If I am?"

"I would counsel caution." Simon harrumphed. "Although, to be blunt, it would be a rare lady who would pass up being a duchess in exchange for a night in your bed and the humiliation that would follow. She would be ruined and for what? Ralston will only find Thornbury another heiress to woo and marry."

"That makes me sound like a bastard."

"It does, doesn't it?" Simon tilted his head to catch Damien's eye. "Why give Ralston and the rest of society the satisfaction of proving them correct? You might have been born on the wrong side of the bed, but you aren't a bastard."

Damien had lived his life with the yoke of his parentage around his neck. His time at Eton had been fraught with insults and beatings. It weighed on him even as he stood in a ballroom with the upper echelon of society.

Only a few trusted friends had insight into what motivated him, but even they couldn't understand him. Simon had inherited a dukedom before he was out of short pants. He was unable to fathom what Damien's mother had endured. "You didn't see the way my mother suffered. He deserves to suffer too."

Simon laid a hand on Damien's shoulder and squeezed, saying nothing. Damien appreciated the lack of platitudes.

Finally Madeline emerged from a group of young ladies all wearing white. She was in a fetching blue gown the color of a summer sky. Her blond hair had been twisted and pinned up, but tendrils had escaped to curl with artless charm against her temples and neck. Her hair matched her personality. It was impossible to tame her vivaciousness.

At Madeline's side was a tall young lady dressed in a russet-colored gown the color of a fallen leaf. Although the color was muted and the cut severe, the lady exuded an elegance that was impossible to deny.

THE COURTSHIP CALCULATION

Arm in arm, they promenaded along the edge of the dance floor, their heads close as they conversed. Madeline glanced in his direction, meeting his gaze with a boldness that didn't surprise him. Only when they were lost in the milling crowd did they break eye contact.

He felt loosed from his moorings, adrift and uncertain.

"How is Jessica?" Damien asked in order to find more solid footing.

"She is excellent." Simon tipped his chin toward the entrance. Jessica chatted with Lady Drummond and Mrs. Masterson. The smile on his face was full of the mysteries of wedded bliss.

Damien suppressed a shudder at the notion, but he was happy for his friend nonetheless. Simon was a good man, an even better friend, and deserved the contentment he'd found.

With Simon's attention focused on his wife, Damien stole another glance around the ballroom. Madeline and her companion were making steady progress in his direction. Her gaze was singular and intense and aimed at him.

Damien's collar tightened and the room grew hot. "What in the devil is she doing?"

"What the devil is who doing?" Simon asked.

"Madeline. I mean, Miss Barnes."

"Which one is she?" Simon craned his neck.

"The one with absolutely no sense of self-preservation."

Madeline moved inexorably closer. Damien sidestepped in an attempt to escape but bumped into Simon.

"I would think this was a boon for your dastardly plans." Equal parts amusement and censure weaved through Simon's voice.

He was right. Damien should be pleased at the turn of events. Except he had the distinct feeling that instead of being the predator, he was the prey. With the suddenness of a pouncing cat, she was in front of him with no possible retreat unless he gave her the cut direct.

79

Already they were garnering looks. He bared his teeth, hoping it would pass for a smile. "What are you doing, Miss Barnes?"

"I would like to introduce you to my friend, Miss Adriana Coffey. She is the recipient of your good deed in the garden. Adriana, this is Mr. Northcutt. And you are?" Madeline looked quizzically at Simon.

"Miss Barnes, this is most improper." Damien couldn't believe the priggish words came out of his mouth. "You and I have not been formally introduced."

"That's ridiculous." She unfurled her fan and spoke softly over the top. "We got to know one another intimately in the garden the other evening."

"Miss Barnes!" His voice was as forceful as he could manage in a whisper.

"Introduce us, Damien," Simon said on a wave of poorly suppressed laughter. "I've always enjoyed the frankness of Americans. After all, I married one myself."

"May I present Miss Madeline Barnes and Miss Adriana Coffey? Simon, the Duke of Bellingham," Damien said through clenched teeth.

Curtsies were dropped by the ladies along with a practiced and graceful bow from Simon. Damien glared at Madeline, but she merely tilted her head and granted him a smile. A sunny smile that made him feel hot and cold at the same time. Was he becoming feverish?

"Ah, I know your father in passing, Miss Coffey. He recently joined my club. An avid outdoorsman, if I recall," Simon said smoothly.

"Yes, Your Grace. He would prefer to be tramping across his estate rather than escorting me around London for the season. It is lovely to make your acquaintance as well, Mr. Northcutt. I've heard so much about you from Maddie." Curiosity but also wariness was stamped on Miss Coffey's striking features.

Madeline exhibited no such wariness even though she would

be smart to do so. Her grin was open and made her eyes sparkle with mischief. As Simon and Miss Coffey chatted about country living, she tapped Damien on the chest with her fan. "Thornbury doesn't like you."

"As you know, the feeling is mutual." Damien tried to hold his tongue but couldn't. "The two of you seem awfully cozy this evening. I was under the impression you did not hold him in high regard."

"Jealous, are you?"

He reared back slightly at her accusation. "Of course not."

There was no way jealousy was at the root of his earlier frustration and anger at watching Thornbury dance and squire Madeline around. She was merely a means to revenge.

"Good. Jealousy is such an unattractive quality in a gentleman."

"I'm no gentle—"

"Yes, yes. As you've proclaimed about a hundred times, you're no gentleman." Madeline waved his protest away like an annoying gnat.

"Now see here, Madeline—"

"Oh, are we on a first-name basis now, *Damien?*"

Hearing the intimacy of his given name sent a not unpleasant shock through him. Gathering himself, he smoothed the lapels of his jacket. Across the ballroom, he caught the duchess's glare. If looks could kill, he would be a pile of smoking ash. "The duchess does not look pleased."

"May I have the next dance?" Madeline asked.

"Maddie!" Miss Coffey's whisper was scandalized.

"It's not done to ask a gentleman to dance." Damien tried to keep his voice stern.

"But I'm not asking a gentleman to dance; I'm asking you."

Damien ignored the stifled laugh from Simon. "I can't dance with you."

She was the picture of innocence from her demure frock to her pink-tinged cheeks to her beguiling smile. All except for her eyes, which dared him to leap off the cliff with her. "Do you not know how to dance? I can teach you if you like."

"I know how to dance," he said with a huffing laugh he couldn't silence. "What I meant was that it is completely unacceptable for a young lady to dance with a man like me."

"If you are so terrible, I doubt a paragon of society like the Duke of Bellingham would associate with you. Isn't that correct, Your Grace?"

"A paragon, am I? Do you hear that?" Simon elbowed Damien in the arm.

Damien was never going to hear the end of this interaction. "Don't let it go to your head, *Your Grace*." He made sure the honorific was dripping with sarcasm.

Simon merely laughed. "In answer to your query, Damien has atrocious manners, hates to lose even simple parlor games, and can be careless with his wit. However, he is a fine man and a good friend."

"I am not." Petulance made him refuse the compliment.

"We must agree to disagree, Mr. Northcutt." Madeline looked up at him through her lashes. "A country dance is next. Or if you prefer, I believe I still have a waltz free."

Simon sputtered a laugh. "You'd better take the lady dancing, or tongues will wag."

Damien suspected tongues were already wagging. More than wagging, they were running amuck and probably leaving messes on the floor. He hadn't wanted to tip his hand this early in the game, but it seemed that Madeline was calling his bluff.

"This is a terrible idea." Damien cast his eyes to the flickering candles above their heads.

Simon turned to Miss Coffey and offered his arm. "May I introduce you to my duchess, Miss Coffey?"

"That would be lovely, Your Grace." Miss Coffey and Madeline exchanged a long look. Finally, Miss Coffey rolled her eyes heavenward and put her hand on Simon's arm.

Dancers assembled on the floor. Madeline left him to stand

in a long row of ladies. He could hardly leave her without a partner, so he joined the line of gentlemen, directly across from her.
He did not recognize the young lady on her right, but Lady
Waltham was staring at him with a combination of shock and
vitriol from where she stood at Madeline's left.

His relationship with Lady Waltham had begun as a light flir-
tation and proceeded to a brief affair. She had fancied herself in
love with Damien, which had been impossible. She didn't actually know him. She was acquainted with the mask he presented
to society. The affair had begun and ended years ago. Surely the
lady didn't still harbor ill feelings, but based on her cutting stare,
she had hoarded her resentments.

Hers wasn't the only incredulous glance he intercepted. The
back of his neck warmed, but he refused to give credence to the
stares by trying to glare them down. He would merely act as if he
danced with innocents all the time.

In the early days, he had partnered widows and experienced
ladies who had seen a dance as a precursor to further intimacies.
Young ladies with marital expectations were to be avoided at all
costs. But he had danced with no one for several seasons now.

How then did he find himself on the dance floor, staring into
Madeline's laughing eyes and trying his damnedest not to smile
back?

Lively music energized the room. The steps came to him as if
he performed them every day, thank goodness. He did not relish
embarrassing himself if the ton was indeed watching. While he
kept his movements sedate, the same could not be said for
Madeline.

She danced with an exuberance that the duchess would try to
quash. If the duchess didn't succeed, Thornbury or someone else
of his ilk she was forced to marry would. It was a damned shame.

Her cheeks flushed and her hair bounced. His gaze drifted
lower. Her bosom quivered with her steps, and he wished he had
claimed a waltz instead. He would have been able to hold her
close and enjoy the view.

The gentleman next to him in line jabbed an elbow into his arm. Damien reluctantly spared him a glance. It was Lord Burchett, a dim-witted earl who had been at school with Damien and Simon. Burchett hadn't rolled out a welcome for Damien, but neither had he been unkind. He wasn't a gambler, therefore Damien had rarely crossed paths with him since their schooldays.

"I say, Northcutt, who is the lovely creature you are dancing with?" Burchett asked in a low voice.

The dance took them apart as they circled the women diagonally, which meant Burchett and Madeline came together in the dance. When Burchett returned, Damien said, "She is under the watchful eye of the Duchess of Ralston. I would stay far away."

While Damien would try to thwart any plan Ralston had to marry Madeline to Thornbury, he shouldn't be feeling this antagonistic toward Burchett. Another pass in the dance occurred, and Madeline aimed her sunny smile in Burchett's direction once more.

"You're not staying away, old chap," Burchett said when he was once more at Damien's side. "She seems delightful."

She *was* delightful, dammit.

It was Damien's turn to squire the lady diagonal him even as his gaze remained on Madeline. A throat cleared. Damien returned his attention to the dance before he trod on toes. His partner was Lady Waltham. He pasted on a tight smile. She did not attempt to return it.

The steps of the dance brought them close, and she whispered, "Ruining innocents now, Northcutt?"

"It's just a dance, my lady."

"It's never *just* anything with you. You are always scheming." The disdain in her gaze was surprising.

He had assumed the women he dallied with were as distant and heartless as he was. Perhaps that wasn't the case with Lady Waltham. Had he truly wounded the widow with his careless attitude?

An unfamiliar feeling of remorse welled up in his chest. They came together once more in the dance, and in a low voice he said, "I apologize, my lady, for any hurt I might have caused you. It was not intentional, I promise you."

"It never is with men like you, is it?" She transferred her attention back onto her partner, effectively dismissing him.

Even as the dance brought him and Madeline back together, Lady Waltham's accusation scrolled. What was his plan for Madeline? Could he seduce her? It would be child's play for a man of his experience. He would make sure she enjoyed herself thoroughly.

In fact, he would do his damnedest to ruin her for any other man. He would make sure when she closed her eyes it was Damien she imagined, not some milksop husband who wouldn't know her clitoris from her elbow. But could he leave her ruined and heartbroken? Was he arrogant to even think he could break her heart?

Their hands pressed together as they turned, and he cursed the glove she wore.

"You are glowering. What are you thinking about?" she asked.

He could hardly confess the lurid images of rumpled sheets and his head between her legs running roughshod over his control. "Nothing to concern you."

"Oh really?" Her eyes narrowed. "I rather think you are fibbing."

"Why would you think that?"

"Because of the way you are looking at me."

He was a master bluffer at the gaming table. He could fool anyone into thinking he had a pair of twos when three aces graced his hand. Could she really intuit his thoughts? Did she know he wanted to throw her over his shoulder and find the nearest horizontal surface?

He leaned closer and injected an edge of warning into his

voice. "If you had an inkling what I was thinking, you would hide behind the Duchess of Ralston's skirts, Madeline."

Far from being cowed, she raised her brows. "Don't underestimate me, sir."

The dance ended with his bow and Madeline's curtsy. One of the milksops from her earlier introductions—Lord Stratton, he thought?—swooped in to claim his dance.

Madeline shot Damien a smile that spoke of secrets shared and made him feel like he was covered in warm, wriggling puppies. It would never do. He turned on his heel and stalked away, ignoring the whispers in his wake. It might not have been a cut direct, but it had been rude.

He was collecting his cloak and hat when Simon strolled up. "You're making a hasty exit."

"I grew weary of the dull company." He folded his coat over his arm.

"You weren't exactly a bucket of laughs this evening either," Simon said dryly.

Where was Damien's smooth charm? He was ruffled by the challenge in Madeline's forthright gaze. "Yourself excluded, of course. You and Her Grace are always a delight."

Simon shook his head. "You're not weary; you're scared."

"That's ridiculous." Damien stalked out the front door.

Simon kept pace with him down the wide front steps to the pavement. Damien craned his neck, but Alcott was nowhere in sight.

"Are you attending Ralston's masquerade?" Simon asked.

"I would never be allowed through the front doors."

"What if I can procure you an invitation under a different name? You will have to remain masked, of course."

Suspicions raised Damien's hackles. "Why are you helping me? I thought you didn't approve of my quest for revenge."

"I don't, but I do approve of Miss Barnes. I like her. Do you want the invitation or not? This is the only time I will offer, so don't come begging when you change your mind later."

Damien's black carriage made an appearance, Alcott deftly steering around stationary vehicles. Damien swung himself inside without lowering the steps but stuck his back head out. "Get me the blasted invitation."

Damien shot a vulgar hand gesture toward the satisfied smile on Simon's face, but his best friend just laughed.

7

The next morning, Maddie was still mildly shocked Damien Northcutt had accepted her outrageous invitation to dance. He could have given her the cut. The duke Of Bellingham *should* have given her the cut. That would have been the end of her, but as suspected, the duke wasn't a stickler for the niceties. He couldn't be if he was friends with Damien.

What on earth had possessed her to approach him? Had it been his intense stare while she was on Thornbury's arm? Was it because she knew Thornbury and the duchess didn't approve of him? Or had it been the way one glance from him had made her body hum and spark?

Unsurprisingly, he had been an excellent partner. He performed the steps with the perfect amount of power and masculine grace. Even so, something dark had festered between him and Lady Waltham. Had they been lovers? Probably. A sick feeling invaded, and she did her best to push it away.

For the next five days, she spent her mornings in the still-room and her afternoons doing her best to make coherent conversation with the constant flow of visitors the duchess received. Of course, many were curious about Maddie and fished for information on her family, her status, and what she might bring to a marriage. The duchess usually demurred with a smile and heavy-handed hints that Maddie's future had already been secured.

Damien did not make an appearance. Was he afraid of the antipathy he would receive from the Ralston household if he called? He might have been a rogue and a gambler, but she hadn't thought him a coward.

He found her interesting. She was sure of that. Did he find her attractive though? She smoothed her hair. Had she forced her attentions upon him? She was inexperienced compared to a woman like Lady Waltham although only because of opportunity, not choice. What did she have to offer a man like him? Nothing. She pressed her hands against heated cheeks and let out a sound of distress.

What was she doing pining for him? He was not suitable marriage material. He had told her this more than once, and she was in agreement. Yet... she couldn't stop herself from wanting to be near him. It was a stupid, dangerous pursuit that wasn't furthering her goals in the least.

Panic sent its tendrils around her stomach and made her feel queasy. Time was ticking away, and she had done nothing to encourage a single gentleman who might be interested in marrying her away from Thornbury.

She didn't have time for histrionics. The household was in an uproar preparing for the upcoming masquerade ball, and the duchess wanted Maddie looking her best, which never quite felt up to the Ralston standards. She would do her best though. Hope that Damien would make an appearance bubbled through her panic. Everyone who was anyone was invited.

The afternoon passed in a flurry of washing and plucking and coifing that left her exhausted before the party had even begun. When she saw herself in the looking glass, she gawped. She had never looked so sophisticated.

Her hair had been curled and pinned within an inch of its

life, but the result was an artful coiffure that twisted and curled its way around her crown. It was a welcome change from the detestable sausage curls so popular at the moment.

Her dress was a saturated dark lavender satin that brought out the color in her cheeks and lightened the golden color of her hair. She had fought hard for something other than white or cream and won the skirmish. A thick, stiff ribbon of deeper purple circled her waist, and the skirts flowed to the floor with an overlay of embroidered netting. The hem was heavy with matching purple ribbons weaved into lovely swirls. She swished the skirts and enjoyed the effect.

"Let me tie your mask on, miss." Sally held a beribboned, jeweled mask in her hands.

Maddie dutifully held still while the maid tugged and adjusted the fit. Her peripheral vision was obscured, but Maddie couldn't deny that the effect was rather spectacular. The mask was winged and embossed with pasted stones of lavenders and whites that caught the light and sparked off her eyes.

She wasn't unrecognizable, but she felt like one of Adriana's caterpillars emerging from a cocoon and allowed herself to preen for a moment.

"You look beautiful, miss." Sally stepped back with well-placed satisfaction.

"Only because you are so skilled." Maddie met the maid's gaze through the looking glass.

"That's kind of you to say." Sally blushed becomingly and fluffed Maddie's skirts. In a more hesitant voice, she said, "I would be very pleased to accompany you once you and the marquess marry."

It was like being doused in icy water. Maddie didn't want to be reminded of Thornbury. "I will keep that in mind."

With a last pinch of her cheeks for color, Maddie descended to the main floor. The sounds of a seven-piece ensemble warming up lured her to the ballroom, which ran the length of the back of the house. It had been transformed from a dim echo chamber into a dazzling scene of fresh flowers with the inlaid wood floors polished to a high shine. Even with the three large chandeliers overhead being fitted with candles, the large room had a shadowy intimate feel.

Fighting the urge to twirl across the dance floor as if she were a child, she left the magic for the drawing room where she had been instructed to gather. Only Thornbury was waiting with a drink in his hand. He wore a black-and-silver mask that emphasized his weak jawline. She hesitated in the doorway, but he had already spotted her.

"Mother and Father will be down shortly. Would you like a drink to fortify yourself?"

Maddie knew the duchess would not approve, but her nerves sent her to the sideboard to pour herself a glass of port. It was easier to ask for forgiveness than permission after all. Although that philosophy had not stood her well after the incident that had sent her to England, had it?

She finished the glass in two swallows and poured another before turning to Thornbury. He lifted his glass to her in a silent toast before downing his spirits with the air of a man facing a firing squad.

"Tonight presents another opportunity for us," she said.

"Are you still hopeful about possibly finding a groom to take my place?"

"Of course I am. We have hardly had the chance to put our plans into action. We do not yet know whether we will succeed or fail."

"But you are still willing to try?" The tiniest spark of hope helped alleviate the gloomy expression dragging his mouth into a frown.

"I won't give up until we are shoulder to shoulder in front of a clergyman."

He barked a laugh. "I'm not sure whether to be insulted or relieved at your tenacity to escape my detestable clutches."

"I don't find you detestable, my lord." Maddie was surprised to discover it was true. She didn't find him attractive or particularly interesting or possessing a backbone, but he wasn't detestable. He was as much a pawn as she was. "We simply don't suit."

"No, we do not," he said emphatically before emptying his glass.

Maddie sipped on her glass and meandered the room to help control her nerves. The sound of voices had her setting her almost-empty glass aside to greet the Duke and Duchess of Ralston.

They made a handsome couple. The duke wore an impeccable evening suit, and his simple black mask emphasized the wings of silver hair at his temples. An emerald stickpin winked from his snowy cravat.

Where the duke's clothes were severe in cut and color, the duchess was a showy flower in her rose-colored gown embellished with a lace overlay and delicate embroidered details around her neckline and the bottom two feet of her hem. Her mask was equally elaborate. Pink and white feathers erupted from one side to bob over her curled hair.

The duchess's gaze landed on Maddie. She tried not to shift or squirm under the critical examination.

"You look very elegant, Madeline." The pronouncement was made grudgingly but with a nod of satisfaction.

"Thank you, Your—" At the tightening of the duchess's mouth, Maddie redirected her tongue. "I mean, Aunt Elizabeth."

"Guests will be arriving soon. We will form a receiving line in the entry to welcome them. Madeline, you will stand to Justin's right. Ralston and I will begin the dancing. You and Justin will wait but a few moments and join us on the dance floor. Every eye will be upon you, so smile and look happy."

Look happy, not *be* happy.

Maddie nodded and only half listened to the stream of instructions that consisted of whom to welcome warmly, whom to curtsy to, and who ranked a mere nod of acknowledgment.

Some names were familiar, but they all muddled together until Maddie was certain she would make a hash of it all.

It didn't matter. Excitement buzzed through her. She should be focused on the opportunity to meet moldable, eligible men, but she could only think about Damien. Would he attend? How could she keep from greeting him familiarly in the receiving line? Would her smile give her away?

It turned out not to be a worry because Damien did not make an appearance. She did, however, welcome the Duke of Bellingham and his wife. She only had the chance for a single whispered question while she graced him with a curtsy. "Is he coming?"

Bellingham's eyes went wide when he cast a look toward Ralston. "I don't know."

Her anticipation fizzled, and she went through the motions with Thornbury to open the ball with a waltz. Did she look happy enough to be in his arms with her stiff shoulders and pasted-on smile?

Couples flooded the floor, and it was easy enough to slip away before the next dance began. Adriana was standing with her stepmother in the corner of the ballroom. Even Lady Coffey appeared overwhelmed by the opulence.

Maddie joined her friend and gazed toward the dance floor. She nodded at the young girls promenading past them, their color high and their giggles uncontained by the fans they used to cover their mouths. Was she feeling a stab of jealousy at the uncomplicated excitement they exuded? "Bellingham doesn't expect Mr. Northcutt to make an appearance this evening."

"I'm sorry to hear that. I know how much you were looking forward to furthering your acquaintance," Adriana murmured.

"It's better this way. I can concentrate on finding a moldable young man more suited to my needs. Or perhaps I should marry an older gentleman like Geneva did. The freedom of widowhood would be welcomed."

Adriana cast an exasperated glance toward Maddie. "That is a callous thing to think. Do you not long for a connection of hearts? Or at least minds?"

"Not all of us has a Lord Cyrus waiting in the wings." Maddie tried to keep her voice light but feared a hint of dryness had slipped in.

She had never met the young man who held Adriana's heart and could only hope he deserved the faith and constancy Adriana afforded him. The longer he was away sowing his oats, the more doubts gathered on the horizon.

For once, Adriana did not jump to her sweetheart's defense. "Surely there are options beyond settling for a loveless marriage."

"Loveless marriages seem the done thing in the ton."

"Then why not just marry Thornbury?"

"Because I would not just be marrying Thornbury. His mother controls him and by extension would control me. My studies would become a bitter memory."

"You'd eventually be the Duchess of Ralston and could spend your time as you wished."

"I wouldn't count on that happening anytime soon." Maddie leaned closer to Adriana. "I suspect the duchess has made a pact with an evil witch to live forever in return for her soul."

Adriana's laugh was husky and quickly stifled behind her hand. "Yes, I see the difficulties. I suppose you must find a suitable substitute."

"Indeed. Wish me luck." Maddie squeezed Adriana's hand and entered the fray.

Thornbury was true to his word and introduced her to more eligible gentlemen than she could keep straight. Her cheeks hurt from smiling, and her brain hurt from the inane small talk she was expected to make.

With each dance, her steps grew heavier at the realization she could not imagine herself settling for any of them. With excuses of needing a rest, she sidled her way around the edge of the dance floor to the double doors leading to the entry and escape.

The duchess's sitting room had been outfitted as a retiring room for the ladies, but Maddie did not relish the thought of facing questions from the curious gaggle of women. Instead, she slipped into the shadows behind a leafy ficus. It offered more camouflage than the useless mask she wore.

From her vantage point, she could observe the room, and the frenetic energy was different than any other ball she had attended. It was odd because the masks did not truly conceal anyone's identity. No one was going unobserved by society, yet there seemed a collective agreement to pretend otherwise. The laughter was more raucous, the glances more flirtatious, and the behavior bordering on scandalous.

As she watched the tableau, a gentleman, who Maddie knew very well to be married, skated his hand from a lady's waist to give her bottom a quick squeeze. Instead of slapping him silly, the lady, who was *not* his wife, merely laughed and tapped his chest with her fan as if he were a naughty schoolboy.

"Why are you hiding?" a low masculine voice asked.

Maddie started and swung around, her tongue tripping for an excuse.

The man wore a more concealing mask than most. It was velvety black and covered not just the top half of his face but was tied over his hair as well, leaving only his jawline and lips visible. Dark eyes appeared even darker against the luxurious fabric. She stared at the well-formed lips quirked into the hint of a smile.

"Damien," she said on an exhale that was part relief and part happiness. "Bellingham didn't think you planned to attend."

"He doesn't know what I'd dare to do to get what I want." The darkness in his voice only served to titillate Maddie's senses. "I expected to find you in the middle of a bevy of suitors or sweeping around the dance floor."

His gaze flicked to the ballroom, and hers followed briefly

before returning to him. How long before they were noticed lurking behind a potted plant? Would the loosened strictures extend to her? She doubted it.

"Would you care to dance?" she asked.

"I would not."

"Oh." Her face heated at his abrupt refusal.

"That is to say, I would like to dance with you, but I would not care to be unmasked in the middle of Ralston's ball."

"The antipathy between you and the Ralston family is rife." Although it wasn't explicitly a question, her tone was meant to draw more information.

"An understatement," he said dryly, offering no further insights. His lashes came down and shadowed his eyes as he leaned closer. "Is there somewhere we can retreat to for some privacy?"

"Yes, of course." Her mind riffled through possibilities. The garden? Too exposed and probably too crowded considering the rambunctiousness of the gathering. Her chamber? Too intimate by far, yet her stomach squirmed at the thought. "Ralston's study?"

His expression was less of a smile and more a baring of teeth. "Perfect. You go first. It would not do to be seen together."

"You know where to go?"

"I do." He brushed a kiss along the back of her gloved hand before melting into the crowd at the back of the ballroom. The barest hint of heat touched her skin through the satin.

A moment of disquiet held her still, but she brushed it aside. If no one observed them leaving, no one would know they were alone together. Anyway, he was not eager to be caught either. As casually as possible, she made her way up the stairs, bypassing the retiring room to continue to the end of the hallway and the duke's study. For a second that felt much longer, she worried it would be locked, but the latch gave with a well-oiled quiet snick, and she slipped inside.

It was dim. The only light came from a fire long burned to

embers. She shuffled across the floor to the windows, pulling the draperies open to let in the moonlight. The back window looked over the garden, and she opened the sash enough to feel the night air on her face.

While she could smell London's soot and sewers, it was the earthiness of loam and the sweetness of the flora that made her take another, deeper breath. She missed tramping through the countryside collecting cuttings for her tinctures and poultices. While her last act was one of ignominy, she hoped those she'd helped through her work balanced the scales.

If only she'd been more circumspect with her power, she might still be home, her feet planted on familiar ground instead of stumbling through the unknown, her future a mystery. Or perhaps a tragedy.

The soft latch of the study door closing brought her around. Although the figure standing there was cloaked in black from his mask to his shoes, she had no doubt it was Damien Northcutt. He wasn't her savior. He might even be her downfall, but she couldn't make herself care about the future. A moment in his arms would be worth the coming heartache.

8

Damien's heart skipped along in his chest, too fast and furious for the mild subterfuge he was engaged in. He had kept many nighttime assignations with ladies and escaped more fractious games of chance than he could count. Never had he felt this unsettled though.

Madeline turned from where the moonlight glinted off the jewels of her mask and the breeze stirred her hair against her nape. She was lovely, yes, but even more, she was... alive. He wasn't sure how else to describe her. She was the sun, full of light and warmth, and he the moon, comfortable in darkness. They should not coexist in the same sky, yet here they were, their orbits coming ever closer.

Her invitation to Ralston's study had presented him with an unexpected opportunity to search out information he could later use, but now that he was here, he couldn't seem to loosen his grip on the door latch and force himself toward the desk. His heart thumped, and his usual cool thinking was hot and muddled.

She didn't seem to wrestle with the same indecision. She swept toward him in a rustle of skirts and the scent of flowers, not stopping until she had twined her arms around his neck.

"Damien." She breathed his name on a sigh before rising to her toes to brush her lips over his.

She did not play the games he was used to. The games he counted on winning through cunning and logic. Yet he didn't feel as though he were losing when her warm curves pressed into him. His clutching hand loosened from the latch to instead fist in the skirts at her hip to draw her closer.

"You are reckless," he whispered before claiming her lips in a long kiss that left them both breathless.

"I have nothing to lose." Her head fell back to reveal the pale column of her neck.

She gave him no choice but to slide his lips across the soft, scented skin along her jaw to nuzzle her ear. "You have every-thing to lose. Your innocence for one. Your reputation for another."

She tensed in his arms but did not pull away. "Losing one doesn't have to affect the other."

Was she implying the unthinkable for a young woman in search of a husband? Unthinkable except he had thought of little else but bedding her since their meeting in the garden. First as a means to ruin Ralston's plans for her and later because he lusted for her night and day. He could at least admit that much to himself.

He cupped her nape and lifted her chin with his thumb even though it was too dark to read her expression. "How did your husband hunt proceed this evening?"

"Fair, I suppose. Thornbury has subtly planted information about my dowry. It has made some of the more fastidious gentlemen overlook my heritage and oddness."

"Are there disappointed men even now who are expecting to partner you on the dance floor?"

"Throngs of them, I'm sure. My dance card was full."

A bolt of satisfaction had him tightening his hold even as he stifled an answering smile at the humor in her voice. "Good. Let them pine for you while I enjoy your favors."

He walked her backward until her bottom bumped into the large desk dominating Ralston's study. Unable to help himself, he cast a glance over Madeline's shoulder, but the duke had cleared the surface of papers and had left only two ledgers stacked neatly in front of the chair on the far side.

A tug on his cravat had him returning his attention to the woman who had parted her legs to allow him greater access. He sat her on the desk and pushed the fabric up past her knees to gather like rippling ocean waves.

With hands that trembled slightly, he ran them up her silk stocking-covered calves to rest on her knees. She pitched back and propped herself on her hands. The position tightened her bodice, and her quickened breaths made him pray her breasts would make a bid for freedom.

"Are you going to defile me?" she asked with more enthusiasm in her tone than was befitting a lady, which of course only made him more eager to do just that.

"On a duke's desk? Steps away from a ballroom full of the crème of the ton?" He inched his fingers higher until they reached the ribbons holding her stockings up. He grazed his fingers along her bare skin. Shivers erupted along her thighs.

"You make it sound quite thrilling. We must take advantage of our opportunities."

"You would not prefer a slow seduction in a soft bed and no risk of interruptions?" He tightened his grip on her thighs and leaned forward to kiss the top curve of her right breast. His knees wobbled slightly.

"Of course, but I don't have that luxury if I want you, do I?"

She wanted him. He knew it, but it hit differently hearing her say it aloud. He had been born a secret and kept a secret. It meant something to be openly wanted.

She continued, unaware of the tumult of feelings churning in his chest. "If you called upon Thorn House, I would welcome you."

"I cannot do that," he said hoarsely.

"I know you are not interested in anything as mundane as marriage to a woman such as myself. I would not expect it of you. Not even afterward..." She touched his cheek below his mask.

She had misunderstood him, of course. He would have loved to call on Madeline and woo her with flowers and pretty words. Marriage? He wasn't sure that would ever be in the cards for him, but to be able to make asides and laugh together and dance in front of the ton without stares and condemnation would be a dream. The sort of dream he never allowed himself to nurture unless unconscious in sleep and unable to stop the churn of his wants and needs.

He could take what she offered. No guilt required. No strings. He could unbutton his trousers and drive himself inside her. This ill-advised, all-consuming desire would be slaked, and he could return to ruining Ralston after he ruined Madeline.

Dammit. There would be guilt after all even if no one else found out. He could feel it like gutter muck coating his soul even before he acted on her invitation. She deserved more than a quick fuck on a desk. However...

Could he give her a taste of pleasure without taking her maidenhead?

He hooked a finger in the bodice of her gown between her breasts and tugged the fabric gently down. She shimmied her shoulders to help his effort until it sat beneath her breasts, her arms caught by the cap sleeves. Her stays were cut low, and it was a simple matter to free her breasts.

What was not so simple was controlling his reaction. His cock throbbed and begged to be freed in kind. He gripped the edge of the desk on either side of her hips to keep himself from acting on the urge. Her breasts were lovely. Full and round, they were tipped by nipples already peaked and eager.

"Damien?" In her voice was the uncertainty of the innocent. One of her hands fluttered over her chest in an attempt to cover herself. As intelligent and brash as she could be, this was a new experience and one she needed guidance through.

"You are beautiful." With his hands still braced on the desk, he leaned in to nose her hand away and brush his lips across one peaked nipple. Her sharp intake of breath was gratifying.

With his ardor back under his control, he cupped her breasts and nuzzled first one and then the other, finally pausing to flick her nipple with the tip of his tongue.

Her back arched, her breasts an offer to him. "That feels quite extraordinary."

"This is only the beginning of the pleasures I can introduce you to." Why did he feel like a wolf herding a lamb closer to the cliff's edge?

"Knowledge is power, and there is nothing I hate more than being ignorant." There was no uncertainty in her pronouncement, and his guilt was overshadowed by her eagerness.

"I would be honored to be your teacher in this." He sucked her nipple into his mouth, his tongue lashing the point. She squirmed closer, her knees clamping his hips, and threaded her gloved fingers through his hair.

"This is beyond anything I've read about," she said breathlessly.

He lifted his head only long enough to ask, "What sort of books have you been reading, my sweet?"

"Nothing *too* scandalous."

He chuckled before sucking her other nipple deep. He straightened and stroked his fingers over her breasts, lightly pinching her nipples simultaneously. "But a little scandalous?"

Her hips jerked closer as if her instincts knew exactly what she needed. Was she wet with desire? He must know. He slipped one hand up her thigh. Like most ladies she did not wear pantalets under her gown, which he very much appreciated in this moment. His fingers brushed against the soft hair of her mons.

She tensed and grabbed his biceps. He stopped with one

hand squeezing her breasts and the other so close to her core he could almost feel the dampness.

"I thought you were going to..." Her voice petered out into a whisper, "...defile me."

"I am not going to fuck you on my—" Dear Lord, he'd almost said "father's desk." "I can give you pleasure without defiling you."

"Fuck me." She repeated his words almost contemplatively but continued to clutch his arms. "That is crude, yet I can't deny I find the sentiment titillating. Is that shocking?"

"Your desire is natural."

"If you're not going to fuck me, then what are you going to do?"

Hearing the raw language fall from her plump lips was making it difficult to stay on the semirighteous path. "I would like to touch you, stroke you, bring you pleasure with my fingers. You will experience *la petit de-mort*."

"*Mort?* Doesn't that mean death?"

"Indeed. You will die from pleasure."

"That sounds intriguing." She was breathless.

"May I?" he asked.

Her grip on his arms eased, and she skimmed a hand up his shoulder to grip his nape. "Yes."

His fingers made contact with the silky, very wet folds of her core. His knees trembled, and he shifted his feet farther apart to brace himself. The motion pressed her legs wider.

He explored her folds, finding her clit and massaging it firmly with his thumb. Her body had more than readied itself for his cock. His fingers felt like a poor substitute. He slipped the tip of a finger inside her, not daring to press too deeply. She gasped and tilted her pelvis to allow him even greater access.

He didn't deserve her trust, especially as he had not told her the truth behind the animosity between him and Ralston. Still, what was happening between them was the most honest moment he had experienced in years. All he could focus on was their combined wants and needs. That was truth.

He continued to massage her clit. Her breaths came faster and turned ragged. She squirmed with what he recognized as frustration.

She needed more. So did he.

He surrendered and fell to his knees. Before she could react to his sudden action, he replaced his fingers with his mouth and feasted. She tasted divine. Sweet and earthy and intoxicating.

"What are you—? Oh!" She cut off her own question and slumped back against the desktop on her elbows.

He curled his fingers into her buttocks and held her to his mouth, her legs resting on his shoulders. He alternated between lashing her clit with his tongue and nipping it with his teeth. When he felt the muscles of her thighs tense and quiver, he sucked her clit into his mouth. She shattered, and he cupped her core, torturing himself by imagining how her pulsing flesh would have felt around his cock.

Only when she went limp did he rise. Her skirts were gathered around her waist, her pussy exposed and plump. Her breasts bobbed with her quickened breaths, and her nipples were peaked into sharp points. The picture she made etched itself in his memory. He planned to revisit it often.

"Did you enjoy your defilement, my sweet?"

She propped herself up on her elbows. "Why are you calling me your sweet?"

The unexpected question made him blink dumbly for a moment before he found a sly smile. "Because that's what you are. Very sweet."

Slowly he raised the fingers that had stroked her in the aftermath and sucked her wetness from them. Her eyes were impossibly wide.

"Would you like a taste?" Before she could answer, he leaned over her and claimed her mouth.

When she flicked her tongue over his wet chin, he nearly

embarrassed himself in his trousers. He would find release alone in his chamber before he washed her off his skin.

While he would have preferred to remain locked away with her the rest of the night, she would be missed, and if they were caught, he did not want her to bear the brunt of his vendetta.

He gave her one last kiss before drawing her off the desk and to her feet. Her skirts swished around her ankles. "It's time for you to return, or awkward questions will arise."

"Awkward questions? I'm sure not I remember my name right now." As he adjusted her stays and bodice, her mouth went in search of his and landed on the corner of his smiling lips.

"Madeline. You must return and act normally."

"That is impossible." Frustration had inched its way into her voice.

"You must put on a convincing act."

"This isn't fair. I want more." She stomped her foot.

"*You* want more?" He guided her hand to the front of his trousers where his erection pressed prominently. "Be glad I have a modicum of self-control."

She didn't snatch her glove-encased hand away but measured his outline. Too much fabric separated their skin. "I would have gladly welcomed you."

The soft huskiness of her admission nearly changed his mind. Unfortunately for his reputation, it would have only taken moments to complete her debauching. And yet he held himself still, both enjoying and enduring her fumbling touch until he couldn't take it any longer. He pushed her hand away and turned her around to neaten her coiffure. Luckily, her maid had used a copious number of pins. He tightened her mask and then checked his own.

"You'll pass muster. If the Duchess of Ralston questions you, blame the dancing and the crush of the ballroom." He led her toward the door.

"Will you claim a dance?"

Instead of repeating his oft-claimed declaration of never

dancing with debutantes, he said with true regret, "I will not be returning to the ballroom. You should carry on interviewing gentlemen as to their suitability for a husband."

Although he'd kept his voice light and teasing, she whirled on him and jabbed a finger in his chest. "You are a bastard for saying such a thing to me after... after..." She gestured toward the desk.

"I am a bastard and a cad and a bounder. I've never pretended to be anything else." He took several steps backward as if the shadows might cover the regret and anger roiling inside him. If his life were different, he would waltz her in front of the ton without whispers or condemnation. It wasn't different. He was quite literally a bastard.

"I know, but—" She tossed her hands in the air before letting them fall limply to her sides, the fight gone out of her. "You have never portrayed yourself falsely. I do appreciate that."

That was not entirely true, but he wasn't in a confessional mood. In fact, it would be best if their acquaintance ended here and now. The risks he was taking were not worth the gain.

"Go now," he said as coldly as he could manage while still nursing a cock-stand.

"Will I see you again?"

It was his chance to sever the chaotic connection. With the word *no* resonating in his head, what came out of his mouth was, "You can bet on it."

9

Madeline didn't arise until nearly noon the next day. Her dreams had been dominated by Damien. She felt like she'd survived a tempest, and her knotted sheets testified to her restlessness.

Damien. His name went on repeat in her head. Dark and dangerous. Her stomach wiggled in a way that was both pleasant and anger inducing. He'd basically kicked her out of the study half-sated, half-frustrated. She had offered herself to him with no expectations, and he hadn't seized the advantage. What did that say about him? What did it say about her?

She had been expecting solitude in the dining room to ponder the implications, but instead, Thornbury, the duchess, and duke were already seated at the table. The duke especially was an unusual sight. Maddie hadn't been in the same room with him more than a half dozen times since her arrival in England. He was a busy man who spent his time in his study or at his club.

"Fix yourself a plate from the sideboard, Madeline, and join us." The duchess issued commands not invitations, picking at her food while opening a stack of correspondence.

Maddie's nerves were of a different sort now, and she bobbled her plate into her teacup when she took her chair. The others had finished, and every clank of her teacup or fork seemed to ring out and increase her awkwardness. No one spoke.

The duchess let out a gasp, drawing everyone's attention. "We have been invited to an intimate house party to celebrate the holidays by the Duke of Bellingham."

Three sets of eyes—the duke, the duchess, and Thornbury—swung to stare at Maddie.

"What do you know of this, Madeline?" the duchess asked frostily. Although, to be fair, the duchess's usual tone would have frozen a lake.

The bite of toast turned into glue in Maddie's mouth. She chewed and took a sip of tea to attempt to wash it down but got strangled and coughed into her serviette. Daubing at her watering eyes, she managed to say, "I know nothing of it, Your Grace. I was introduced to His Grace the evening of the Haversham's ball, and we merely exchanged cursory greetings last evening in the receiving line."

"Perhaps this is an attempt to woo your vote." The duchess directed the comment toward her husband.

With Ralston's narrowed eyes still on Maddie, he said, "We agree on little, and this invitation won't change that."

"Do you think it has to do with... *him?*" Thornbury asked his parents.

The duke and duchess exchanged a glance before turning once more to examine Maddie as if she were an insect under glass. "Bellingham wouldn't be so bold as to invite him as well as us. That would be beyond the pale."

By their tones, the him they referred to might have been the devil himself. However, she recognized the same vitriol in Damien's voice when he spoke of Thornbury. She had assumed her cousin and Damien had crossed swords over a gaming table. After all, Damien wasn't a highflier or an influential member of Parliament. He wasn't even a gentleman.

Not a gentleman, and yet... He had attended Eton. He

moved through polite society and called peers his friends. How and why would a common gambler be welcomed by the ton?

She avoided Ralston on a daily basis because she found him austere and intimidating. For perhaps the first time, she studied him. His aquiline nose and strong jaw were familiar. His dark hair was still thick, although his temples were silver. If Maddie squinted, she could convince herself she was seeing Damien three decades down the road. Except for their eyes... Instead of the hard, cold slate of the duke's eyes, Damien's were as warm as a summer's night sky.

Realization hit her like a punch in the chest, prompting her heart to jolt and beat faster. The duke and Damien were related. A nephew? More likely a son. Illegitimate and unacknowledged. Damien certainly favored Ralston more than his heir, Thornbury. And hadn't Damien admitted as much the night before. He had claimed to be a bastard. Maddie had assumed he'd meant metaphorically, but perhaps...

Her curiosity would have to be appeased later. Even she wasn't so bold as to ask the questions skipping around her head.

"Bellingham left the invitation late. It would not be rude to beg off because we have accepted another." The duchess laid the invitation to the side, but a crinkle appeared between her eyes.

"But we have not accepted another, and they will surely hear we merely retreated to our own estate," Ralston said.

"Then you wish me to respond with an acceptance?" Surprise lifted the duchess's voice high.

Ralston tapped a finger on the table. Usually he was unruffled and unrufflable. One might even say emotionless. For the first time, Maddie sensed agitation behind his stoic mask.

"We must attend. Perhaps the Duchess of Bellingham merely wishes to further her acquaintance with another American. It would appear churlish and insulting if we sent our regrets." The duke sounded more like he had received a sentence of hanging rather than a gracious invitation from one of his few equals in the realm, the Duke of Bellingham.

Thornbury half rose from his seat, leaning on his hands. "It's obvious his hand is in this."

The duchess shushed him. "Your father has the right of it. A refusal would be akin to a cut direct. That would be even more damaging."

"Why?" Thornbury asked with derision. "You are the same rank as Bellingham."

The duke threw his napkin on top of his half-finished breakfast and rose. "Send our acceptance today. We can work the party to our advantage."

"How?" Thornbury had retaken his seat when his father had risen like an animal ceding dominance.

"By announcing your betrothal to Miss Barnes." The duke walked out of the room without noticing the emotional carnage he left behind.

"No!" This time it was Maddie who rose half out of her chair. "It's too soon. I haven't... We haven't..."

What could she say? Their plan to find her someone more suitable hadn't borne fruit yet? The duchess would hardly prove sympathetic to that argument.

Thornbury propped his elbow on the table and his forehead on his fist, defeat written across his slumped shoulders.

The duchess poured herself another cup of tea and sipped, her eyes narrowed on Maddie over the rim. Feeling self-conscious, Maddie sank back onto the edge of the chair.

"Ralston's idea has merit. An announcement would quash any machinations at the house party. I realize the two of you would prefer more time for affection to manifest, but I see no reason to delay the inevitable."

"I can think of one very good reason," Maddie said.

"What's that, my dear?" The duchess's voice was cool and distant.

"I don't want to wed Thornbury, and he most certainly doesn't want to wed me."

"That is not a good enough reason. Not even close." The

duchess daubed the corners of her mouth and rose gracefully. "Marriage is not about love; it's about power and connections and wealth."

Should she encourage Mrs. Courtright to spread her poison? Would that be enough to scuttle an engagement between Maddie and Thornbury? Or was it more likely to lead to a quick wedding?

It depended on how important wealth was to the triad of power and connections. Her father was willing to pay a pretty sum in order to get rid of her. Looking around at the opulence of Thorn House, it didn't seem like the duke needed money, but was something rotten lurking underneath the gilding?

She wasn't standing in front of a clergyman yet. She had time to find a way out. Doing her best to calm her nerves, Maddie said, "Yes, I understand."

Her agreement seemed to mollify the duchess slightly.

Maddie cleared her throat. "I would like to beg a favor, however."

"Yes?"

"Can you wait until the end of the party to make an announcement?"

The duchess's gaze flitted from Maddie to Thornbury and back again. Maddie did not glance over to see Thornbury's reaction. Speaking of power, he had none.

"I suppose we can wait until the final ball to make the announcement. It would make more of a splash then anyway. Then, when we return, we will plan an engagement ball. It will be the most coveted invitation of the season." The duchess seemed to be speaking more to herself than either Maddie or Thornbury. They were merely observers to their future.

The duchess gave a decisive nod and swept out of the room. Silence settled over the room like a pall. Neither she nor Thornbury seemed inclined to break it. Was her life to be endless mornings of silence with this man over the breakfast table? Would they even share breakfast? Or anything else for that matter? Except a bed. The breeding expectations of a ton lady were rarely discussed but well known. An heir and a spare. And the English called Americans barbaric.

Maddie shuddered. She wouldn't allow her life to be reduced to livestock. "We must redouble our efforts."

"What's the point? It's over." Thornbury's mien was pure misery. She ought to be offended.

"No, it's not. We have two weeks to change our fates."

"You will never thwart Mother."

"I refuse to give in so readily. There is still time to find me another suitor."

"The situation is impossible." Shaking his head, Thornbury stood and made his way to the door. He stopped with his hand on the door latch. "But, as you know, I wish to avoid a permanent entanglement as much as you do. I will not hinder any plans you devise."

It was the most she could hope for. She had to get serious. No more daydreaming about Damien, especially now she had her suspicions about his parentage. She did not care whether he was a bastard by birth, but her father would cut her off without a penny.

Her head spun with possibilities. She could elope with another man, although the only one who sprang to mind—Damien—would never consent to whisking her away. For just a moment, she imagined kidnapping him instead. The laugh she had at her own expense was more bitter than expected. She groaned and tapped her forehead as if that could banish Damien from her head.

What were her other options? She could put a post in the paper offering her services as a nanny or governess. If only she knew anything about children. What about joining a traveling show full of freaks and acrobats? She possessed no unusual talent to draw a crowd or coin, unfortunately.

The clock on the mantel struck the hour and made her start. She was due to meet Adriana and her stepmother for a carriage ride in Hyde Park soon. Levelheaded Adriana could offer sage advice.

Maddie changed into a claret-colored walking dress with gold cordage decorating the military-style bodice and the hem. The neck was high and the bodice snug. The rich color suited her and brought a rosiness to her cheeks. While Hyde Park was a poor substitute for the country, it at least offered fresh air and sunshine.

And who knows? Perhaps she would meet an interesting, eligible gentleman. Someone who would appreciate the fact she had interests outside of dancing and embroidery and breeding heirs. A girl could dream.

Before the butler had a chance to open the door for Maddie and her maid, the duchess swept down the stairs to the entry. "Where are you going, Madeline?"

"I was invited to join Miss Coffey and her stepmama for a carriage ride in the park. I'm joining them at their town house."

The duchess narrowed her eyes. "That won't be necessary. Justin will escort you in his phaeton."

Maddie's fingers tightened on her reticule. "No, that's not—"

"Send a footman with word to the Coffey residence that Miss Barnes will no longer require their company," the duchess said to the butler.

The duchess's high-handedness was infuriating, but throwing a fit in front of the servants would only cause talk. She must be patient. It took another half hour for Thornbury to ready himself. Their combined resentments darkened the mood, which was in stark contrast to the blue skies and puffy white clouds overhead.

It seemed as if half of London was out enjoying the lovely weather. Freshly bloomed flowers offered their varied colors and scents as tribute. Maddie couldn't enjoy them. Thornbury was taking out his frustrations on the horses and driving recklessly.

They were perched high, and Maddie clutched the edge of

the seat on every turn. "Stop this instant. You're going to tip us or run someone over."

Thornbury looked like he wanted to whip the horses even faster, but they were approaching a cross path where pedestrians strolled, and even he had to take care.

"I had other plans," he gritted out.

"As did I, you oaf. This was your mother's idea."

"Watch your tongue." There was a hard edge so like the duchess's it took Maddie aback. Thornbury was not kind or funny or particularly charming, but she hadn't thought him cruel. Would bitterness through the grind of years turn him into someone like his mother? Indifference she could bear; malice she could not.

After maneuvering around the pedestrians, he slapped the reins and the horses increased their pace to a trot. The carriage felt like it tipped on two wheels around the next turn. Her heart pounding in her throat, she grabbed Thornbury's sleeve. "Stop right now and let me out. I refuse to perish because of your foolishness."

"Death would offer a satisfactory way out of this mess, wouldn't it?" Thornbury said grimly, but he pulled the phaeton to a stop.

"Satisfactory for you, perhaps," Maddie muttered as she hiked her skirts. Her knees were shaky, but her experience in trees served her well on her clamber down from the high perch to the graveled path.

"Where do you think you are going?" he asked.

"I will find the Coffeys."

"Mother would not approve."

He was right about that. Should she heed the warning in the words? "Don't let me keep you from your plans. What say we reconvene at the entrance in two hours, and you can escort me home as if we enjoyed a delightful outing together?"

His eyes narrowed, but he nodded curtly. "Try not to get into any scrapes."

He rode off without a backward glance. Once she was alone, she slid her bonnet backward a few inches and lifted her face until the sun kissed her cheeks. While the breeze still held a chill, spring had arrived. Her steps grew lighter, and she stopped to examine the blooms on a pink azalea bush, plucking one to tuck into her lapel.

Back home, she would think nothing of taking a walk by herself, but the askance looks she was receiving from passersby made her pull her bonnet forward again and quicken her pace. She was not fast enough. Two dandies crossed to block her path. One was in robin's-egg blue trousers that fit his slim legs too snugly, and the other wore a yellow jacket with a comically high collar. They were attempting to impress through their plumage.

"What do we have here?" The blue-trousered one spoke in a voice full of affectation.

"I would think that's obvious. I'm a lady," Maddie retorted tartly.

The yellow-jacketed young man still had spots on his face. "A *lady* wouldn't be walking on her own. Mayhap, you're looking to sell your charms?"

"I'm not," she said firmly yet couldn't stop herself from adding, "And even if I were, I wouldn't be desperate enough to offer them to either of you."

With three brothers, she had observed certain things about the male species. Men liked to proclaim women were the weaker sex, but it was the male ego that was so easily shattered. Their reaction to such damage was generally not a retreat to lick one's wounds but a lashing out.

"Then perhaps we'll take what we want." The man in the yellow jacket grabbed her arm and yanked her toward a stand of evergreens.

She dug her heels into the gravel and was dragged a few inches. A hearty scream would summon help but also the kind of scrutiny that would infuriate the duchess and possibly bring ruin upon her. She would have to deal with the miscreants herself.

She quit fighting, her body moving closer to the man who held her. She smiled up at him, and her sudden acquiescence made the man hesitate, his brows knit in confusion. She raised her knee, aiming between his legs. With her skirts hampering her movement, she dealt him a glancing blow. Still, he dropped to the ground with a groan.

"And what about you then?" Maddie asked the blue-trousered man, her hands set on her hips. He stared at his friend with his mouth agape.

The clomp of a horse grew close until she could tell it had stopped behind her. Oh dear. The last thing she needed was a witness who would spread gossip. Her only hope was whoever it was had no idea who she was.

Keeping her face lowered, she half turned to ascertain how much trouble she was in. Her gaze settled first on a polished black boot, which led to a firmly muscled thigh in buckskins. She swallowed and continued farther up to observe a deep chest and broad shoulders encased in a tailored navy-blue frock coat.

Damien Northcutt cut a fine figure on horseback. His hat was black and not as tall as some. It shadowed his eyes, but she knew them to be warm and dark. She could see his mouth though, and a bolt of heat shot through her, remembering exactly where it had been the night before. Why hadn't she thought to bring a fan?

Luckily, he hadn't noticed her unladylike perusal of his person because his attention was on the two men. Although compared to the potent masculine energy emanating from Damien, they barely earned the classification of men.

"Are you harmed?" Damien asked without sparing her glance.

"I am not. However, a less accomplished young lady might not have been so fortunate." All of a sudden, she was trembling, but it was difficult to tease out the reason. Shock? Relief? Excitement? Desire? To be certain, it was a confusing stew.

"Look what the doxy did to poor Williams, sir," the blue-trousered man said, pointing to Williams, who was still clutching the vulnerable organ between his legs.

"I knew your wits were dull after I fleeced you at the tables, Manchin, but I underestimated just how stupid you are." The anger in Damien's voice was even more potent because it was icy cold. "The lady is wearing a fine dress in Hyde Park during the fashionable time. What should your conclusion be given the facts?"

"Uh... I think she might be a lady, sir?"

"She *is* a lady, you absolute tosser. I should whip you both, but Williams already seems the worse for wear. Leave now, and if I hear even a whisper of what occurred here, I will ruin you both. Is that understood?"

Damien watched Williams and Manchin stumble away still mumbling their acquiescence. Then he dismounted and grasped her forearms in a gentle hold. "Are you certain you are well?"

"Well enough because of your timely arrival." Her heart rate hadn't slowed, but at least her trembles had abated.

One side of his mouth ticked up in a way that made her want to touch it... with her lips. She couldn't tear her gaze away from the charmingly quirked corner. "I'm not sure you needed me."

"I do need you," she whispered. She blinked as the words squirmed into her consciousness. "I mean, I did need you. Sort of."

"Dare I ask where you learned to fell a man so thoroughly?"

"My brothers. My eldest in particular."

"Ah, of course. You did warn me upon our first meeting. I'd better watch myself."

She hoped he was joking but wasn't sure. She playfully punched his arm. "That's right, you'd better."

He glanced around. "Are you truly alone? Not even your maid?"

"I was with Thornbury, but we went our separate ways. I'm hoping to locate Adriana at the Serpentine." They fell into step side by side, his horse trailing sedately. "I'm sorry to interrupt your ride."

"I much prefer your company to my horse's."

"That is an unusual stance among ton gentlemen."

His laugh made her feel like she had discovered a new species of flora. She would name it Squirmous Tumnous, because that's what hers was doing. A lightness came over her, and her feet skipped as if she could actually leave terra firma.

"Won't the duchess be upset if you return without Thornbury?"

"We are meeting in two hours' time and will arrive at Thorn House together with the duchess none the wiser."

"You hope."

"You're the gambler. What are my odds of success?" She tried to keep her voice teasing.

"Low. The duchess is many things, but dim is not one of them."

A pit formed in Maddie's stomach and weighed her back down. "She wants to announce our engagement soon."

The horse shied as if upset at the news. The beautiful black mare tossed her head, and Damien stopped to stroke her cheek and whisper in her ear. She settled.

"Before the season ends?" he asked, not meeting her eyes.

"At the Duke of Bellingham's house party. Shockingly, we were invited." She shot him a narrowed look. "Did you have anything to do with the invitation?"

"I am an inveterate gambler and rake. Why would you think I would be invited?" He continued to gaze at his horse.

"Because you and Bellingham are friends."

"Even Bellingham wouldn't be so bold as to invite me. I would weaken his position. The house party is a means for him to exert influence in Parliament."

Maddie made a scoffing sound. "Weaken him? He is a duke. Anyway, you are not besmirched, and contrary to your prostrations, you continue to demonstrate you are a true gentleman."

"Oh really? Was I acting the gentleman with my head between your legs last evening?"

A flush raced up her neck and into her face. She gasped and clapped a hand over his mouth, but there was no one to hear them. If anything, it was her strange behavior drawing looks. She dropped her hand and continued walking, keeping her gaze cast down.

"I can't believe you said that," she whispered.

"I thought you preferred to speak frankly."

"I do, but—" Bereft a fan, she used her hand to try to cool her cheeks. "My brothers would kill you and throw me in a nunnery if they were here."

"They sound unreasonable and bloodthirsty."

Maddie laughed at his assessment. "Do you know what we call my eldest brother?" At his raised eyebrow, she said, "Duke."

It was Damien's turn to laugh. "Why?"

"Obviously we have connections to British aristocracy, and Duke is... well, the antithesis of what we thought of as genteel and gentlemanly. He is a bruiser who likes trouble. The opposite of Ralston and Bellingham. In fact, he reminds me more of you." A pang of homesickness hit her with enough force to bring the sting of tears to her eyes. "I miss him."

"Once you marry, you can invite him for a visit."

"Perhaps." She didn't want to think of marriage.

The clop of horses and the sound of gravel underfoot filled the silence between them. She cast several side-eye glances in his direction. His good humor had departed with the mention of marriage as well.

She argued with herself before asking, "Do you really prefer frank talk?"

"I do, but you don't have to tell me how much you enjoyed our interlude. I can still taste your honey."

"You are incorrigible, sir." Her blush had returned and made her feel incredibly out of sorts and gauche. She wanted to wipe the smirk from his face. "Ralston is your natural father, isn't he?"

Damien stopped as if hitting a wall, his horse neighing and shaking his head. "Who told you?"

His nonanswer was answer enough, but she regretted the abruptness of her question. "No one has spoken of it. In fact, I wasn't sure until this moment. I noted a similarity between you and Ralston, and the antipathy between you is too deep for a superficial connection."

"I am not spoken of or claimed because I was a mistake. Everyone's lives would have been better if I hadn't been born." His voice had grown as cold as his obsidian eyes.

Did he really believe what he said, or was he repeating what others had told him? The moment was heavy with portent. With vehemence, she said, "Not my life."

🎴 10 🎴

Damien stared into Maddie's guileless blue eyes. She seemed to have a difficult time accepting that he was a bastard in every way imaginable. Everyone else in her life was using her, including him. He was no better—and probably worse—than Ralston and Thornbury.

As a matter of point, after she'd left him in the study the night before, he'd taken the opportunity to rifle through Ralston's desk. It seemed the duke had made a series of unfortunate investments that had left him in tightened financial straits.

He had attended the masquerade in order to obtain information on his father, yet on arrival, he had sought out Madeline like nothing else mattered. It was unthinkable to allow her to transform from his pawn to his weakness. It had to stop.

Instead, the blackened coal of his heart sparked and heated his chest at her words, and when he spoke, his voice was rough. "If you never saw me again, it would scarcely matter."

She took his hand in both of hers. "That is not true."

Instead of snatching his hand free, he curled his fingers around hers and held fast. "I will bring you nothing but heartache and tragedy."

She sighed and rolled her eyes. "That is absolute nonsense. You sound like one of the melodramatic novels I've read."

Caught somewhere between laughter and frustration, he said, "I'm trying to save you from me."

"I thought we were in agreement. I don't need saving." She thumbed over her shoulder as if marking a point in her favor.

If he dwelled on the incident, he would turn on his heel, track down the two fops, and beat them until they were unrecognizable. The outcome could have been dire, yet Madeline didn't seem cowed. Her confidence in herself was unusual and surprisingly attractive.

Most of the women of his acquaintance looked to him for protection of one sort or another. Although, as he cataloged the women he wasn't romantically or sexually involved with, he came to a different conclusion. They were fierce and strong and, frankly, intimidating. Even the Duchess of Ralston, whom he loathed, was a force to be reckoned with.

"Why are women considered the weaker sex, do you think?" He disentangled his hand from hers and restarted their stroll.

"Because for the most part, we are weaker physically and the world has been ruled by war. Men fight the wars and seize the power. They also write the histories and choose who receives the glory." She linked her fingers behind her back and continued while gazing at the branches overhead. The leaves danced in the crisp spring breeze. "However, there will hopefully come a time where wars do not determine who is in power. It will be intelligence and logic and the ability to promote equality among the classes and the sexes."

"It doesn't sound like you are enamored with our monarchy or peerage."

"And you are?" She raised her brows but didn't wait for his answer before adding, "An accident of birth should not consign someone to poverty or wealth."

He wanted to burn the bloody peerage to the ground. Men like Simon and Drummond would be successful with or without their titles. It was men like Manchin and Williams who were born thinking they could take what and whom they wanted with impunity. Men like his father. His anger was like a river of magma beneath a dormant volcano.

And yet, hadn't Damien himself benefited from the very same system? If the duke hadn't sent him to Eton, he would have become one of the many orphans roaming the streets as sweepers or pickpockets. He would have most likely died before reaching manhood.

"As much as I detest the British system, I must admit to having used it to my advantage. The young bucks have provided me with an ample living thus far," he said.

She tilted her head and looked to the trees shading the path. "You are like the mistletoe we gathered."

"How so?"

"You need an established tree to live on but aren't truly part of it."

"You're saying I'm a parasite?" He was torn between feeling offended and amused.

"Oh no! I didn't mean to imply... I'm so sorry..." A blush raced up her cheeks, and in a smaller, less confident voice, she said, "Mistletoe is only hemiparasitic, if it makes you feel any better. It does rely on photosynthesis for a portion of its energy."

"But it can't live away from a host, can it?"

"No." She bit her bottom lip. "But it's a very useful plant. It has many healing properties. It treats apoplexy and painful joints and heart issues. I kept it cultivated at home to make elixirs."

"In that case, I'll take your comparison as a compliment."

She let out a sigh. "Good, because that's how it was meant."

Their path was intersecting a more crowded thoroughfare. "The Serpentine is not far ahead. You will be safe from here if you'd rather not be seen with me."

"Please accompany me." Her cheeks were still rosy, and tendrils of hair had escaped her bonnet and framed her face. There was no guile in her pretty eyes.

"If you're sure."

A smile was her answer. His horse protested the sedate pace with a chuff and shake of her head, but Damien soothed her with a pat on her neck and a promise for a rousing ride later.

The looks the two of them garnered didn't seem to register with Madeline. She was too busy craning her neck on the lookout for her friend. She pointed. "There she is!"

Madeline quickened her pace, and Damien did his best to keep up, but the graveled walks were becoming more crowded, and his horse was growing skittish. Miss Coffey stood with her stepmama. While he couldn't tell how warm or cool Miss Coffey's welcome would be at his presence, her stepmama looked ready to garrote him. Even worse, she might inform the Duchess of Ralston, who her niece had been with at the park.

"Madeline, wait." When she didn't turn, he said more forcefully, "Miss Barnes!"

She returned to where he had stopped. "What's the matter?"

"My horse is growing restless for her promised ride. Now that you've been delivered to your friend, I will take my leave."

"Oh, but you are most welcome to stay. Adriana would be pleased to see you."

"I really must depart."

"When will I see you again?" The certainty in her voice was unsettling.

"We must hope chance will cross our paths once more," he said noncommittedly.

Of course, as a skilled gambler, he left nothing to chance. Chance was a fickle demon. The note he'd received over his morning coffee had informed him Madeline was expected to join Miss Coffey for a stroll in the park, and instead, he had watched her drive off with Thornbury himself. That had certainly crimped his plans.

The scene with Manchin and Williams had been another chance encounter he couldn't have anticipated. The variables out of his control made him nervous. However, it had all worked out in the end. The time they had spent together had been engrossing. Too engrossing. He was losing sight of his goal. He was beginning to care more for Madeline than his plans to destroy Ralston.

When Madeline reached the Coffeys, she turned back to raise a hand in farewell. He gave her a small bow and forced himself to walk away. Why was it so difficult to leave her?

After all, he would see her again soon as long as Ralston accepted Simon's invitation to the house party. Already anticipation bloomed. There would be ample opportunities to lure Madeline away from the watchful eyes of the other guests. House parties were notorious for mischief.

He wouldn't be an official guest, of course. What he'd told Madeline was entirely true. He was a liability to Simon. Jessica was none too pleased with his plan to stay in one of the estate's follies for the duration of the party, but like many a foolish endeavor, he'd talked Simon into saying yes.

He mounted his horse and rode away, but the tug he felt toward Madeline lingered long after she was out of sight.

addie kept her face at the carriage window, wishing the Bellingham estate to appear over every hill. Dark clouds had encroached the blue skies and squatted low, heavy with rain. A drop splatted on her cheek, a harbinger of the deluge that began moments after.

"Close the window before we all get a soaking," the duchess said without opening her eyes. Her head was resting on the back of the squab, her face tipped up.

She looked pained, and Maddie wondered if she was suffering from motion sickness or was simply bored. Ralston sat next to his wife with a small desk on his legs to compose letter after letter. Surely his penmanship suffered on the rutted road.

Maddie shut the window. At least the passing scenery had offered a distraction from the thick silence in the carriage. Her only consolation was the fact Thornbury was traveling on his own and not arriving until later. The duchess had not been pleased, but Thornbury had somehow managed to piece together the semblance of a spine and defy her.

"This must be miserable for those riding outside," Maddie said. Rain pelted the carriage. The driver and a footman sat in the front and a groom on the back. At least the maid and valet they brought were following inside a second carriage with their luggage. "Should we stop at the next waypoint to allow them to get warm and dry?"

The duchess deigned to look up at Maddie's question, her expression incredulous. "Are you mad? We must arrive in time to dress for dinner."

Maddie opened her mouth to ask if dinner was more important than the servants' health and comfort but closed it and slumped to rest her chin in her hand when she realized the answer would have been a resounding yes from the duchess.

"How much farther must we travel?" Maddie asked after another five interminable minutes.

"As long as we don't find ourselves stuck in muck, not more than another hour," Ralston said.

Maddie hadn't thought the duke was paying attention to anything but his correspondence. He sanded the letter, folded it, and tucked it into a leather case. His gaze rose to fix on Maddie, and the intensity was such that she sat up straighter and smoothed her skirts. It felt like an inspection, and going by the look on his face, she had failed to pass muster.

"Have you received word from your mother or father lately?" he finally asked.

The question was unexpected and unwelcome. Had the duke caught any rumors of her troubles back home? What choice did she have but to bluff her way through?

"Just a brief letter from Mother soon after my arrival."

"And?"

"Everyone is well. My eldest brother, Duke... erm, that's his nickname. His given name is James." She took a breath. "Anyway, he is traveling."

"Does Mr. Barnes have plans to visit England?"

"Not that I'm aware of, Your Grace, but he's not one for correspondence. He's more likely to turn up on the doorstep with fantastical stories of his adventures. I would be most happy to see him though." Homesickness had turned her voice wistful.

The thought of her brother being welcomed into the Ralston drawing room and introduced as Duke Barnes would have garnered a hearty laugh from him. He enjoyed more than a bit of mischief.

"I hope you learn to embrace London and your new family here. Once you and Justin wed, you will be busy hosting events and learning to become a duchess. My son will be an important member of Parliament. You must support him in any way possible." The duke's voice was cold and solemn.

"And you must produce heirs," the duchess added.

"Yes, of course," the duke said as if that went without saying.

The life they plotted was her nightmare. There would be no room for any interests of her own. All she could do was nod because the panic roiling in her stomach made her want to sick up all over the carriage.

"I'm glad we understand one another." The duke turned his attention to the window, but the duchess kept her narrowed gaze on Maddie.

She wanted to hide, but the best she could do was squinch her shoulders to make herself small and turn toward the window to watch the rivulets of rain streak down. By the time the carriage turned onto the long drive leading to the Bellingham estate, her muscles had grown stiff from the tension hanging over them darker even than the storm clouds outside.

It was a relief to disembark from the carriage even if she got damp from the torrential rain. The entry was a flurry of activity with footmen in their silks carrying trunks and hat boxes hither and yon.

The Duchess of Bellingham descended the stairs in a gown of flowing blue that brought out the auburn highlights in her hair. She was very pretty and not much older than Maddie, yet she seemed more polished and much more regal than Maddie could imagine becoming.

The Duchess of Bellingham was also an American by birth, although she had been in England since she was a young girl.

Still, when she took Maddie's hands in both of hers and bestowed a wide smile, the warmth calmed Maddie's frayed nerves. Perhaps she could count the young duchess as an ally.

Maddie trailed their trunks up one side of a curved double staircase. At the top, a footman led the Ralstons down a hallway to the right while the Duchess of Bellingham slipped an arm through hers and swept her in the opposite direction. Maddie cast a glance over her shoulder and caught her aunt's glare. The warning to behave was as clear as church bells ringing on a Sunday.

From the front, the Bellingham's manor house appeared large, but it was even more enormous than Maddie had realized. A wing extended around the corner, making her feel like she was entering a maze she might never find her way free from.

"You will be on a hallway with other unmarried young ladies. Couples will be along the main hallway, and the young men will be sequestered on the opposite side of the house and one floor up. I would prefer not to be blamed for any debauchery, but there is little I can do if the parties are determined." The duchess's tone held a warning. Was it directed in a general way or specifically at Maddie?

"This is my first real house party. Back home, we might spend the day with our neighbors, playing games and whatnot but never the night." Maddie didn't add that no one had a house as grand and fine to host such parties. Her family was considered wealthy and owned a country house and a townhome in the city, but neither compared to the homes of the ton.

Maddie studied her hostess. She was very pretty to be sure, but there was an edge to her demeanor that spoke of a strength under the delicate lace of her dress. Where had her strength been tempered? In the womb? Or in childhood?

On the cusp of letting her curiosity get the better of her, Maddie was wrought speechless at the room the Duchess of Bellingham escorted her into. It was the last room on the hall, cozy and beautifully appointed. A creamy coverlet puffed like a cloud on the four-poster bed, embroidered with blue and pink flowers around the edges.

The rug underfoot was plush, and two blue-velveted chairs sat before a grate already prepped with kindling for the chilly night ahead. A brace of books lined the mantel. The papered walls complemented the delicate embroidery on the coverlet with vines running in neat lines up cream paper.

"The room is lovely." Maddie barely resisted the urge to launch herself into the middle of the four-poster bed to wallow in its softness.

"The room overlooks the garden. My husband assures me the weather will break by this evening. I myself was not blessed with a green thumb, but our master gardener would be happy to give you a tour. There is also a hedge maze beyond the gardens that can be entertaining on a sunny day." The duchess made no move to leave. "Your trunk should be along shortly. Was the trip tiresome?"

Unable to catch herself in time, she said, "The company certainly was."

The duchess's eyes widened, and Maddie's face burst into flame. "Please pardon my loose tongue. I didn't mean—"

"Of course you did." The duchess lost her guarded expression, and her brown eyes twinkled. "I heard from my husband and Mr. Northcutt that you spoke your mind with an ease that is sorely lacking in society."

"Is he here?" The eagerness in her voice betrayed her, but she couldn't help herself. She never would have asked about Damien outright, but since the duchess had mentioned him...

"My husband? I certainly hope so since this was his idea. I would pummel him if he left me to entertain this lot by myself."

Maddie mumbled a few "ums" and "ohs," not sure how to respond.

The duchess's eyebrows lifted. "But you are probably more interested in Mr. Northcutt's whereabouts, aren't you?"

"I mean, not *interested*. At the most a bit curious."

The duchess turned to rearrange the books on the mantel, leaving Maddie to stare at her perfectly coiled hair and straight spine. "He was not formally invited. You are savvy enough to understand why."

Maddie did understand. Inviting the bastard son of one of your guests would create a maelstrom of gossip and ill will. Ralston might be a pompous ass, but he was still a duke and therefore held a great deal of power. "My aunt is curious why the family was invited. Ralston and your husband don't see eye to eye on most issues, do they?"

"They do not, but compromise is important for progress." The duchess moved to smooth the plush throw blanket folded neatly at the foot of the bed. Why was the duchess so restless? "Do you miss your family, Miss Barnes?"

A dagger of homesickness pierced her, made worse by the lingering nostalgia over her brother. "I do. My brothers drove me to distraction growing up, but I miss them."

"I have a brother as well. He's younger and away at school. It is easier to bear now, but when he first left, it felt as if I had lost a limb. I am very protective of him just like your brothers are of you, no doubt."

"Indeed. Too protective by my reckoning." The rueful smile she found did much to banish her sadness.

Strangely, the duchess's restlessness looked more like worry now. "Miss Barnes, I feel I must—"

The door bounced open and a red-faced footman carried her trunk inside, setting it down with a clatter. Galloway, her aunt's maid, was on his heels. "A bath is coming, miss. I'll unpack your trunk."

The duchess inclined her head. "That is my cue to retreat. I will see you at dinner, Miss Barnes."

The duchess left before Maddie could even offer her thanks. Maddie and her aunt would share Galloway for the duration of the house party. Maddie fully expected Galloway to spend the bulk of her time with her aunt, which suited Maddie fine.

Galloway hung dresses in the corner wardrobe and folded her unmentionables into drawers with swift efficiency.

Maddie fell back onto the bed and sighed. The bedding was as soft and comfortable as it looked. She had been left with a disconcerted feeling about her encounter with the Duchess of Bellingham. What had she been about to say?

Chewing over her worry had to wait. The bath arrived, and Galloway informed Maddie she had a half hour until it was time to dress her hair. Maddie enjoyed the brief solitude and soaked, making sure her hair stayed dry. Dinner would offer an opportunity to meet new gentlemen. Without Damien to distract her, she could focus on finding someone tolerable to shackle herself to for the rest of her life.

Maybe she should just drown herself right now. If she didn't succeed, Galloway would finish the job if she returned, and Maddie was still in the bath. After toweling dry and slipping on her dressing gown, she looked out the window.

The rain had stopped as Bellingham had predicted. A small balcony let out from her window. She was on the second floor, but her view was obstructed by a large oak tree. Still, the earthy scents of plants and flowers, as freshly washed as she was, beckoned. She wished she could skip dinner and explore.

Upon first arriving in England, she might have done just that, but it seemed her aunt's decorum lessons had taken root. Maddie shivered at the thought of losing herself to the strictures of society.

Galloway returned just in time to distract her from her morose thoughts. Although she was none too gentle in her ministrations, Galloway had Maddie's hair pinned elegantly in mere minutes. She was dressed and descending to the drawing room well before the gong.

Dinner was a subdued affair. Or as subdued as a dinner for twenty or more could be. Not everyone had arrived, and those who had traveled from London or beyond were tired. On one side of her was a young man whose interests were limited to horses and horse racing. On the other was an older man who was hard of hearing. The result being by the time the fish course arrived, she was silent and wishing herself anywhere else. Would the entire week be this tiresome?

As soon as the ladies retreated to the drawing room, she took the opportunity to escape to the gardens along with a few other guests. Two young women who were obviously well acquainted with one another walked arm in arm, their heads close together. They did not include Maddie in their confidences, and she was left to trail behind them, feeling like ballast. She missed Adriana and their easy conversations.

Maddie stooped to inspect the emerging small pink buds among lush green leaves. It was a tea rose bush. The leaves were veined and slightly rough. The bush itself lacked prominent thorns. Had it been bred in such a fashion? Was this a new type of rose? She plucked one to take back to her room to study closer.

She straightened. The two ladies were rounding the corner of a manicured hedge. She could catch up to them. She *should* catch up to them. Her aunt would not be pleased to find out she had been left alone. With only a small niggling of guilt, she turned the opposite direction and walked deeper into the garden.

The solitude was intoxicating. How did the young ladies live being dogged by maids or footmen or chaperones? Did they not understand what they were missing?

Her parents were many things, not all of them admirable, but they had not been controlling. Perhaps she had her brothers to thank on that score. After raising three rambunctious boys, Maddie had been easy by comparison. She had been allowed to roam the woods and fields around their country home. The silence in which to grow her thoughts and dreams had been something she had taken for granted. They probably regretted giving her so much freedom now.

Solitude was a rare commodity, and she would relish it. She ducked between two hedges into the shadows. The exhilaration of escape and the cool night air revitalized her, and she found herself humming a bawdy tune her brother Duke would play on the pianoforte when their mother went to town to shop and left them with the run of the house. Where had Duke's travels taken him? No doubt his roguish smile was winning him friends wherever he went.

She needed to worry more about herself than her brother right now. A fact that became more immediate when the shadow at the edge of the bush materialized into a man.

12

Damien held up his hands. "I apologize for startling you."

"You didn't." By the way Madeline had taken a step back and clutched her wrap closer as if it could offer protection, he had surprised her at the very least. Her surprise didn't last long. She closed the distance between them. "I thought you weren't invited."

"I wasn't." Only two feet separated them. He was close enough to smell the scent she had daubed behind her ears. Where else did the scent linger? Between her breasts perhaps?

"Does Bellingham know you're here?" she asked.

"He does."

"His duchess?" she asked with more suspicion.

"Yes," he said in the same light tone. Jessica knew and didn't approve, but damned if he would admit that to Madeline.

She hummed thoughtfully. "I believe she tried to warn me, but we were interrupted. Why would she warn me against you? I thought you were friends."

How did she cut directly to the question he preferred not to answer? "We are friends, but she worries one of us will do something foolish."

"Like what?"

Like everything he wanted to do to her—*with* her—because he had no doubt Madeline would be an active participant in whatever foolishness they got up to together. She would bring the same curiosity and energetic playfulness to the bedchamber as she did to everything else. Intimacies between them would be for his selfish pleasure and not for revenge. But it was difficult to untangle the two motivations at this point.

There was more to his desire, yet he couldn't name exactly what he yearned for. Which was why Jessica had fixed him with a disapproving stare when they had discussed his subterfuge.

When he didn't answer her, she asked, "Won't your father be furious when he finds you here?"

"Ralston sired me. He is not a father." After so many years practicing his indifference, he was surprised to hear the bitterness in his voice. He cleared his throat. "With any luck, I won't be seen by him or anyone else. I will not be taking part in the insipid drawing room games Jessica has planned."

"Are you not planning on studying Ralston to determine his weakness?"

It was a valid question. Perhaps he should make plans to feed Simon questions he wanted answered, but heretofore, Damien had only been focused on seducing Madeline back into his web. He hadn't expected to catch her this easily though.

"I would rather study you." He didn't even have to try to work insinuation into the words.

Her blush was evident even in the shadows. "And how will you do that if you don't plan to take part in the house party?"

"I intend to lure you away every chance I get." Although he declared his intentions in a teasing tone, he was being entirely honest.

"Easier said than done considering how closely the matrons watch us." She laughed and waved a dismissive hand toward him.

"No one is watching you now," he said.

"Only because of my own recklessness."

THE COURTSHIP CALCULATION

He was counting on that very trait to aid his efforts.

They strolled to the edge of the gardens where the plants and flowers met a manicured lawn. Jessica had planned archery and croquet for her guests as long as the spring rains didn't force them into charades every day.

"Is Ralston your only family?" she asked.

Damien hesitated, not relishing the change in subject, but he supposed there was no harm in telling her the truth. "I have an uncle. My mother's younger brother. He is in service."

"He is still in service?" She glanced over at him with a hint of accusation.

Damien held up his hands. "I've tried to talk him into retiring and taking up residence with me, but he'll hear nothing of it. He is Lord Drummond's London butler."

"Do you see him often?"

"As often as I can. Drummond is often in the country, and his father, Earl Winder, has been on health sojourns, which leaves my uncle with time on his hands."

"I thought Ralston sent you to school? Isn't that how you and Bellingham became friends?"

Her questions stirred old memories. Memories he did his best to suppress. The coldness of the stones in the tiny room in the church where he had lived with his mother. Sitting next to his mother's body in shock and fearful of being sent to a workhouse for orphans. Workhouses were a consignment to hell.

"My uncle saved me from the workhouse, but he couldn't keep me with him. He was only a footman at the time. I'm not sure if my uncle threatened Ralston or if somehow Ralston found a shred of decency in the moment, but he promised to see to my education."

An owl broke the silence before she did. "I'm sure your uncle would have kept you close if he was able, but he couldn't give you what Ralston could."

A deep wound he had plastered over oozed feelings of abandonment and grief as though a quarter century hadn't passed.

From his heart to his mouth came truths he had never put into words. "I should be grateful, I suppose. But I'm not. I was so angry with my uncle for washing his hands of me. Angry at Ralston for shipping me off to Eton without even a word of kindness or sympathy for the loss of my mother."

No one had wanted him. He had been a burden to his mother, his uncle, Ralston. Something to be endured or dealt with or ignored.

Maddie's hand brushed his. His fingers unfurled as if she offered water to a thirsty bloom. She weaved their fingers together and squeezed. "It was not fair."

"What was not?"

"All of it. Your uncle was young and without prospects. Unable to care for a child. I'm sure if you asked him, he would tell you how much he wished to keep you. He was doing what he thought best to secure your future. You have done well on the path he set you on, haven't you?"

"I suppose." He had much to be thankful for, and yet he nursed an unhappiness that had been with him since he could remember. "Even so, I will never forgive Ralston for tossing my mother to the wolves of London after she was ruined."

She stopped him with a tug on his hand. "Women should not be solely judged for a sin that is equally shared at the very least, but it is the way of the world. Even in America."

Her gaze slipped away. If he was reading her at the card table, he would name the emotion guilt. In her voice there was the bitterness of knowledge. A protectiveness reared. He took her chin between his thumb and forefinger and forced her to meet his eyes. "Has someone overstepped and treated you without decorum, Madeline?"

"Besides you? No. The incident didn't involve me directly." Her expression was rueful and secretive. "What is that?"

He followed her pointing finger to see the burnished white stone of the gazebo at the edge of the lawn. The hedge maze stood starkly dark and forbidding beyond it. He recognized her

attempt to steer the conversation elsewhere and would allow it—
for now. "Perhaps you'll tell me how you were involved another
time. Would you like to see the gazebo? I believe we should leave
the maze for another time."

"I would." She would have led them straight across the open
lawn, but he steered them to the edge to keep on the gravel path
and near to the line of fruit trees to offer as much concealment
as possible.

"I have often ruminated on the question of sin." She plucked
a leaf from the limb of an apple tree and traced the veins with
her finger.

"I hadn't thought you a particularly pious lady." At her raised
brows, he gave a laugh. "That was meant as a compliment, by the
way."

Her laugh was husky. "I suppose after our evening in
Ralston's study I can hardly claim the moral high ground."

"Do you regret it?" He kept his voice light, but his shoulders
tensed.

"Not at all. I suppose that brands me a woman of easy virtue,
but I would prefer to view it as collecting experiences of the
natural world." Her smile made him feel gooey inside. "In fact, I
would question whether it is even a sin."

"The *it* being lying with a man out of wedlock?" Once again,
she had surprised him.

"In the natural world, animals mate whenever they feel the
biological urge. The goal is to produce offspring. Obviously." She
shrugged as if this fact should be common knowledge among the
debutantes vying for husbands. "Can following one's natural
instincts really be sinful?"

"Have you shared these beliefs with your morning callers?" he
asked dryly.

She rolled her eyes toward him. "I have learned not to speak
my mind in polite society."

"Am I not polite society?"

"If you were polite society, you wouldn't be skulking around gardens outside a house party you weren't invited to luring young women to sin."

He chuffed a laugh. "Very true."

She stopped along the path to examine a bush with large green leaves and small white flowers. "I can't wait until I can explore Bellingham's gardens in the day."

She pulled back, but a branch had snagged her hair. Her jerk only managed to tangle the elaborate cluster of curls.

"Oh bother. I do not enjoy fashionable hairstyles," she muttered.

He fought another smile and lost, surrendering with surprising ease. "Let me free you."

Did he have to move within a hairbreadth in order to untangle her from the dastardly branch? Certainly not, but it was delightful to be standing so close to her. Her scent reminded him of a spring garden—roses and evergreens and earth. It was intoxicating.

"Your theory is not entirely correct, you know," he said softly. He plucked the pins out on the pretext of freeing her but tangled his fingers in the thick, soft locks, trapping her as surely as the branch had.

"What theory is that?" The breathless response was gratifying.

"Mating between a man and a woman is not always about producing a child."

"No?" She lifted her face to his, her head settling into his palm with a trust he did not deserve.

"It can merely be about satisfying a hunger with unbearable pleasure." He lowered his face to hers and skimmed his nose alongside hers, not quite letting his lips touch her skin. "I could taste your hunger on the duke's desk."

"Your hypothesis must be tested." The hitch in her voice supported his theory, but he was more than happy to play along.

It was with a smile on his lips that he lowered his mouth to hers. Their kiss in the garden the night they met had taken him by surprise. He had been aware of the other couples milling about and the consequences of being caught.

Tonight they were alone. He could sink into her mouth and take his time. Any other woman, even experienced ones, might play coy, but not Madeline. Her enthusiasm outpaced her experience, but he had a feeling that wouldn't be the case for long. Her arms found their way around his neck, her fingers into his hair. She squirmed closer, and a jolt of arousal had his cock hard in an instant.

While one hand cupped her head, he skimmed his other hand to her bottom, fitting her closer, his erection cradled against her soft belly. He tried not to think how soft and tight and wet her grip would be if he could sink his cock inside her. Would she even protest if he hiked her skirts up and tested her will?

Instead, he swept his tongue against her lips and pressed for entry. She welcomed him with a moan that came from deep within her. He was not surprised when her tongue sparred with his and then tentatively delved between his lips. She was forever seeking more from life.

He was happy to offer encouragement, nipping her bottom lip playfully before sucking the soft flesh. She was on tiptoe and attempting to get even closer. He squeezed her bottom and her back arched, her wrap falling away and revealing the plump, pale curves of her breasts above her gown.

He trailed his mouth down her neck, dropping tiny kisses along the way. Tracing the tip of his tongue along her neckline left her gasping for breath.

"Are you hungry?" he asked.

"Yes. Are you?"

He had not expected the question in return. Even more surprising was the hand she trailed to the front of his breeches. His hips bucked against the pressure. "I'm starving."

"You satisfied me on the duke's desk. I would like the chance to do the same for you." She laid soft kisses along his jaw. The sensation was sweet and hot and nearly undid him.

He should take her back to the house, give her a chaste kiss on the forehead, and send her to her room. The one thing he shouldn't be doing is considering her offer.

Madeline was the most dangerous kind of woman on earth— a curious one.

He took her hand and led her toward the gazebo. She didn't resist. In fact, by the time they reached the three steps leading inside, she was ahead and pulling him into the shadows.

The gazebo was meant for picnics or to shelter from a sudden rainstorm. It was not meant for lovemaking. The floor was oak planks and the pillars white stone.

He spun her around and settled her back against his front. Her head settled into the notch of his neck, and her hand came around him to clutch the back of his thigh. He grabbed her skirts and lifted.

"Let me touch you again. I want to satisfy your ache." His lips were at her temple.

"Stop." Her sudden tension drew her away from him.

He stilled. Was she entertaining second thoughts? Could he blame her? Why would she throw away something so precious to society as her innocence on a blackguard like him?

13

It felt selfish to allow him to bring her unspeakable pleasure a second time without giving him the same in return. Maddie looked over her shoulder. His face had blanked of emotion. For a moment, he appeared a stranger, and it filled her with disquiet.

"Life can be unfair, but this doesn't have to be," she said softly. "I don't want to take selfishly."

A warmth stole over his expression and lifted the corners of his mouth. "Touching you is a gift. Allow me the pleasure."

"But—" Her argument was cut off with a gasp when he notched his pelvis snuggly into her bottom and rocked. "Is that your cock?"

"Miss Barnes!" His scandalized exclamation escaped on a guffaw. "Where have you heard such language?"

"My brothers didn't realize I eavesdropped on occasion." Her voice was embarrassingly breathless. "You feel rather hard."

"Rather hard?" he murmured in her ear before nipping her earlobe and grinding his hips against her.

A shiver went through her body, but she wasn't cold. In fact, her skin was flushed and heated, and her blood raced through her veins. "Very hard. Incredibly hard. Like an iron bar in fact."

"It is a testament to your beauty and power over me." He glided his hands up the outside of her thighs, drawing her skirts higher.

In anticipation, she shuffled her feet apart and clutched the rail tighter, the satin of her gloves catching on the grain. Had one bout of pleasure with him already trained her body to get what it wanted? It was a question for another time. Her brain was too busy processing the stimulus from his touch.

His forefinger slipped through her core with the lightness of a butterfly. She didn't want to complain about his gentleness, but a knot of desperation expanded in her chest. She squirmed her bottom even closer against him. "Are you going to put your cock inside me this time?"

His hand stilled, which was the opposite of the reaction she wanted. "Do you want me to?" he asked.

The longing to be filled by him was animalistic. Animals didn't care about tomorrow's consequences, and neither did she. "Yes."

He hummed, pressed his lips against her neck, and instead slipped the tip of his finger inside her. It was not nearly enough. "I've told you already that you deserve more than a rutting."

"What's the difference between your finger and your cock?"

"Several inches in length and width, love."

Instead of scaring her, the thought spun her arousal higher. She reached behind her to clutch his hip. "But you are ruining me either way, aren't you?"

He drew in a long breath before saying, "You are a temptress, but I will not fuck you here."

"But you will fuck me? When? Where?" Later she could be mortified at the begging tone of her voice, but she was under his spell. She was coming to understand how easily a woman could fall prey to a man. How vulnerable she could become to his whims. She wanted to be strong and deny herself the pleasure he could bring her. Instead, she grabbed his wrist and pushed his hand farther between her legs.

His other hand went to her bodice and slipped inside to cup her breast. The gentle squeeze spiraled pleasure to her core. He hadn't answered her question, but she would have to revisit it later when her thoughts reorganized themselves.

"Will you kill me again?" she asked.

His laugh was husky. "Do you mean experience *la petit de-mort?*"

"Yes. That. Again."

His thumb moved to circle the loci of her need, but before a satisfied sigh could escape, he reentered her with a finger. This time he didn't tease her with the tip. Slowly, but inexorably, he slid deep inside her. The fullness didn't entirely satisfy her craving, but it was enough. For now.

He nibbled on the side of her neck while one hand teased her breast and the other was driving her mad between her legs.

"You are very coordinated." What on earth was she babbling about? Her ability to control her thoughts and tongue had disappeared.

He hummed a little laugh against her neck. "I only wish I had more hands to touch you with."

Her imagination went askew. "I suppose that's why orgies are so popular."

He lifted his mouth from her skin, but the finger between her legs drove even deeper, drawing a throaty moan from her. "I hesitate to ponder how you know about orgies. Surely not from your brothers."

"A book on ancient Greece mentioned an orgy but not in any great detail. I had to research them. Have you ever been to one?"

"No."

She glanced around at his profile to see his brows raised.

"You seem surprised," he said.

"I suppose I am after your repeated warning about how debauched and ungentlemanly you are. It seems to me a true blackguard would be less concerned about my pleasure and more concerned about fucking me." Using the naughty language was becoming less embarrassing and more arousing.

"I could ruin you with my cock in ways you can't even imagine." His voice edged toward a growl.

"I realize you probably mean that as a dire warning, but all I hear is a promise you refuse to fulfill."

"For tonight, let me pleasure you with my fingers."

She nodded and spread her legs wider. "If it will feel like what you did on the duke's desk, I am selfish enough not to deny myself."

The fullness intensified. Had he added another finger? She lost the breath to ask when he began pumping his fingers in and out of her. The friction and pressure made her feel like her skin was too tight and uncomfortable. Did she want him to stop, or did she want more? It was even more intense than in Ralston's study. While he wasn't being rough, he wasn't being gentle either.

"I feel strange," she said.

"Tell me." The command was given in a husky voice.

"Like my body is too small to contain what I'm feeling. Like I might break apart."

He hummed as if he had some understanding but only redoubled his attention on her body. He pinched her nipple and pressed his thumb more firmly against where she was most sensitive.

"Let go. I've got you," he whispered.

Her trust in him was absolute. Even as she recognized the danger, she surrendered. The pleasure that had been winding tighter and tighter inside her unspooled. She bucked against his hand, any sense of self-consciousness or embarrassment at the moans or movements wiped away.

He eased his fingers from her channel and righted her skirts. She was thankful for the steadying arm he kept around her waist. She turned in his arms and peered up at him.

He spoke first. "It is time to—"

"—give you the same pleasure." She didn't give him the chance to finish.

"That's not what I was going to say." His voice held notes of apology and regret.

She didn't want either emotion to interfere with the warm feelings coursing through her. "I know."

He laid a too-chaste kiss on the tip of her nose. "You should return to your room. What if your maid alerts your aunt?"

"My aunt and I are sharing Galloway, and I already told her I wouldn't be needing her this evening. I am perfectly capable of getting myself into a night rail. Or perhaps I'll sleep without any clothes on." She slid one hand to his nape and the other to the disks of his fall.

Her satin gloves were a hindrance in countless ways, but in this moment, they were making it impossible to maneuver the disks free.

"You cannot, Madeline," he said in a gentle but regretful voice.

"I can sleep in the nude if I wish it, sir." She would play obtuse to prevent from being deterred from her goal.

She sidestepped and reversed their positions so he was boxed between her and the wooden rail. Without breaking eye contact, she peeled off one glove and dropped it to the floor.

"What are you doing?" The question came out hoarsely. He took a step back, bumped into the rail, and grabbed hold, half sitting.

She removed her other glove, taking her time, tugging at each finger before she stripped it off and it joined its mate at their feet.

"That's better." She closed the distance between them, laying her hands against his chest.

He flinched. For the first time, uncertainty overshadowed his confidence. The confidence wasn't a facade. He had to possess more than his fair share in order to make a living at the gaming table. The uncertainty gave her a hint of the boy he'd once been, tossed in the tempest of the world with no control.

The tears that stung her eyes were unexpected and not welcome. If he got a whiff of the tenderness growing inside her for him, he would run to catch a ship to another country.

She was beginning to form theories about him that might prove to be true. He had been left and abandoned by everyone—his mother, his father, even his uncle. Accepting love was too risky, so he only allowed himself the most superficial of physical encounters with women. For Damien, sex was the only safe way to care for someone.

Or she might be completely wrong. He might be a rake and a scoundrel with no redeeming qualities. Right now she didn't care.

She curled her hand around his nape and brought his face to hers for a sweet yet devastating kiss. He didn't deepen it or try to take control. She walked her other hand toward his waist. This time, even though her fingers were trembling, she slipped the disks free.

He clasped her wrist and held her hand still before it could delve farther south. He swallowed and gazed down at her. "I fear you will be shocked."

"At the size?"

His laugh was more pained than amused. "That is the wish of most men but not what I meant. I am on the edge of control."

"I will anchor you through the chaos."

His breath hitched. He lowered his head to press his forehead against hers the same time he let go of her wrist.

Giving him no time to nurture more excuses, she delved into his breeches. Her fingers brushed over his erection. He was right. She was shocked but in a wondrous way. The skin was velvety soft over the stiff length of him. The tip was flanged, and her thumb brushed over a slit on the very end.

She understood the basics of copulation, of course. She wasn't a ninny-headed innocent who accepted remaining in ignorance. When she had observed mating in the natural world, her curiosity had been piqued.

Women often went to their wedding bed without a clue what was to happen. It was appalling and traumatic for some women. They in turn were initiated in silence, and the cycle continued. No gently born woman of Maddie's acquaintance, her mother included, had offered any useful knowledge.

Finally Maddie had found a woman willing to divulge the secrets. That she had been a woman of ill repute hadn't bothered Maddie. After all, who better than to be experienced with the nature of men.

The differences in hearing about the literal ins and outs of sex and experiencing the act was overwhelming to her senses. Maddie had not expected the give and take of pleasure or the shifting dynamic. She had assumed as the weaker sex, the female would be dominated by the male, but it was Maddie who currently held the power.

She wrapped her hand around his shaft and squeezed. He gasped and shifted his feet farther apart, granting her better access. She was eager to learn the mechanics of what he wanted.

"Teach me what you like." She leaned forward to nip his earlobe and was gratified when he shivered slightly.

"Stroke over the head and down the shaft."

She pulled slightly away from him, not in disgust but so she could see better. Afraid she might hurt his silky skin, she kept her grip soft. He covered her hand with his own to teach her the rhythm he wanted—fast and hard. She was strong and her fingers slightly callused from her work using a mortar and pestle. As she worked him, he plucked the remaining pins from her hair so it streamed over her shoulders.

Her thumb glanced over the tip of his cock. It was wet and eased her strokes. His hands twisted in her hair and forced her face up. Her scalp tingled pleasantly. He kissed her roughly and with little control. She returned his kiss in equal measure.

His hips jerked, and he repositioned her to his side, breaking their kiss. His curse was muffled in her hair. His cock throbbed in her hand and fluid spurt from the slit on top. She gasped but continued to stroke him through his climax.

He sank against the rail as if the act had exhausted him. His cock throbbed rhythmically in her hand. What did he taste like? Damien had feasted between her legs and seemed to enjoy it. She had been told men paid women to use their mouths on their cocks. Was it the done thing for a lady to do to a gentleman? She had no idea, but Damien was no gentleman, and she was only playing at being a lady.

She bent over and swiped her tongue across the tip of his cock. His spend was earthy and slightly salty. She looked up at him through her lashes to judge his reaction and licked her lips. His face was a mask of incredulity, but she could sense a dark satisfaction at her boldness.

Feeding on his reaction, she continued to look up at him and sucked the flanged tip of his cock into her mouth. His head fell back with a moan, and he pulled her away with a firm hand fisted in her hair.

"You are a temptress." He produced a handkerchief and offered it to her.

While she wiped his sticky spend off her hand, he righted his appearance. She avoided meeting his gaze, which wasn't difficult because he seemed to be avoiding hers as well. After the unbearable intimacy of the interlude, the awkward aftermath made a blush intensify through her body. Had she overstepped?

"Was that beyond the pale? Did I offend you?" The questions stumbled out of her mouth.

"It was most certainly beyond the pale, but far from offensive, I found your actions delightfully bold and sensuous." He took her upper arms and gave them a gentle squeeze. Finally she looked up at him but found no judgment. "However, it is time to get you back to your room before your reputation is truly damaged. Did Jessica put you in the corner room by the large oak?"

Maddie nodded, and they began the trek back to the house. Damien scanned the grounds ahead and kept them to the shadows.

"What does it matter? Am I not ruined?" she asked.

"As long as we are not caught, your reputation will remain pristine in society's eyes."

"And if we are caught, your reputation would only be burnished by debauching an innocent. It's not fair."

He glanced down at her with a grim frown. "We established earlier how unfair life is, especially to women."

"Why is my purity more precious than yours?" Even as she spoke with a decided sense of petulance, it was a serious question.

"The peerage has to guarantee blood lines from father to son. Once that is accomplished, the lord and his lady-wife can seek their pleasure with whomever they fancy."

"Breeding is a transaction." She let out a huff to cover the despondency and panic welling up. "I suppose I should be grateful. Once I produce an heir, my obligations are finished. I will only need to tolerate my husband for a short time."

They reached the back corner of the house where her room was camouflaged by tree branches and flanked by a sturdy iron trellis on which nothing grew. It was if it had been designed by a profligate.

She spun on him. "Did you have a hand in which room I was given?"

Was that a blush tingeing his cheeks? It was difficult to tell in the shadows. "I might have mentioned to Jessica how much you would enjoy the furnishings."

"It had nothing to do with a ladder leading to the balcony hidden by a tree?"

"Of course not." Damien cleared his throat. "If you are averse to the climb, I can show you where the servant's stairs are located, but it would be riskier."

She was used to climbing trees. Ascending the trellis was a

simple feat, and she was up and over the stone rail onto her small balcony before Damien could tell her to take care.

She peered down at the dark figure almost hidden under the branches. This wasn't Shakespeare, but the moment did feel dramatic. Their talk of her marriage to someone else had left a dark cloud over their parting. "Goodbye, Damien."

A long moment passed. As softly as the call of a whippoor-will, he said, "Sleep well, Madeline."

14

G alloway informs me you've already soiled the hem of one frock. I repaired to our room early with a headache, but I was told you did not join the group in the drawing room for games and conversation." The Duchess of Ralston was smiling for the benefit of the gathered ladies, but her voice held not a trace of warmth.

Maddie's aunt had cornered her as the group was assembling to take carriages into the village of Everleigh. The gentlemen of the party had left early for a spot of shooting.

"I took a walk in the garden with two of the other young ladies," Maddie said.

Her aunt's gaze sharpened. "Who?"

Oh dear. Maddie tried to recall their names, but introductions had taken place before supper and there had been too many to keep track of. Her time in society had been brief, and even being sponsored by the Duchess of Ralston could not erase the taint of being an American.

"A tall girl with fair hair and her bosom friend. The one who favors feathers."

"Lady Eleanor and Miss Evelyn?" her aunt asked.

No wonder Maddie hadn't been able to keep them straight. "Yes."

"You should continue to cultivate a friendship with them both. It is rumored that Lady Eleanor will marry Lord Egbert Fernsby-Sallow."

"No. You must be making that up." Maddie covered her mouth to keep a guffaw at bay.

Nary a hint of amusement crossed her aunt's features. "Fernsby-Sallow will inherit one of the oldest earldoms in the country. He will be influential. As a future duchess, you must learn to show the proper respect. I will not allow you to bring embarrassment to the Ralston name."

With the pit in her stomach yawning to swallow her amusement, Maddie nodded. Seeking to deter her aunt from discussing marriage or the previous evening, Maddie searched for a safer subject. "It's a lovely day. We should walk instead of waiting for carriages."

"Where you grew up, walking might have been necessary, but here you must make use of the carriage. Your skin has seen too much sun, and your limbs are much too strong for the tastes of an Englishman."

"Men prefer weak women?" Maddie asked without a hint of the bite she felt in her chest.

"*Gentlemen*"—she emphasized the word as if Maddie was a simpleton—"prefer their ladies to be soft and pliant. Your bosom is acceptable, but your limbs are not at all the thing. You will understand once you are married. Less time in gardens and still-rooms is what is prescribed. Your embroidery could use practice."

Before Maddie could voice her dismay, the carriages arrived. In the commotion, she managed to take a seat in a different carriage than her aunt. The morning proceeded much as Maddie anticipated. Long stretches of small talk punctuated by jolts of excitement whenever she glimpsed a tall man with dark hair and followed by disappointment.

If Damien wasn't staying at the Bellingham estate, then it was only logical he had taken rooms in the village. Yet she had not spotted him on the road to and from the village. She had not spotted him at the inn where the group had taken refreshment. She had not spotted him in any of the shops or along the boardwalk. Her frustration was acute.

"Are you not enjoying yourself, Miss Barnes?" The Duchess of Bellingham fell into step beside her as they made their way back to the carriages to return to the house.

"I am enjoying myself immensely." A lie, of course.

"Your frown would say otherwise." There wasn't the same sort of sharp accusation in the duchess's voice that her aunt would wield. In fact, she sounded amused. "Is it the activity or the company that is lacking?"

A slight on either would reflect poorly on their hostess. "Neither. Just my mood, I suppose. I would rather be exploring your beautiful gardens."

"You are a botanist."

Maddie swallowed down a slug of emotion at the casual pronouncement. The typical conversation about her interest usually went the way of a disparaging assessment such as "I heard you enjoy collecting leaves," or "I understand you fancy yourself a gardener."

"I am a botanist. My particular interest is in the medicinal uses of plants, but I enjoy all aspects of flora. There is such a diversity of plant life." She gestured around them before stopping to point at a weed struggling from between the crack of the planks of the boardwalk. "Look at how resilient plants can be. That is chickweed. It may not be noteworthy for its beauty, but it finds a way to thrive in the harshest of environments. A splash of green among the wood and mud."

"I find resilience to be a more admirable trait than beauty, don't you?" the duchess asked.

"Indeed. Usefulness even more so." Most of the party had made it back to the carriages and were being loaded in by the attending footmen. As they continued on, Maddie matched the duchess's unhurried pace. "Medicinal plants are hiding in plain sight in the fields and forests around us."

"How so?"

"*Inula helenium*, for instance, is common. You might know it as elfwort. The roots can be used to soothe sore throats, or tinctures can be used for a variety of skin ailments. Mosses can have healing properties. *Filipendula ulmaria* or meadowsweet can heal sores. Of course, one must be careful. Some plants that heal in small doses can kill if given too much."

Only faced with the duchess's laugh did Maddie realize that playing hostess did not come naturally for her. Maddie could image the house party was an ordeal for the young duchess.

"Remind me not to cross you, Miss Barnes."

"Oh, I would never—" Maddie cut herself off. Except she had used her knowledge to harm, no matter how deserving. She was relieved when they parted ways to climb into their respective carriages.

After arriving back at the house, most of the ladies retired for a rest. The men had returned from their shooting expedition and were enjoying cigars and port while entertaining themselves with cards or billiards.

Without an obligation, Maddie heard the gardens calling. She had almost made it to the garden balustrade when her aunt caught her arm. "You will not go out in this sunshine. Tonight we play charades. You must rest."

"But that's hours away." Maddie was drawn toward the stairs by her aunt's implacable grip.

"You can read or nap." Her aunt escorted her all the way to her room. "I don't want to see you out of your room, Maddie. Is that understood?"

"Yes, Aunt," Maddie said grudgingly.

Maddie entered her room on a sharp push from her aunt. By the time she caught her balance and spun, the door closed in her face.

Being ordered about had never set well with Maddie. Perhaps it was because she was the youngest and a girl and had been overlooked until her bosom had sprouted. She cast a sly glance toward her window. She really shouldn't.

But she would.

It wasn't the first time she'd snuck out from under watchful elders. Plumped pillows under the coverlet would fool anyone who peeked in to check on her. She wished she'd been able to slip one of her tramping dresses into the trunk, but the blue walking dress she wore would suffice.

With bubbling resentment, she tied on a straw bonnet. If she returned with sun-pinkened cheeks, her aunt would know Maddie had defied her. Not a soul was in sight when Maddie descended the trellis.

Freedom made her feel giddy. It had been too long since she had been surrounded by such natural beauty. London held an appeal for those who thrived in bustle and excitement, but Maddie's spirit was fed in the countryside.

While she would have loved to explore the garden and discuss plantings with the head gardener, she couldn't risk word of her escape reaching her aunt, so she set off in the opposite direction toward a copse of hardwoods on the other side of a grassy meadow.

Once concealed in the boughs of the trees, Maddie paused to enjoy the sensations around her. The newly sprung leaves shushed in the slight breeze, providing a backdrop of sound for the scurry of squirrels overhead and the rustle of a small animal in the undergrowth.

Fallen dry leaves crunched underfoot as she navigated the copse. The gentle flow of water tickled her ear. The tree line ended at a narrow stream but not narrow enough for her to leap over. She sat on a flat rock to unlace her boots and roll her stockings off. With her boots tied together and hanging around her neck, she fisted her skirts and lowered herself to the stream.

The cold water licking her ankles elicited a gasp of surprise.

The sun's warmth had tricked her into thinking summer had arrived. A fool's summer, the farmers called it. If one planted their vegetable patch during a fool's summer, chances are a frost would wither the tender shoots.

The water wasn't deep but was fast moving and the stones underfoot slippery. Maddie was careful to test each foot placement before shifting her weight. She was more than halfway across when the rustle of footsteps drew her gaze to the other side.

Damien Northcutt appeared like a fairy king. He wore breeches and a flowing white shirt undone at the neck and with the sleeves rolled to the elbows. His hair was mussed in a way that was charming instead of messy. He carried a rod and a fish basket, which he set at the side of his well-worn Hessians. She stood in the freezing cold water while her feet grew numb staring up at him.

The Damien Northcutt of London was polished and urbane and witty. This Damien was earthy and rumpled and even more attractive than the buttoned-up Damien with his perfect cravat and polished boots.

"Hello," she said inanely.

"I wasn't expecting to catch a water nymph today." He stepped to the edge of the bank and held out a hand.

She juggled her skirts and took a step, reaching for his hand, her gaze fixed on him. The algae-covered rocks left her flailing. Her skirts fell into the water, the current catching them and tugging her even more off-balance.

She grabbed harder at Damien's hand, but instead of pulling her in, he followed her into the water with a curse. She released his hand to try to catch herself, but before she could even prepare for the shock of cold, she was sitting in the stream, the current sweeping her skirts to her knees.

Damien ended up in the water, but at least he wasn't on his arse like she was. The knees of his breeches were wet and splotches of water had glued his shirt to portions of his torso.

The sun haloed his head. All she could do was stare up at him.

"Are you hurt?" He took her by the elbows and lifted her to her feet.

"I don't think so." Her hands and feet were numb, and her wet skirts were stealing the rest of her body heat.

Damien helped her clamber back onto dry land. "You'll catch cold if we don't get you dry and warm."

"Then I should return to the house." She pointed a shaking finger toward the opposite bank.

"It is my fault that you are soaked." It was partly true. If he hadn't been standing there all godlike and knee-weakening, then she would have been concentrating on where she put her feet and probably made it safe and dry to the other side.

"You're wet too. I don't want you to catch cold." Her teeth were beginning to chatter.

"I can't in good conscience send you back in this state. What would you tell your maid?" He made an excellent point considering she was supposed to be snug in her bed. "I'm staying just over the hill."

Once again, she found herself alone with Damien. She couldn't think what else to say than, "Oh."

They crested the hill, and on the other side stood a stone folly in gothic style. Vines wound around the columns, and wildflowers grew right up to the walls. A stone-ringed well with a bucket was only feet away from the stone carved steps leading inside. Apple trees stood sentinel in rows on the far side. Fields and forests surrounded the folly as far as the eye could see. It felt like the dwelling place of some minor Grecian god.

"It's somewhat rustic, I'm afraid, but there is a fire and food and drink while we wait for your clothes to dry."

If her brain was working, he meant her to strip naked. He also would have to change from his wet clothes. "This is dangerous," she said softly.

"Are you implying I won't be able to control my ardor?"

"I have no doubt you can exert an iron will over your urges, but what if I cannot control mine?"

His laugh came from his chest and kindled warmth in her belly. "Your candor is delightful."

"Most find it off-putting."

"That's because the ton as a whole does not place a high value on honesty."

"And you do? Does that mean you do not bluff at cards?"

He shook his head, his lips twisted in a rueful half smile. "You've caught me out, I'm afraid. If we are speaking honestly, I learned at a young age how to lie and charm and convince people I am something I'm not—one of them."

"It must be difficult to have to pretend all the time."

"There are some I don't have to pretend with."

"Bellingham?"

"Yes, and a handful of others." He led her up the steps and inside the folly.

Gauzy white draperies hung over wooden rafters under a ceiling that soared overhead. On a dais in one corner stood an enormous four-poster bed piled high with pillows and blankets, all in white. The room gave the impression of the light airiness of a cloud but retained a shadowy chill even with the coals burning in the hearth.

The fireplace was located close to the bed, and Maddie walked over to gather what warmth she could. "It must get cold at night."

"Under the covers and with a fire blazing, it is quite cozy." He knelt to stoke the embers and feed it fuel. Soon enough a proper blaze enveloped her in warmth. "Get out of those wet clothes." He handed her one of his shirts and a blanket. When she hesitated, he asked cheekily, "Would you like me to assist you, or shall I wait outside?"

"Outside please." She tried to keep her voice prim when she really wanted to ask him to stay even though she was capable of undressing herself.

He bowed and retreated. Her fingers were not as nimble as usual, and she fumbled with her lacings, but she peeled off the layers of wet frock and petticoat and chemise and dropped his shirt over her head, already feeling warmer. She dragged two wooden chairs close to the fire and laid her clothes over them to dry. Luckily, her boots had escaped a soaking.

His shirt fell almost to her knees, and even though she tied the neck closed, it slipped down one shoulder. After wrapping herself in the downy white blanket, she went to open the door to invite him back in.

"You should get out of your clothes too."

"Is that an invitation?"

She chuckled. "I'll wait outside as is proper."

"You don't have to," he said with a dark edge, holding her gaze.

She opened her mouth to respond but decided nothing she could say would make any sense with the jumble of her thoughts. She slipped outside and tightened her hold on the blanket.

Dark clouds had spun up on the horizon. Spring weather was unpredictable and variable. A moment of panic had her heart racing. Could she beat the storm back to the manor house? She made it halfway down the steps when she recognized her foolishness. If she were seen barefoot and in nothing more than Damien's shirt, her reputation would be worth nothing. Anyway, walking back in a chilly rain in already wet clothes might lead to a lung infection.

Her aunt would probably prefer her dead to ruined. Thornbury would have a tragic story to share with any rich, young ladies he pursued. After all, they weren't formally engaged—yet—so there was no need to formally, or informally for that matter, mourn her. A laugh escaped at the absurdity.

"What do you find amusing?" Damien asked.

Maddie swung around, her hand over her heart. She hadn't heard him join her. His dry breeches hugged muscular thighs like a glove. They were well-worn and looked buttery soft. His shirt was a twin to the one she wore and hung untucked over his hips. His feet and calves were bare. She stared at his hairy limbs and large feet.

Of course, she'd seen her brothers in a state of dishabille many times, but she'd never taken notice of their particulars. Her stomach had certainly never dipped like she was in an out-of-control carriage.

She pressed a hand to her belly and turned away from him to look at the darkening sky. "It's going to storm."

"Yes," he said simply. After a moment, he asked, "And that's funny?"

"No, it's actually very inconvenient. I was wondering if I should try to beat the storm back to the house and risk catching a chill. I have a feeling my aunt would prefer me dead over ruined."

"That's not amusing. I don't want to even think of you ill."

She felt his warmth before he actually touched her, sliding behind her and wrapping an arm over her chest. Her body vibrated with nerves and awareness. With a clarity that belied her inexperience, she understood what would happen if she didn't run for the house right this second. If she followed him back inside the folly, it would earn its name this day.

"What do you want from me?" Her voice was barely a whisper. Yearning and fear tangled.

His chest expanded against her back in a long sigh. "I enjoy your company very much."

It wasn't a proper answer, but what did she expect? A marriage proposal? Even if he did offer his hand, she couldn't accept. Her father would cut her off, and he would be saddled with a poor wife. He would come to resent her, which she couldn't bear to think on.

"I hope this is not an elaborate plot to force me into marriage, because my father will refuse my dowry if he does not approve."

"I would never force you to do something you did not wish to do." He brushed his lips across her temple, and she relaxed into his body. "Nevertheless, should I be offended?"

She twisted her neck to look back at him. "Probably. Although it's not your fault. I approve of you. That's all that should matter. But that's not why you have pursued me, is it?"

"What do you mean?"

"You want to provoke your father and half brother by taking what they consider theirs."

He made a humming sound. "I won't deny my initial interest was driven by thoughts of revenge."

"And now?"

"And now I find myself enchanted by you."

"Pretty words. Be careful or I might get the idea you cared for me."

His arm tightened around her, and his mouth dropped to her ear. "You deserve love, Madeline. Don't settle for anything less."

"I fear I won't have the choice." The Duchess of Ralston's words came back to her. Maddie's wishes did not matter. She was chattel to the Ralstons and a burden to her parents.

To Damien, she was merely a dalliance. An amusement. Although she suspected a large part of his enjoyment was because he would know her intimately before Thornbury or any other man. Was he using her?

Perhaps, but there was a difference. She wasn't being forced to do anything. She was choosing Damien for herself. She wanted him and wanted to experience sex with him before having to endure it in the marriage bed.

The certainty of what was about to happen settled upon her. What should she be feeling in the moment? Any decent young lady would be battling shame, but all she could summon was the satisfaction of guiding her destiny even if it only lasted for a stolen afternoon.

She wanted Damien, and she would have him. "Take me and show me what I'll be missing."

15

Damien's cock throbbed at Madeline's declaration. He had a long list of debauched things he wanted to do to Madeline. Yet the sad resignation in her tone made his heart ache. Marriage had never been in the cards for him, but if he ever succumbed to the terminal condition, he would want a woman like her.

Their bed would be a place of passion and play. Their days would be filled with teasing and conversation. She would serenade him with her husky laughter, and he would bask in her sunny smile. No. Not a woman like Madeline. He would want Madeline.

But it wasn't practical, and he had learned practicality was essential. Only those who had always had full pockets didn't understand the importance of money. Chiefly, having enough of it. She didn't want to get married, and he was against the institution entirely. Anyway, he would never ask her to debase herself by marrying a bastard gambler.

However, there was no reason they couldn't enjoy themselves now. Tomorrow was not a consideration. He couldn't give her love or marriage or reassurances of happiness, but he could give her the freedom to satisfy her curiosity. In return, he could take satisfaction in knowing no other man, especially Thornbury, would enjoy her awakening.

He had thought her a pawn in his revenge, but she was no one's pawn. She was the most powerful piece on the board—the queen. And she had put him into check.

The patter of rain picked up and provided a curtain of solitude from the outside world. It felt as if the gods themselves approved of what was about to happen.

He slid his hand down her arm to take her hand. "Come then."

She was unusually docile and silent as he led her toward the bed. "You will show me everything?"

"Everything," he promised.

Her eyes were wide, but he could sense no fear only a nervous excitement. She clutched the edges of the blanket together on her chest. A light touch on the back of her hand had her grip loosening. He drew the blanket away and tossed it on the foot of the bed, leaving her in his shirt. Her nipples were budded and shadowy under the fine lawn.

He plucked the pins from her hair. The blond waves tumbled around her shoulders, and he ran a hand through the springy locks before tilting her face to his. Her cheeks were flushed, and her lips parted. Her chest rose and fell on quickened breaths, and his hand trembled in her hair with the force of his longing.

"No one will ever know?" She cupped his nape before fisting his hair, the tug more erotic than he could describe. It was as if they were making a pledge. The intensity scared him, and at the same time, he was grounded without the urge to run.

"This is only for the two of us," he whispered.

"For us."

He kissed her then with an inevitability that settled deep within him. This was exactly where he was meant to be. She tugged on his hair harder and nipped his bottom lip. Lightness burst through him, and laughing, he gathered her in his arms and tossed her on the bed.

He followed, straddling her hips and toying with the tie of his shirt on her collarbone, desperate to see her naked. "Are you ready to be shocked?"

At her vigorous nod, he ripped his shirt down the front. Her gasp was delicious, and he leaned down to kiss her lips before exploring her with his gaze. Her breasts quivered. Color flushed over her chest and into her face.

"I love your blushes." He lightly brushed his fingertips down the side of her breast.

"I hate them. It makes it difficult to hide my feelings." She tugged her bottom lip between her teeth and arched her back.

His cock jumped. Was she driving him mad on purpose? "I spend my life bluffing. To see someone who wears their emotions so openly is enviable."

She caught his hand in hers. "You don't have to bluff with me."

He swallowed hard, unable to form a reply that wasn't too telling.

"Now you," she said.

"What?"

"Rip your shirt off. I want to see you." Her confidence was growing before his eyes.

With a smile, he tugged his shirt over his head and tossed it aside. "I can't afford to ruin two shirts."

The way her gaze perused his torso made his chest puff out. He'd thought after all these years he was immune to female admiration, but he was wrong.

"You are very"—she rubbed her lips together, plumping them—"hairy."

Her conclusion was so unexpected he burst into laughter. He propped himself over her on one hand and cupped her breast with the other, brushing her nipple with his thumb. "And you are thankfully not hairy in the least."

With his gaze on her face, he leaned down to lick the hardened peak of her breast and pull it into his mouth for a gentle suck. Her hands were on his chest, tracing every line and ridge and inciting shivers down his spine.

Craving skin-to-skin contact, he repositioned himself, his chest against hers, his hips pressing her thighs apart. Her breasts were soft, and by the way her knees clamped his body closer, she was enjoying the sensation as well.

"Will it hurt?" she asked.

He hesitated to answer.

She lifted her head and stared into his eyes. "We agreed to not bluff one another."

"Fair enough. It may hurt since this is your first time, but I'll prepare your body for me. You can tell me to stop if it becomes too uncomfortable."

"You'll stop?"

"Of course. I am not an animal."

"I don't know... this feels very primitive." She ran her hands down his back to his buttocks and squeezed. Unfortunately, he still had his buckskins on. "Very instinctual."

She was right. While they weren't wild animals, there was something primal about how he felt. He wanted to claim her in the most basic way possible.

She slid her hands inside the waistband of his breeches. "It's time for these to come off."

"You're awfully bossy for a virgin." He rolled to his back to comply, but before he could, she was straddling him, his ripped shirt barely hanging onto her shoulders.

He pushed the shirt down her arms, and she slipped free, letting the white lawn puddle around her hips and over his thighs.

"Allow me," she said huskily. She scraped her fingernails from his collarbones, over the sensitive skin of his nipples, and down his flanks to his fall of his breeches.

The disks of his well-worn buckskins slid out with ease. She opened the flaps with the careful eagerness of a child with a present, her tongue caught between her teeth and her lips curled into a knowing smile.

Considering she'd thoroughly explored him the previous night, she was more knowledgeable than the average virgin. His cock sprang up, and she took him in hand, grazing her thumb over the top slit. His hips jerked in response.

"You will put this inside me and release your sperm?" Her gaze was fixed on his cock.

If he watched her ministrations, he might spend in her hand again, which was not his plan. "Actually, no."

Her gaze flew to his, her eyes wide. "No? You will not take my virginity?"

"I am very much planning on taking your virginity, but I will not spend inside you. While it doesn't eliminate the risk for a babe, it does reduce it. I assume you do not want to bear my child."

She tilted her head and regarded him, her hand still lazily stroking him, driving him mad. The fact she seemed to be considering his statement as a question prodded his heart faster. Did she want his child? A bastard's bastard. His cock grew harder even as the thought should terrify him. He didn't want to father a bastard, and neither did he want his child to be a cuckoo for another man to claim and raise.

"A child would complicate matters. Although, don't forget, I have knowledge of herbs. I can take care of myself."

What she was insinuating would have made her an outcast in times gone by. Knowledge was power, and he had underestimated hers. His respect for her knew no bounds. If his mother had known someone like Madeline, her life might have been different.

He cupped Madeline's nape and pulled her down to him. Her soft breasts pressed against his chest, and he had to stifle a moan. Her gasp at the roughness of his hair against her nipples was equally arousing to him.

"You are a marvel," he whispered before claiming her mouth in a kiss.

With a heave of his shoulders, he reversed their positions. He kicked off his breeches and settled himself on top of her. His cock was pressed against her folds, and he rotated his hips, slipping against her wetness and grinding against her clit.

Her head was thrown back, her eyes closed. Fingernails dug into his shoulders. He wanted to rut her right then and there until pleasure drove out any thought of the past or future. He resisted. Barely.

Right now he needed to ready her body to take him. He sat up on his knees and let himself take her in. Her blond waves spread out on the pillow like the halo of a fallen angel. Her breasts were quivering and tipped with hard pink buds. Her folds were plump and wet. He stroked her with a finger and hummed with satisfaction. Very wet indeed.

He rubbed the head of his cock against her folds and pushed slightly inside her. "How does that feel?"

She grabbed his biceps and tried to pull him close. "Like it's not enough."

The strain in her voice matched the way his muscles held him back when he wanted to plunge balls deep inside her. First he had to see to her pleasure. With the head of his cock still stretching her entrance, he manipulated her clit with his thumb, pressing his palm against her pubis to keep her hips from bucking.

From the glassy look in her eyes to the softness of her parted lips, he could tell she was close. He eased another inch deeper while rotating his thumb more firmly on her clit. Her back arched a moment before she cried out.

Feeling her walls grip him while she came apart was a siren's call he could not deny. He pushed slowly but inexorably deeper, passing through her maidenhead, until he was buried inside her. Her climax was intense and bathed him in wet heat. He savored the feeling and remained still until her spasms ended.

Her cheeks and breasts were flushed with color, and she blinked languidly up at him. "It didn't hurt."

"I'm glad."

She raised her head to look down at where they were joined. "Did you...?"

"Not yet. I was waiting for you." He gritted his teeth, his legs trembling from the effort of holding back.

"Join me then." She ran her hands up his arms and pulled him down to her.

He slipped a hand under her buttock and tilted her pelvis toward him for what he hoped would bring them both greater pleasure. The first slick stroke nearly drove him over the edge. His only consolation was that Madeline in her inexperience would not realize how out of control his ardor was for her.

He grimaced and reined himself in enough to take another stroke and another. Her gasps and cries were ones of pleasure, and his movements became more desperate and less gentle until his thrusts were sharp and pounding.

He couldn't hold himself in check a moment longer. Breaking their embrace, he retreated from her body, took himself in hand, and pumped. Long spurts of his spend crisscrossed her belly. It was the most erotic moment of his life.

He sat back on his heels between her legs and settled his hands on his thighs, breathing like he'd run a mile. The urge to rub his spend into her skin was strong. He wanted her to carry his scent into the drawing room and to the dinner table. It would mark her as his.

But she wasn't his and never would be. Both of them had accepted the inescapable reality. He rose and retrieved a wet, clean cloth. Her eyes were huge and questioning, but did they hold regrets? He was afraid to know the answer.

"I apologize for the coolness of the water." He touched her belly with the cloth, and her muscle rolled with the shock. Once she was clean, he rejoined her on the bed and pulled a cover over them.

The patter of rain was slowing outside. Their cocoon would soon be breached by reality. Gathering her in his arms, he stoked her hair back from her face. "How are you?"

"I feel—" Her gaze wandered as she searched for a word. He tensed, but she smiled when their eyes finally met. "Wonderful. Energized. It feels like I've taken a magic elixir."

"I've never had my cock referred to as a magic elixir before," he said dryly.

She shoved his shoulder playfully, but her expression darkened. "Have you been with many women like this?"

He opened his mouth, then closed it. He had, of course, had sex before. Yet he had never been with a woman like this. He had never lounged and talked and teased in the aftermath. It was a novel experience for him. He would sound like a lovesick fool if he confessed how rare the moment felt. It was safer to answer superficially.

"No bluffing. You promised," she said.

"I am experienced, yes. Does it bother you?"

"It shouldn't. After all, I am now more experienced than the average debutante."

"You might be surprised. There are always a surprising number of healthy fat babies born a month or two early."

It took but a moment for Madeline to understand his meaning. "Oh. Sexual relations before marriage are not uncommon?"

"Not as uncommon as one might think. Especially if an engagement has been set."

"What about the Bellinghams?"

"Simon nearly broke his neck scaling a town house to get to her room in the dead of night to debauch her."

Madeline's giggle kindled warmth in his chest. "That is wonderfully romantic."

"Is this romantic?" He couldn't believe he'd even asked. Sex had nothing to do with romance.

"Extremely." Wiggling her eyebrows, she ran her fingertips down his side to his back and lower still to cup his buttock.

"I've wanted to be able to touch you freely for some time now."

Damien had never been with a woman as delightfully playful in bed as Madeline. Or maybe he'd just never given any of his partners a chance to be playful. He'd made it a point to never linger afterward.

"I was afraid losing your virginity would leave you in dismay."

"Not in the least," she said matter-of-factly. "It is a stricture I am well rid of. I prefer being ruined to being ignorant."

It was good she would have knowledge of the marriage bed before having to endure one. He didn't want to speak of another man in a different bed. Instead, he kissed her, long and slow. His cock stirred against her belly, but he ignored it.

Breaking the kiss, he gathered her close and did his best to memorize what her body felt like against his. Would this be their one and only time together? Desperation wasn't a new feeling. It had been intertwined with hunger and loneliness when he was little. Yet he'd never experienced desperation with a woman. It terrified him. He needed more of her like he needed food. His breathing shallowed, and a panicked heat prickled his body.

Madeline groaned, rolled away from him, and sat up, clutching the sheet to her breasts. "The rain has passed. I must return or I'll be missed."

Keeping his back to her, he rose to dress. "I'll escort you to the edge of the back gardens."

"It's unwise to be seen together. You're not supposed to even be here."

"More unwise if you fall in the swollen creek and are swept away. Allow me to escort you across the creek, at least." His voice was hoarse.

He wanted to sweep her back into bed and keep her. Or run away with her where no one could find them. Instead, he helped her finish dressing and led her into the misty afternoon to a destiny that did not include him.

16

Madeline was under no pretense. This wasn't love. It couldn't be. Yet the way he had cared for her and put her pleasure before his own stoked dangerous feelings in her chest. Feelings she was unfamiliar with and therefore wary of. Using Damien to satisfy her curiosity was one thing, falling in love with him was something else entirely. Something she couldn't afford.

He was a distraction, not an escape from her current predicament. This was the last time she could allow herself the weakness of being with him. Except how would she deny herself knowing he was so close?

At the far edge of the stream, she buried her face in the crook of his neck and took a deep breath, imprinting the memory of his scent. Soon, very soon, memories were all she would have left.

"You'll be fine from here. No one has seen us," he said into her hair. He seemed as reluctant as she was to break their embrace.

With a deep breath, she did what he seemed unable to do and stepped away, focusing on what was next. Her skirts were still damp but not noticeable from a distance. She would not have much time before Galloway would arrive to dress her for the next interminable dinner she would be forced to endure.

How was she supposed to act like nothing had changed? No one would be able to look at her and discern a difference, but she didn't feel the same. She was Eve after having tasted the forbidden fruit and found it addicting.

"Goodbye, Damien." She backed away.

He didn't follow but stood at the edge of the swollen creek in breeches, boots, and a black greatcoat, his white shirt loose at his throat. If she had Adriana's artist hand, she would paint him like this.

"Until we meet again, Miss Barnes." He gave her a polite bow.

She laughed slightly at his sudden formality considering how they had passed the afternoon. He smiled in return, but it was a sad smile. Her heart ached to see it. Would they meet again? The thought stopped her cold, but he had looked away from her as if he couldn't bear to watch her go.

Finally she turned and began the trek back to her window trellis to scale back inside of her room. All was as she'd left it. It appeared as if she had succeeded in her subterfuge. Less than a quarter hour after she had stripped off her dress and crawled into bed, Galloway scratched on the door and entered without an acknowledgment from Maddie.

Dinner provided the opportunity for her to cultivate an acquaintance with an eligible young man who had the makings of a potential match. Mr. Johnson was the son of a local landowner and had been invited for dinner and games. Not well connected enough for her aunt, but perhaps her parents would approve. His father was a blustery fellow but seemed jolly.

Mr. Johnson had a high forehead and weak chin but was pleasant to converse with. He had knowledge about farming and plants that was admirable. She should be excited to learn more about him. Instead, she couldn't concentrate on what he was saying.

She kept a smile on her face and nodded when it seemed appropriate, but her thoughts were in the folly with Damien. What was he doing? Was he lonely? Were his feelings hurt he wasn't considered acceptable to socialize with by the Bellinghams?

Thornbury didn't join the group for games or music in the drawing room, preferring the company of gentlemen and access to large amounts of brandy. He appeared to be resigned to his fate as her husband.

Maddie should be pursuing friendships among the ladies in attendance, but she was terrible at the sort of witty small talk that came naturally to the others. Most seemed to be acquainted from childhood or through family connections. She felt unable to puncture the ties that bound them. Or perhaps she was being purposefully ignored because of her American background.

She took up residence in the farthest corner from the pianoforte, hoping to avoid being called upon to actually play it. Her lack of skill would only ostracize her further.

Her Grace, the Duchess of Bellingham, approached holding two small glasses of port and offered one with a slight smile. "I find a bit of liquid courage helpful when confronted with a room full of people."

Maddie took the glass gratefully and chucked it down in one go. The duchess's smile grew into a laugh, and she exchanged the empty glass with the full one. "Sip on this. It helps to have something to hold. Keeps you from fidgeting."

"Do I appear that awkward?" Maddie murmured.

"Only to someone who understands how you feel. It has taken me some time to learn to circulate and not embarrass myself or Simon. My stomach was in knots for weeks leading up to the house party."

"Everyone is having a splendid time, and you have been the epitome of grace and welcome." Maddie toasted the young duchess before taking a small sip.

"I fall into bed exhausted every evening. It does not come

naturally, but being a duchess and a helpmate to a man so highly engaged in politics means I must learn to cope with the responsibilities. It is all worth it though."

The port had fuzzed her inhibitions, and she spoke with more heat and forthrightness than her aunt would approve of. "Is it? If marriage means I must abandon my study of medicinal plants, then I can't see how it would ever be worth it."

"Perhaps the trick is finding someone who won't make you abandon your studies."

"An impossibility, I fear." Maddie sipped the port. "The gentlemen I have met all want an acquiescent wife who has no interests beyond them, the household, and whatever children she is forced to bear."

The duchess's eyebrows raised. "You have very strong feelings on the institution."

"When has any institution run by men benefited women?" The man who denied Maddie entry into the Chelsea Physic Garden flashed into her head. The unfairness was a painful thorn in her psyche. And she knew that Adriana and Geneva had experienced the same in their pursuits.

"You would do well to watch your tongue among this group." The duchess cocked her head and considered Maddie long enough to make her shift on her feet, wondering what judgment was about to befall her. "However, there are others who feel the same. None that would ascribe to be a scientist but those who use their power, no matter how limited, to help those who are truly powerless."

"But *I* am powerless."

The duchess shook her head. "You are connected to one of the oldest titles in England, and you have a dowry. You have power; you just need to learn to wield it."

Maddie opened her mouth to confess what had sent her scurrying to England to seek the protection of a husband. If she chose judiciously, she would have a dowry. Otherwise, her parents would cut her off like an infected limb.

"I suppose I must practice," Maddie said lightly.

"I can see why he likes you." The duchess's smile was wider now and more natural-looking.

"Thornbury? I believe you are mistaken, Your Grace. He barely tolerates me."

The duchess's throaty laugh drew the curious gazes of those around them, including her husband. "No. Mr. Northcutt, of course."

"Oh him." Heat suffused her face. "He is an unusual gentleman."

"He would never claim the title."

"He has warned me to not consider him in a good light countless times now."

"Yet you haven't listened?"

"Titles mean little to me. It is character than counts for more, is it not?"

"A very American sentiment, which I happen to agree with. Mr. Northcutt is a gambler, a scoundrel, and a rake, but he is a good man."

From the corner of her eye, Maddie spotted her aunt making her way toward them. The duchess gave Maddie a small smile before gliding away to join her husband. The knowing, intimate look they exchanged hollowed out a place in Maddie's chest. Loneliness, desperation, and a certain amount of envy jostled to fill the space. She couldn't imagine ever exchanging such a loving glance with Thornbury or any other man for that matter, except maybe—

Her aunt huffed a sound of frustration at Maddie's side. "I can't seem to engage Bellingham's wife in any meaningful conversation. Garnering her support for the ladies' league charitable foundation would be a coup for me."

Most married ladies of the ton involved themselves in charitable works. It was even more important for wives of gentlemen with political aspirations to take part in order to give their husbands the luster of generosity and good will even if it were all for show.

"The duchess is very busy as our hostess." Maddie offered the placating excuse.

"More pressing matters are upon us." Her aunt waved her hand as if clearing smoke from the air. "We must discuss the ball."

Maddie had tried to avoid thinking about the final event of the house party. Her plan to find a potential match at the party had been obliterated by Damien's presence. So far, her free time had been spent either in Damien's company or reliving her time in Damien's company. Not at all productive but very enjoyable. Her body twinged at the memories, and she glanced at her aunt, hoping the new experiences were not writ large on her face and body.

Her aunt didn't seem to notice anything different about her and continued on. "Ralston will make the announcement before the final waltz."

"Are the Bellinghams aware you plan to hijack their ball?"

"They should be thrilled. This announcement will have everyone in town talking for weeks. Otherwise, no one would even mention this dull little party. It has proved quite boring thus far. The village was mundane, and the rains ruined the afternoon activities."

Hadn't that been lucky for Maddie? "Rain will ensure the gardens are beautiful come summer and fall."

Her aunt rolled her eyes. "Always about the plants. It's quite maddening."

The port and her talk with the duchess had stoked Maddie's courage, although it still took some effort to expel the words. "I don't wish to marry Thornbury, Aunt Elizabeth. We will never suit."

Her aunt shot her a sharp look. "My son doesn't wish to marry you either, but he understands his wishes don't matter and neither do yours. This is bigger than the two of you. The future of the dukedom is at stake."

Options gave one power, and Maddie had none that seemed viable. She could not return home, and she couldn't stay under the Ralston's protection without marrying Thornbury.

Yet if the rumors reached ton ears about why she had been banished to England, no one would marry her and she might be cast out or, worse still, sent to an asylum for dangerous women.

Would Lady Geneva Dorn take her in? Perhaps, but Maddie's letters had gone unanswered since Lord Dorn's death the previous year. Guilt twinged. All she had done was answer questions. What Geneva had done with the knowledge should not fall on Maddie's conscience. Yet she feared if the full accounting of what had transpired was to come to light, it would be catastrophic to them both.

Like Maddie, Adriana had few options and no power. Her beau was wandering the continent with only vague reassurances of marriage, while her father and stepmother favored a match with her stepbrother in order to keep the inheritance in the family. Could Maddie and Adriana forge a life together as spinsters? Adriana could sell portraits, and Maddie could turn her hand to making poultices and healing syrups. More likely they would end up in the poorhouse.

By rules of elimination, that left one option. Marriage to Thornbury. At least they would both be miserable. It was something they would have in common.

A sharp pinch on her arm made her exclaim and swing her attention back to her aunt.

"Quit your woolgathering and focus. I want you looking your best for the ball. I had Galloway pack the Ralston sapphires. You will wear them with the silver gown."

As her aunt continued to strategize, the noose tightened around Maddie's neck, and she could see no escape.

A TEMPORARY RESPITE PRESENTED ITSELF THE NEXT afternoon. The morning was spent shooting arrows at straw bales painted with varying circles. All the ladies except for Maddie seemed to possess the skill as if they'd trained to repel a horde at the gates.

Maddie's third arrow went askew and almost resulted in injury to a footman. The teasing she was subjected to had a sharp edge, and she was grateful to be sent back to the house. She had promised to practice her embroidery, but she had no such plans.

She paced the floor, trying to talk herself out of going to the folly. Her willpower lasted mere minutes before she was grabbing a straw bonnet and setting off. This time she left from the back door with a pair of secateurs and a basket in case she was questioned. Cutting blooms was an acceptable pastime for a young lady. She even snipped a few spring flowers along the way to stuff into the basket.

The stream had receded, and she had an easy crossing this time. A sudden crimp of anticipation and worry had her stopping on the crest of the hill. Damien might very well be off fishing or visiting the village or any number of places. It would be better if he wasn't there. The last time was supposed to be the last time.

The doors were open and the white drapes stirred in the breeze. A bolt of excitement had her hurrying down the hill. Damien stepped outside and shaded his eyes to watch her approach. He was barefoot and dressed simply in buckskins and a white shirt, loose at neck and exposing a deep vee of his chest. He was a pagan god, and she was ready to sacrifice herself on his alter.

"I wasn't expecting you," he said as she closed the distance.

"Am I welcome?"

"Very much so. I had expected Jessica would keep you busy."

"She tried, but I almost killed a footman with an errant arrow."

His laugh boomed and made her smile in return.

She set the basket and secateurs down and untied her bonnet, letting it fall haphazardly to the ground. She was starved for him, and he must have felt the same, because he wasted no time in pulling her into his arms and kissing her with a bruising intensity that fired her need.

She knew too much now. She knew how his naked body felt against hers. She knew what he could do with his fingers and cock. She knew she needed him like she needed air.

She was suffocating in her clothes and began tugging at her ties and tapes with a mewl of desperation. With deft fingers, he brushed hers away and made quick work of her dress. It pooled at her feet. She was just as desperate to rid him of his clothes and tugged his shirt free from his breeches. It joined her dress.

Her stays slipped over her hips. The sound of fabric tearing only made her laugh, especially as it meant her chemise had left her body in a flurry of cotton. A button on his breeches popped off and pinged against the stone floor. He kicked free of them, leaving him naked.

Damien made a rumbling sound that was so animalistic she wanted to howl in return. His cock was hard against her hip, and she ground against it with an instinct that felt entirely good and natural.

He lifted her, his hands under her buttocks, and buried his face in the curve between her neck and shoulder. He took a bite at the tender skin and tendon. A frisson went through her, part shock but mostly arousal. She threaded her fingers through his hair and tugged sharply. His intake of breath might have been pain, but she felt no contrition, only power and satisfaction.

"You little minx." His voice was almost a purr.

He carried her inside and dropped her on the bed crossways, his body between her legs. He took her by the calf, his hand warm and slightly rough, and unfastened her half boot, tossing it carelessly over his shoulder. He did the same with the other. Her stockings went next.

He put his knee on the edge of the bed and loomed over her. She backed up, and he followed like a wildcat on the prowl. "Are you trying to escape me, my love?"

"Never." The word came out with a vehemence that erased their burgeoning playfulness. Their gazes held, and she felt naked in a way that was even more intimate than shedding her clothes.

His dark eyes were alive with heat, and he narrowed them slightly, his voice dropping into a register that bordered on menacing. "You'll never be rid of me. I'll live forever in your memories. When you close your eyes, I want you to remember this."

He took her wrist and pressed her hand against his chest. The hair was rough under her touch, the muscle hard. She curled her fingers slightly to score her nails against his skin. With his grip tightening, he forced her hand lower until her palm brushed the thickening hair at his pelvis. Then her hand was circling his cock without any prodding from him. She stroked him, her grip tight like he'd taught her in the gazebo.

He broke her hold on him and flipped her, positioning her on her hands and knees. This was how animals mated. She arched her back and spread her knees even wider. He gripped her hips and pulled her back toward him. His cock slipped through her folds. She was more than ready for him.

She cried out in frustration. Pandora's Box had been opened, and now that she had experienced the pleasure, she wanted him inside her.

"Tell me what you want." He thrust his hips against hers again, his cock once more sliding against her but not inside her. Leaning over her back and wrapping a hand around her neck, he said in a softer though no less compelling tone, "Tell me what you want, and I'll give it to you."

"I want you to fuck me." The scandalous admission came out in an embarrassingly begging whine.

His answering laugh sent a shot of indignation through her,

but she didn't have time to nurture it. He drove his cock inside her. There was none of the slow easing of the day before, and there was no pain, only an intensity that had her fisting the coverlet, her mouth open on a soundless cry.

He gave her no time to adjust to the taking. He pulled nearly out of her and then thrust back in, his hips bumping into hers hard enough to send her forward an inch. With his hand still on her neck, he pushed her head and shoulders to the bed, leaving her bottom high in the air.

It was a position of powerlessness. Unable to touch him, she could only lay there and take him thrust after thrust. A moment of disquiet flitted into her conscious thought at how easily she surrendered to his domination.

His wandering hands brushed away any reservation. They cupped her breasts and squeezed them, pinching her nipples in a way that only sent pleasure skittering through her. Too soon, he moved to her buttocks to play, his fingers brushing forbidden places. Finally he found the bud he had expertly manipulated the day before and kindled a similar alchemy today.

Her climax was sudden and wracked her body with pleasure. His movements grew jerkier, and he pulled out of her. Warmth spurted over her buttocks.

Their harsh breathing mingled in the stillness of the aftermath. Her legs trembled, unable to hold her up a moment longer, and she collapsed flat on her stomach. He crawled from between her legs to lie on his back next to her, their faces close. They stared into one another's eyes.

The intensity of their coming together had not eased with their pleasure. Would his earlier declarations prove an omen? Because she would never be rid of Damien. Her marriage bed would be dominated by his ghost.

He was not smiling. She couldn't not qualify his expression, but it made her want to cry. She closed her eyes and turned her face into the mattress to try to hide the surge of emotion.

The bed moved as he rose, but she remained. Water trickled,

and soon after, a soft cloth wiped her clean. He rejoined her, his fingers tracing patterns on her back. His gentleness was in stark opposition to the rough nature of their joining.

Slowly she relaxed and was finally able to look at him once more. His cheek was propped on his hand, and he raised his brows. "Was that too much?"

"No, it was exactly what I didn't know I wanted."

His lips quirked but didn't continue into a smile. "I should have taken more care with you. Were you sore?"

"It didn't hurt if that's what is worrying you."

"Good."

She stayed on her stomach but pushed herself to her elbows to put their faces level. "Should I have enjoyed that as much as I did?"

Confusion scrunched his brow. "What do you mean?"

A blush suffused her face as she stumbled over an explanation that wasn't even coherent in her own mind. "I mean you... pressed me down and... took me. Like an animal. I was powerless."

"Ah." He brushed hair that had come loose from their pins over her shoulder. "Did you enjoy the domination?"

She shouldn't have, and yet she had. A sharp nod was her answer.

"You might have felt powerless, but I assure you, you were no such thing. In fact, you are only beginning to discover your power."

Power, or the lack of it, seemed to be a theme of her recent conversations and musings.

"You're delightfully pink again. Are you embarrassed?"

"A little."

He leaned in to brush his lips over hers. "Embarrassment has no place between us. Anything that *feels* good *is* good."

It was a simple yet profound statement and the opposite of what was drilled into a woman's head from a young age. Pleasure was at best an indulgence and at worst a sin.

"You are so much stronger than I am in a physical sense. How can I ever hold power over you?" she asked.

"Your very presence is power." He glanced down his body.

She twisted to follow his gaze. His cock bobbed at attention between his legs. "You are hard again?"

"How could I not be with you lying naked in my bed." He smoothed his hand down her back and through the dip of her waist to rest on her buttock. A squeeze sent a bolt of awareness to her core.

Her experience was limited, but when she had stroked him to spend in the gazebo, power had surged through her. He had been left weak. She stared at his cock and rubbed her lips together. What if instead of stroking him to spend, she sucked him to spend?

Before she could lose her nerve, she scrambled to her knees and pushed him to his back.

"What—?" His question turned into a moan.

She had taken his cock in hand and squeezed.

She considered their positions and decided to lie opposite of him, her head at his cock and her legs above his head. On her side and raised on one elbow, she fisted the base of his cock and leaned over to trace the ridge at the tip with her tongue.

His head fell back and his hips tilted toward her as if begging for more. She must be doing something right. She sucked on the tip like sampling an exceptionally large sweet. He took a sharp breath.

She looked up at him, letting him pop free off her mouth. "This feels good?"

"Incredible, but you don't have to. Some women don't enjoy sucking a man off."

"I won't know unless I try." Opening wide, she engulfed the head once more, her tongue tracing along the edge. A mere hint of the earthiness of his spend remained under the light scent of soap he'd used to clean himself after. She pushed farther onto his cock until she nearly gagged and eased away.

He threaded his hand through her hair and drew it into a fist. Her scalp tingled in a way she was coming to recognize as arousal. What now? As if sensing her need for direction, he pulled at her hair, and she raised her head until only the very tip remained in her mouth.

Before she could question him, he pushed her head back down onto him, not deep enough to gag her this time. He guided her again and again. Closing her eyes, she lost herself to the rhythm. This was a mimic of the traditional act of sex.

Except she couldn't take him as deep. As a means of apology, she swirled her tongue along the head and shaft every time she rose and fell on him. He didn't seem disappointed. On the contrary, he writhed under her ministrations.

A throbbing at her core tried to distract her from her mission to drive him wild. She squirmed and cut her legs against one another to ease the ache.

"Are you wanting too, my love?" he asked hoarsely.

With her mouth full of his cock, all she could do was hum. His hips jerked up in reaction, driving his cock deeper into her mouth. She gasped and raised slightly away from him.

He shifted to scoop her on top of him, her knees braced to either side of his shoulders. Her core was so close to his face she could feel his warm breath on her tender, wet flesh. It was too intimate, and she tried to squirm away, but he pressed her down on him.

"Suck me while I feast on you," he said.

The image his words evoked was unbearably erotic. She braced herself on his thighs and closed her mouth over him. He gripped her buttocks and dragged his tongue through her folds, pressing inside her before flitting toward her clit. The pleasure outweighed any embarrassment she had been battling. In fact, she found herself angling her hips to give him greater access.

When he sucked at her clit, she moaned and drove farther down on his cock than she thought possible. As the coil inside her tightened, she sucked him deep.

He plunged a finger inside her as he flicked and sucked at her clit. Her hips moved instinctually, grinding against his mouth. It was too much for her to bear, and she orgasmed on his face.

She groaned and sucked hard at his cock. He tried to move her head, but she was too lost in her climax and took him in another inch. Fluid hit her tongue and the back of the throat. His cock throbbed, and she swallowed reflexively. Another spurt filled her mouth. She raised her head to take a breath and swallow again. His mouth was still buried between her legs, and the friction of his moans against her sensitive folds set off another round of trembles through her body.

She licked the head of his cock as it began to soften slightly and then laid her head against his thigh, utterly satisfied and spent. He must have felt the same because his body went slack under hers and they lay, panting and silent, for a long while.

She was drifting into sleep when he tapped her buttock and rolled her to her back. She felt like a rag doll, loose-limbed and sated. He lay next to her on his side and trailed his fingertip from her cheek, down her neck, to circle her nipple. It puckered into a bud. He gave the same attention to the other breast.

She shivered and looked up at him through her lashes. He had drawn his bottom lip between his teeth and was concentrating on his ministrations. No hint of modesty overcame her in the aftermath of their intimacies, and she marveled at the change in her attitude about her body in so short a time.

A wave of melancholy rolled through her. Would *this* be their final liaison? Maybe. Probably. The ball was only two days away, and once she returned to London, there was no trellis outside her window or folly with a giant bed.

She took his wandering hand and threaded her fingers through his. "I will never forget this." Her voice was rough with emotion.

His gaze rose to hers and held. "Neither will I."

She wasn't sure she believed him. He had shared his bed and body with many women. How soon before he shared such intimacies with someone new? Her eyes watered, and she blinked. She could cry later. For now, she would savor these last moments together.

With a sigh she hoped was tinged with regret, he stood and pulled her up alongside him, their hands still linked tightly. Their bodies were pressed together, her cheek over his heart. It beat strong and steady.

If she didn't break away from him, she would end up begging him to sweep her away from her impending future even if it meant being his mistress. She bit the inside of her lip until she tasted blood and pulled free from his loose embrace to dress.

Neither of them spoke until she had gathered her straw bonnet and basket. The flowers she'd cut were already starting to wilt.

"I don't know if I can get away again." She looked anywhere but at him.

"I understand," he said.

The two words were daggers to her heart. She wanted him to beg her to try or promise he would find her. Perhaps he was too honest to make promises he couldn't keep. He didn't even pull her close for a goodbye kiss. She backed away and finally turned to trek up the hill toward the gardens and manor with her vision blurred by tears she was too proud to shed in front of him.

17

Damien was hidden well behind a pillar and an enormous potted plant whose name was a mystery. Madeline would know the Latin and common name. He plucked at a leaf and sniffed the fresh green scent that he associated with her. If he angled himself just so, he could see half the Bellingham ballroom. The occasional flash of Madeline's silver gown was like a lightning strike, making his heart beat faster.

How pathetic was he? Monumentally. He was betting on Madeline to retreat for fresh air at some point in the evening. The garden held too much of a pull for her to deny. But what if she was on the arm of Thornbury or some other fop? Would he be forced to watch another man dance attendance on her?

His hope was running thin when a lifeline appeared. Simon slipped out the door toward a shadowy corner, a cheroot in hand.

"Psst!" Damien whispered.

"Who's there?" Simon's head swung around to peer in Damien's general direction.

"Who do you think, you dunderhead?" Damien was the only man who could get away with insulting the Duke of Bellingham.

Simon cursed and moved closer, his cheroot still unlit. "Are you mad? What are you doing here? If you're seen..."

Simon didn't have to elaborate. All hell would break loose, and rumors would abound. Simon could lose political influence with Ralston and his set, and the people of Britain would be worse off. Yet here Damien stood, desperate and willing to beg.

"You're right. I'm the dunderhead." Damien edged closer to his friend. "Can I beg a favor?"

"Another one? Jessica has blistered my ears already over allowing you to stay in the folly. She fears you plan to lure Miss Barnes into an indiscretion."

If Jessica knew the extent of their indiscretions, she would do more than blister Damien's ears. "It's the last evening. I need to see her just once more. Can you bring her to me?"

"No. Absolutely not. You are being incautious and, frankly, stupid."

"Yes, all of that, but I can't help it. Please, Simon. Tell her—" Damien looked out over the garden. "Tell her to meet me at the hedge maze. That should offer us enough privacy. I won't keep her long, I promise. No one has to know. Please."

Simon peered at Damien for a long moment. He wasn't sure what his friend saw, but Simon's face softened and he shook his head. "You have it bad, don't you?"

"What do I have?" Damien felt lost and craved illumination.

"It's obvious. You love her."

"No, I don't. That's preposterous." He was flummoxed by the simple pronouncement, but at the same time, he felt like he'd slipped on a perfectly tailored jacket. One that fit him like a second skin. It felt... exactly right. He whispered, "Impossible."

Simon tapped his cheroot on the stone pillar. "Yes, exactly what I thought before Jessica."

"What do I do?"

"You could try being honest. It's just as obvious she loves you too." Simon grinned. "Poor girl."

Damien's head was spinning and confused. Was it love he felt? How was he to know? He'd never experienced it before. Even if it was love, did it make a difference in their fates? Love in the ton was not fashionable or necessary. Love was something reserved for Shakespeare or overwrought novels. It wasn't practical.

"Go to the hedge maze. I'll send Miss Barnes, but you can't keep her long or Ralston and his duchess will suspect something. They aren't idiots and seem more on edge than usual this evening."

"Thank you," Damien croaked out.

As soon as Simon had returned to the ball, Damien made his way to the hedge maze to wait. The moon was bright overhead, and Damien spotted Madeline as she made her way past the gazebo.

She was breathless, and when she saw him, she didn't stop until she was in his arms. He let out a long breath and held her close, breathing in her scent. She soothed him like his own personal elixir.

"I couldn't believe it when Bellingham pulled me aside." Her voice was muffled against his neck.

"What did he say?" He was careful with her coiffure, pressing a kiss against her temple.

"That a dear friend of his would like a word with me. Of course, I knew by the look on his face it was you."

"What look was that?"

"Resignation and worry."

"He thinks this is a terrible idea, but I had to see you."

"I'm very glad to see you too. We leave in the morning. Everything will be different after tonight."

"Yes." It would be difficult to find ways to continue their affair, but he was resourceful and an excellent climber if it came to that.

"An announcement is forthcoming, and I—"

"Yes, about that. What if you could convince Ralston and your aunt that you wish another season? It would not be an outrageous request."

"There's something you don't know. Something I should have told you. I wasn't merely sent to England to find a husband because my parents deemed the prospects better. I was banished. There was an incident." Madeline pulled out of his arms and paced.

Instantly he knew it was the rest of the story she had not told him in the gazebo. The one that had left her troubled. She had been a virgin in his bed, of that he was sure, but men could be vile and abuse women in countless ways. He had nurtured a vow of revenge against Ralston for years. To seek this unknown man and deliver retribution would be swift and sweet.

"Who took advantage of you, Madeline?" The darkness in his voice made her stop and stare at him.

"No one." She glanced away and rubbed her arms. "But a man —a *gentleman*—took advantage of a friend. A woman who was not of the same social standing and therefore had no power."

"He raped her?" He preferred not to use honey-coated words to mask dastardly deeds.

She nodded. "My rage was red-hot, and I did something ill-advised."

"What?"

"I poisoned him."

Shock caught him between disbelief and admiration.

"I didn't kill him," she added hastily. "He lost control of his bowels in front of New York society, which can be as cruel as London's ton."

He barked a laugh. "He deserved worse."

"You don't think I'm a terrible person?" She took a step toward him.

He took her waist and brought their hips together. "You used your skills to dispense a righteous judgment. I would never condemn such actions."

She let out a long breath. "I didn't regret it either until I was discovered. I was sent here to find the protection of a husband as a last resort. It's only a matter of time before word of my misdeed reaches the ears of the ton. Already a young lady and her aunt who I was acquainted with in New York will be circulating and saying who knows what."

Damien's amusement withered. Madeline was in a precarious situation. She couldn't return home, and if she was branded dangerous by the ton, she would never make a good match. Ralston might even be heartless enough to send her to an asylum to wash his hands of her.

She wrapped her arms around his waist. "I'm glad you know and don't hate me."

"I could never hate you," he murmured.

It was worse than that. Simon was right, blast it. Damien loved her.

He blamed her smile. The open sunny smile that she had hit him with the first night in the garden. It had knocked him off-balance, and so he had remained. She tilted her head back to look at him with an even more brilliant version. He tightened his hold around her as if that might steady his wobbly heart.

"Will you take me to the folly?" she asked.

"If only I could steal you away forever." But he couldn't. Could he? His thoughts were too confused to parse. "We only have a little time, but there is something I would like to show you, if you trust me?"

"Of course."

He did not deserve her trust, but he would take advantage of it anyway. He took her hand and pulled her into the hedge maze. The shadows were deeper in the maze, but he had explored the twists and turns on many a school holiday and visit. Within minutes, they emerged into the center of the maze.

It was a small area awash with color. Different-colored flowers weaved together to form a kaleidoscope. It was a wild explosion highlighted by moonlight.

Madeline stepped forward with her arms out as if she could envelop the scene in a hug. "It smells divine. They really shouldn't be called wallflowers, should they?"

"Is that their name?" Damien only knew he loved the chaos and scent of the hardy colorful flowers allowed to run wild in the center of the maze.

She squatted to examine one of the blooms. "*Erysimum*, I suspect. No medicinal value but very pretty."

Damien took her hand and helped her rise. There was much he wanted to say to her, but he couldn't organize his thoughts. They were as jumbled and pretty and sweet as the flowers around them.

He took a deep breath and leaned down to kiss her, gently but with the intention of imparting his feelings. They broke apart, and both of them were breathing hard.

"Oh Damien, why does this have to be so difficult?" she whispered.

She could be referring to countless aspects of their situation. Being away from her was difficult. So was being with her, knowing it was temporary. Imagining a future where she was wed to another was impossible.

"I must return before I'm missed." She took his hand and led him to the opening in the hedges.

The mood between them was melancholy as he led her back through the maze. Their hands remained linked and their bodies close. When they reached the edge of the garden, he stopped.

"You should continue on without me from here," he said.

"I wish..." She looked away, blinking rapidly. "This is the way of the world, isn't it?"

Damien wasn't sure what she meant, but he caressed her cheek with the back of his hand. Her soft skin was intoxicating. "This world can be cruel."

"Indeed, it can." She took his hand in both of hers and pressed a kiss on the back. "I'm sorry."

"What—?"

The crunch of gravel underfoot startled them both. Had they been caught?

His mind whirled. Would that be such a terrible thing? What if he was forced to marry her to save her reputation? For a blink, he imagined it. Then reality broke.

Marriage to Damien wouldn't save Madeline's reputation but blacken it further. They would both be outcasts. Her family would withhold her dowry. He would no longer be welcome at the gaming tables of the rich and powerful. How would he make his living and support those who counted on him?

Picturing Maddie hungry and living in squalor made his insides go cold. Never. He would rather she be unhappy in a marriage to someone else, even Thornbury, if it meant she could be warm and well-fed and healthy. Damien refused to condemn her to a life like his mother had endured.

She dropped his hand and moved away from him.

Simon appeared, looking harried. "There you are, Miss Barnes. I was getting worried Damien had absconded with you. Jessica is waiting on the balustrade to escort you back inside. You two ladies have been discussing the garden the past quarter hour if anyone asks."

"Quick thinking, Your Grace." Madeline took several steps toward the house but stopped for a moment to look over her shoulder at Damien. Then she was gone.

"Did you get what you needed?" Simon asked.

"Yes. No. I don't know what I was seeking." Damien moved farther into the garden toward the house.

Simon followed. "What are you doing? You can't make an appearance at the ball, man."

"I won't. I will take up my spot behind the plants and watch." God, he sounded like a lovesick fool. No. He *was* a lovesick fool.

Simon muttered to himself but left Damien to hide away. He watched Simon rejoin the revelries with smiles and laughter. He could see Madeline and Jessica as well. Everyone looked jolly. None of it was real. Heartache hid under the veneer.

Madeline moved in and out of his line of sight, but he dared not move closer. After another quarter hour of dancing. Ralston climbed the dais to stand in front of the small group of musicians.

He tapped the edge of a music stand until the conversation quieted. Even Damien could hear his words from outside, albeit faintly.

"I know Bellingham won't mind me interrupting his ball with such glad tidings to share." Ralston gestured to someone out of sight. Thornbury joined his father, followed by Madeline, looking pale and serious.

Damien broke out in a sweat, and his heart banged around his chest, drowning out Ralston's toast. He only heard a few words.

"...engagement. My son... married to... welcoming Miss Madeline Barnes... future duchess." Ralston raised his glass of champagne. The crowd clapped, but underneath the congratulations, gossip buzzed.

Damien had stepped forward, nearly pressing his face against the glass like a street urchin left to starve outside. Madeline's gaze clashed with his. Her eyes went wide, and she took a step toward him. That was the last thing either of them needed.

He stumbled backward, huddling in the shelter of the shadows. Engaged. Contracts would be signed if they weren't already. Binding contracts. Madeline would marry his half brother. Ages ago, it might have amused him to have deflowered his brother's future wife, but now his heart was being ripped to shreds.

It was ridiculous to allow his feelings to be hurt over the announcement. This is how it was always going to end. It would have been nice to be informed, but how was she to know that he was going to witness the moment.

No wonder their parting had held such a note of melancholy. Madeline must have known what was planned. After what she had confessed to him in the maze, she didn't have a choice but to make a hasty marriage.

He told himself that as he crashed through the garden toward the folly. All he wanted was to sink into the comfort of a bottle of brandy.

18

This was incredibly foolish. Maddie knew it, yet like lemmings off a cliff, she couldn't stop herself. She had to see Damien. It had been a week since the announcement. She had taken a walk in Hyde Park every day since returning to London, hoping to run across Damien. Once upon a time, he had always seemed to know where she was, but she only gained sore feet and no sightings of her lover.

Damien must know she didn't want to marry Thornbury. She loved Damien, and he... well, he at least cared for her. It wasn't too late for them. It wouldn't be too late until Maddie was standing beside Thornbury facing a clergyman and choking out vows she didn't want to make.

The man's cloak she wore had been pilfered from Thornbury's closet by the red-headed footman who was kindly escorting her to Damien's town house.

"I can't thank you enough for assisting me, Seamus." She pulled the hood of the cloak tighter around her face as a carriage clattered by. Being recognized would be disastrous. Even with an escort, young ladies did not visit unmarried men at night, especially considering she was officially engaged to someone else.

Would Damien even receive her? What if he had already

moved on? Her situation was too complicated and risky. It would be wise to merely send her on her way. What did either of them have to gain by drawing out their connection?

While she huddled at the bottom of the stoop, Seamus rapped the knocker and waited. A black man wearing a well-cut black frock coat and trousers opened the door, his eyebrows rising as he and the footman held a murmured conversation. The butler looked over Seamus's shoulder to her.

"You'd best come in, miss," the man said with the trace of an accent she couldn't place.

She lifted the hem of the cloak so she wouldn't trip on her climb, pausing to look from the butler to Seamus. "I'll require an escort home later. Can my man wait for me below stairs?"

"You may have to wait for some time as the master is not in."

"Oh." Disappointment fed the clog of tears in her throat, and she ducked her head to keep her wobbling chin to herself. Bursting into tears on her lover's stoop was something out of a melodramatic novel. Had she expected him to be wallowing in misery like her? He had a living to make, and the only way to do that was to circulate among the gaming hells and card tables of London.

"I'm sure Mr. Northcutt will want to see you. Are you willing to wait for him?" the butler asked.

"I'll wait—" *Forever.* She bit her tongue before the rest of the thought emerged. In a more demure voice, she added, "I would be happy to wait."

"Very well. Mr. Northcutt will ensure you reach home safely. You can return to Thorn House, young man." When her footman looked to her and hesitated, the butler said in a firmer voice, "It will be fine, Seamus. Run along before anyone questions your absence."

"You'll be all right, miss?" The footman did not look comfortable with the situation, but Maddie was willing to risk everything to see Damien.

"Yes, of course." She tried to sound confident even as her nerves frayed to the breaking point.

The butler took her cloak and led her to a comfortable sitting room. "I'm Costa. Would you like refreshments while you wait?"

Her tummy rumbled, and she gave an embarrassed laugh. "If it's not too much trouble. I pleaded sickness this evening and skipped dinner, but I don't want to put anyone out."

"It's no trouble at all. Make yourself comfortable, Miss Barnes. There is brandy and port on the sideboard. I will have a tray brought up."

"That is very kind of you, Costa. Please thank Cook for the inconvenience."

He stopped in the doorway to give her a thoughtful look before nodding and closing the door softly behind him.

Once she was alone, she paced and gnawed on her thumbnail. This would never do. If Costa was correct, she would be here for some time and her nails would be bitten to the quick. She eyed the sideboard. A spot of brandy might settle her nerves or at least dull them. She poured two fingers in a heavy crystal tumbler and took a tentative sip.

The brandy was smooth with a sweet bite. Her next sip was bigger and settled warmly in the pit of her stomach. She wandered to a stack of books on a side table and picked up the top one. It was a book of children's fables with lovely illustrations.

She barely had time to ruminate on why Damien would have such a book when the drawing room door opened and a little head popped around.

"Who are you?" The boy slipped inside and leaned against the door, his eyes bright and curious.

"I'm Maddie. And who might you be?"

He thumbed his chest, his gap-toothed grin charming. "Timothy. I live here. I'm supposed to be in bed."

The boy was dressed in a long nightshirt and had a stuffed dog with floppy ears tucked under one arm.

"It's lovely to meet you, Timothy."

"Are you a friend of the master?"

Timothy settled himself on the settee and crossed his legs, setting his elbows on his knees and tucking his chin on his hands. Maddie sank into the chair opposite him with her glass of brandy and the book.

"I hope I am still a friend of your master."

Timothy nodded sagely. "I wouldn't worry. He gets quite cross with Alcott and Costa, but he always forgives them."

Maddie's curiosity overcame the slight twinge of her conscience for pumping the small boy for information. "Why does he get cross with your butler? And who is Alcott?"

"Costa gets the blue ruin, whatever that is, and takes to the bed sick as a dog, but Mother says we can't catch whatever he has. Alcott is the coachman, and he has a smart mouth. I'm not sure why that gets him in trouble though. Being smart is a good thing, isn't it?"

"A very good thing. A smart mouth, however, means he talks disrespectfully."

Timothy's mouth formed a circle of understanding. "Oh, then yes, Alcott has a very smart mouth. He tells the master exactly what he thinks."

Maddie drank the rest of the brandy and mulled the new information. Damien employed a drunk as a butler and a disrespectful coachman and a little boy who had the run of the house. "Does your mother work in the house?"

"She's the housekeeper."

Could Timothy be Damien's son? Maddie swallowed a lump. The boy was blond with an honest, open face and a spray of freckles across his nose and cheeks.

"And your father?"

"Dead in the war." The boy shrugged. "I never knew him, so it's hard to be sad."

The boy glanced at the book in her hands and bit his bottom lip. She held the book up. "Would you like me to read you a story?"

His smile lit up the room, and Maddie couldn't help but return it. She moved to sit beside him, and he flipped the pages to a story in the middle. "Here's where the master left off."

Maddie's heart flopped around her chest. "Mr. Northcutt reads to you?"

"When he doesn't go out in the evenings. Or sometimes if he has a spare afternoon. Or if it's rainy outside."

The image of Damien reading to a little boy made tears gather. Whether Timothy was his natural son or not, it wasn't something most gentlemen of the ton would do. Damien was so much more than the rakish figure who cut through the London ballrooms and gaming hells.

Timothy tapped the page a little impatiently, and Maddie forced the words around the lump in her throat. As she read, the excitement of the story took over, and Timothy's gasps and giggles made her even more animated.

A throat cleared from the doorway, and she whipped her head around. A man she recognized as Damien's coachman stood holding a tray bearing a teapot, cup and saucer, and thick-sliced bread and jam.

"Take yourself to bed, Timmy." The man set the tray down on the sideboard with a clatter and turned with his arms crossed and a stern look. "Now."

The boy was gone like a shot, the book abandoned at her hip. She closed it and held it to her chest as she stood. Her aunt would never be intimidated by a servant, but this man didn't act at all subservient. He met her gaze without flinching.

"Where is Costa?" She squared her shoulders.

"Busy. Plus I wanted to see what you were about, Miss Barnes."

"You must be Alcott. It's nice to make your acquaintance."

Her stomach chose that moment to rumble its discontent at her tardiness in exploring the delicious tray.

Alcott's stern countenance broke into amusement even though the man didn't actually smile. "Eat," he said in the same voice that he'd used on Timothy.

She poured herself a cup of hot tea and loaded a plate with fresh bread spread with butter and jam before regaining her place on the settee. Her eyes closed at the first bite, and she made a noise of appreciation. Alcott sat in the chair she had occupied earlier and slumped back, setting his booted ankle on his knee.

"Why are you here, miss?" he asked.

"I need to talk to Damien."

"About what?"

She was hardly going to confess her tumultuous feelings to Damien's coachman. "That is between Damien and me."

Alcott leaned his cheek into his fisted hand and continued to study her like prey. "I can see why the master likes you."

"Does he?" Heat burst into her cheeks from both pleasure and embarrassment.

"It's because you're American. Crazy bastards, every one of you."

Her spine stiffened. "Wait just a minute, Mr. Alcott—"

"Just Alcott. I'm no mister."

"How many Americans are you acquainted with?"

"I've met quite a few down at the docks. I've also observed many ladies of the ton, and you are a very unusual debutante. You got into a carriage with the master—*alone*—the first night you met him."

Alcott was as bad as a disapproving governess, and Maddie rushed to defend herself. "Nothing untoward happened. It's not like I intended to get myself mixed up with someone like Damien. It was a chance meeting in a garden, you see. I had no choice but to accept Damien's offer. My dress... My hair..."

"Is that what he made you believe? Warned the master then, I did, but did he listen?"

"You warned *him* about *me*?"

"Considering you are sitting here eating bread and jam, he obviously did not," Alcott muttered to himself before pointing his finger at her. "And the master leaves nothing to chance, miss. He's a very successful gambler after all."

"He must be. This is a very well-appointed house, and he employs many servants. Wait, what do you mean he leaves nothing to chance?" When Alcott simply stared at her like she had grown an extra head, she moved on to another question she was desperate to have answered. "Who is Timothy?"

"The housekeeper's son. Mrs. Henshaw is her name."

"Timothy said his father is dead, but is Damien his natural father?" She clutched the edge of the settee and leaned forward, preparing herself.

Alcott's expression didn't change. "And if he was?"

Maddie wasn't sure what her feelings were until the question was posed. Her response was instant. "Then I would commend him for taking care of the child and his mother. I know how much his own past pains him."

Alcott seemed to sink into the chair, some of his animosity dissipating. "The master is not Timothy's father. The boy was telling the truth. His father got himself run through with a saber before he even knew he was going to have a child. They would have married otherwise."

Everything became clear in an instant of clarity she'd experienced too rarely since arriving in England. "Damien is trying to save you all from his past. That's why he has a housekeeper with a child, why he keeps a drunk on as his butler, and why he tolerates your forward behavior. I know of no other coachman who would interrogate a guest. You are as protective over him as he is over you."

Alcott's lips pursed as he regarded her. Finally he spoke. "He has been good to us, although I would not tell him that in case his head grew too big for his hat. Nevertheless, none of us will see the master hurt."

"I don't want to see him hurt either." Her retort was swift and hot with emotion. Did she hold that kind of power? He was so worldly and contained and experienced, and she was... none of those. "Could I even hurt him?"

"You don't know?" Alcott narrowed his eyes, not in anger but as if he could see straight through to her intentions. If he found them, she hoped he'd share, because she wasn't sure what she was doing. She was engaged to Damien's brother.

Before he could answer, sounds filtered from the entry and Alcott cocked his head. "That'd be him. I guess he got the note."

Nerves shot Maddie to her feet to brush the crumbs off her skirts. "What if he doesn't want me here?"

Alcott sent her an incredulous look and shook his head in answer. Damien came around the corner and stopped in the doorway. "I thought the note Alcott sent was in jest."

His surprise was to be expected, but there was no anger or unwelcome in his demeanor. She found a tremulous smile to match her wobbling knees. "Hello."

Damien shot a narrowed gaze toward Alcott. "Do I want to know what this brigand has been filling your head with?"

Alcott plucked at a frayed thread at his cuff and said nothing.

"Nothing of import," Maddie said. "He was kind enough to feed me after Timothy went to bed."

Damien stared at Alcott, tension rising. Alcott gave in first, rising and lumbering through the door without a by your leave.

"I don't know why I still employ the blackguard. He's impertinent and oversteps at every turn." Damien was looking toward the empty doorway, his exasperation clear.

Maddie chuckled because the tone and sentiment was dearly familiar. "You speak of him much like I do of my brothers. They drive me to distraction, but I love them."

"That's... that's... preposterous. Outrageous." Damien reared back as if bit. "I don't love Alcott. He's my coachman."

Maddie touched his arm and smiled up at him. "He's your family, Damien. I understand so much more about you now that I've visited your house."

He sputtered denials.

"Why are you getting all worked up? It's very sweet," Maddie said.

"*Sweet?*" Damien's shock was quickly replaced by a much darker expression. Without warning, he swept her into his arms. She yelped and clutched his shoulders as her world went topsy-turvy. "Shall I prove how dirty I can be?"

He laid her on the settee and settled his weight over her, his thigh pushing between her legs. His nose nuzzled hers. "Is this what you came for?"

"No. Yes. Maybe." She was having trouble taking a full breath, and it was only partly due to having him on top of her. He could steal her breath without even touching her. "I came to explain. I should have told you Ralston was going to make the announcement during the ball. I don't want to marry Thornbury."

"But you must," he murmured.

The fact he posed it as a statement hurt. Why was it impossible for them to be together?

He raised himself enough to see in her eyes. "Do you want me to fuck you?"

She didn't even need to consider his question. "Yes."

"How long do we have?" he asked.

"Not long enough. I've been waiting for some time." She threaded her fingers through his dark hair. "I should have considered you'd be out."

He didn't waste any more time. His kiss was aggressive, his tongue plundering her mouth. She welcomed the domination, understanding now that it didn't mean she was powerless. She was starved for him. She sucked his bottom lip into her mouth and nipped the supple flesh.

Their hands pulled fabric and ripped at fastenings until she was left in her stockings, stays, and chemise, and he was shirtless with his trousers unfastened. She welcomed him between her legs and slipped her hand into his trousers to grip his buttocks and pull him closer.

The head of his cock bumped her folds and had her crying out for him. "Please, Damien. I need you."

He took the base of his cock and guided it to her entrance. She expected him to proceed with the same desperation she was feeling, but his experience offered more control. He pressed inside her inch by slow inch. The pleasure was unbearable, and she closed her eyes.

"Look at me." His voice was raw and guttural.

She obeyed. His gaze was burning with intensity and emotion. Emotion he might never be comfortable expressing. But he was a man who cared deeply for the people around him through his actions.

Finally he was buried, yet he remained still. Unsaid words churned between them. She cupped his cheek and stroked his lips lightly with her thumb. His eyes closed, and he nuzzled her hand to lay the softest of kisses on her palm. The sweet gesture while his hard cock was buried inside her left her feeling fragile.

Then he took his first stroke, and the physical overtook the emotional. Each thrust was harder than the last until he was battering her with pleasure. It was rough and wild and out of control. Her climax took him with her. His cock throbbed, and warmth bathed her passage. He had spent inside of her.

His weight pressed her into the cushion. Even as it grew uncomfortable, she didn't want him to leave her. They remained connected in the most primal way possible, their bodies quaking in the aftermath.

He rose and the gush of his spend trickled to wet her thighs. He drew a handkerchief from his discarded jacket and cleaned her. "Dammit, I'm sorry, Madeline. I meant to withdraw."

"It's fine." It was difficult to worry about anything with her body still clenching around the ghost of his cock.

"It's not fine. You could become with child. *My* child." He half reclined on the settee and pulled her into his arms.

She laid her head on his shoulder and let her fingers play along the ridges and hair of his chest. "I can brew a special tea once I return to Thorn House. It is known to prevent such accidents."

"A dangerous woman, indeed." He played with her hair as the silence stretched.

She propped her chin on her hand and looked up at him. His expression was unguarded.

"I like you like this," she said.

He grinned down at her. "Like what? Mostly naked?"

"No. Well, yes, that too." A blush suffused her cheeks. Neither of them had bothered to repair their clothes. His trousers were still open, his cock lying against his leg, and her breast peeked over the edge of her chemise.

He delicately traced her ruched nipple with the pad of his finger. "I curse the day when you stop blushing."

"I hate that my inexperience is so obvious."

"You aren't jaded like me. I envy you that and wish I could protect it. Instead, I can't seem to keep myself from defiling you." There was a wistfulness in his voice that sparked hope.

"I enjoy being defiled by you. Do you ever imagine things turning out differently?" she asked.

"Do you mean with my mother and father?"

"I mean with us." She tensed. The pity and regret in his eyes stamped out her hope, and she dropped her face to his shoulder to hide from the truth she could read. "Forget I said anything."

His chest rose in a long, slow breath against her. "It would never work," he finally said.

If she couldn't have a declaration of love or commitment, then she was at least thankful he didn't pile on platitudes and false promises. She wouldn't have been able to bear it.

"I don't care, you know," she said against his skin.

"Don't care about what?"

"I don't care about any of the trappings. I don't want to be a duchess. I want—" *You.* She couldn't finish. It felt too much like begging.

With her pride in tatters, she rose and stepped into her gown. Her braided hair could be shoved into her bonnet, and the cloak would hide her half-fastened dress. "I must return to Thorn House. I will need someone to accompany me."

Damien slipped his shirt over his head and put his jacket back on, leaving the tails of his shirt hanging out. "I'll send Alcott to escort you home."

When he left her to get Alcott, Maddie pressed her fingertips under her eyes to stop the tears from forming. Damien had affairs all the time. She could imagine women wept and wailed at the conclusion. She wouldn't be one of them. She was stronger than that.

She almost had herself convinced when he returned with her cloak and Alcott.

She donned the cloak and headed toward the door. "I'm ready."

Damien caught her arm when she tried to brush by him. "Madeline, I..." He shook his head as if hoping to rattle some words loose.

"Don't start lying to me now," she murmured while turning away. "Are we taking a carriage or walking, Alcott?"

"Carriage would bring too much attention." Alcott was frowning.

Costa stood at the door, looking equally solemn.

"Thank you for your hospitality, Costa." Somehow she found a smile for him. "Please tell Timothy I very much enjoyed the story we shared."

"I will do that, Miss Barnes." Costa cast a look over her shoulder at Damien, but no matter how much she wanted to, she refused to look back at him.

She marched down the front stairs with Alcott on her heels,

but she could sense Damien watching until they turned a corner. Only then did she slow.

Breathing hard, Alcott came up beside her. "You set a brisk pace, miss."

"I enjoy walking long distances in the country harvesting plants and cuttings."

"Not much of that in London, eh?"

"Actually, London boasts a very famous garden full of medicinal plants."

"You must enjoy visiting."

"They don't allow women through the gates." Life seemed doubly unfair in that moment. "Women are expected to follow rules that make no sense. Is my brain smaller than a man's? Is my heart?"

"I'd say both are a fair amount bigger than most men's." Their footsteps filled the silence before he added, "Servants feel the same, you know. At least the ones who have seen a bit of the world. The lords and ladies of London are only my betters through an accident of birth."

"That kind of talk is positively revolutionary," she said wryly.

"I wager you Americans had the right of it to throw off the yoke."

She kicked a pebble in her path. "How do you stand being subservient?"

Alcott barked a laugh that echoed off the stone around them. "I'm not. I tell my master how it is."

"But you call him master. Isn't that subservient?" This was a discussion she hadn't expected on having.

Alcott shrugged. "I suppose, but Mr. Northcutt is different. As much hell as I give him, I do respect him. He has done right by me and many others."

"I'd rather mull over all his bad qualities right now, if you don't mind."

Alcott made a grunt of what she assumed was understanding. As Thorn House came into view, they paused. The windows remained dark, which boded well. She led Alcott through the mews to the garden gate. She had left the stillroom door unlocked.

"Thank you for the escort," she whispered.

Alcott grasped the gate and held it, stopping her from entering. "You don't have to bow to the rules. Not many have the courage to break them, but I believe you do."

"Damien doesn't want me. I basically offered him my hand, and he told me it would never work. I have no choice but to marry Thornbury."

"Even though he was born a bastard and outside of society, he is still an Englishman and bound by certain rules. I believe he has convinced himself you will be better off without him. Perhaps he needs to be shown another path."

"I'm looking for my own path forward."

"Perhaps you could find that path together, Miss Barnes."

The last thing she needed was the eternal flame of hope that flared at Alcott's pronouncement. "Tonight was our goodbye, Alcott."

"I wouldn't be too sure about that, miss. From the way he was looking at you as you walked out, I doubt the master is done with you."

Before she could ask him exactly how Damien looked, she said firmly, "It's impossible. I'm officially betrothed. It's over."

She pushed the gate open, leaving Alcott and the false hope he offered behind.

19

The next day, Maddie was half-heartedly poking a needle and thread through an embroidery hoop when her aunt swept through the door followed by a red-cheeked Seamus.

Maddie's hand jerked, and the needle pricked her finger. She put the hoop aside and sucked the bead of blood away. Dread and relief fought a battle in her chest. If her aunt knew the truth about her whereabouts the night before, maybe the engagement to Thornbury would be broken.

Her aunt pointed to the red-haired footman, whose shoulders were caving in on themselves as he cowered. "This man has been passing that low-born gambler information about you since your arrival. He was a his townhouse last evening. What did you tell him?"

Panic radiated from Seamus. Sweat beaded his forehead even though the hearth was unlit and the room cool. "Only what parties you would be attending, Your Grace."

"What did he promise you?" Her aunt paced around Seamus like a wildcat.

He craned his neck to keep her in sight. "Only a bit of extra coin to send to my family, Your Grace."

"Did you pass anything besides our social schedule to the *bastard?*" The way she spat out the word made it clear she applied both the literal and colloquial meaning.

"He was particularly interested in any marriage arrangements between Miss Barnes and Lord Thornbury."

"I knew it," the duchess gritted out. "He wanted to keep your dowry out of our hands."

Maddie wanted to defend Damien, but wasn't the duchess was basically correct? Even so, he could have ruined her reputation a dozen times over yet hadn't. Still... Alcott's words came back to her. Damien left nothing to chance. Had their meetings been calculated? Had Seamus received a bonus for delivering her on a platter to Damien the night before?

"You are dismissed. Pack your things and leave this house." Her aunt's voice was cold enough to make Maddie shiver. "I expect you gone within an hour."

"What about my reference, Your Grace?"

"You don't deserve a reference, nor will you receive one. You will never work in a respectable house again."

Seamus's freckles were stark against his ashen face. Without a reference, he would be hard-pressed to find decent work in London, but there was nothing Maddie could do to save Seamus from the duchess's wrath.

Maddie's heart was pounding and her mouth had turned as dry as chalk. "What will happen now?"

"Northcutt's schemes have come to naught in the end. You and Justin will marry." Her aunt's tone held bitter satisfaction as she took up her own embroidery hoop, "Should we consider a special license?"

Something in her aunt's voice turned Maddie's blood to ice. She was frozen.

Her aunt finally looked up and pinned Maddie with a dagger-like gaze. "Should we, Madeline?"

Maddie opened her mouth to try to deny the accusation left unsaid, but only a croak came out.

"I will discuss this with Ralston. No one will look askance if you and Justin marry by special license. Perhaps in a fortnight?"

Maddie's fingers dug into the cushion of the settee. Two weeks. Even after the announcement of their engagement, Maddie had assumed she had time to devise a way out.

Love had been an abstract concept. A theory as yet unproven. Now though, it was real and tangible and she could not marry Thornbury while her heart belonged to another. Even if Damien refused to claim it.

The duchess was spearing the needle in and out of the linen with an ease and grace that did not betray anger or disappointment. "Northcutt only pursued you in order to hurt us. You should ask yourself why a man of his experience would dally with an uncultured virgin."

When Maddie finally found her voice, it was reed thin. "You seem eager to align yourself with me."

"For your dowry." The duchess didn't show the least amount of embarrassment at the notion. "At least you can trace your blood back to nobility even if you possess common manners and pursuits."

"But Thornbury and I do not wish to marry." It was the argument of a child, but Maddie couldn't help but attempt it once more.

"Did you expect Northcutt to whisk you to Gretna Green? He pursued you to hurt Ralston. You are a pawn. Women are always pawns."

Maddie's heart shrank with the realization it hadn't been fate but Damien's calculations that had brought them together. He had not been enamored of her beauty or wit. Their chance meeting in the park had been planned. The invitation to the Bellinghams house party had been orchestrated by him. He had paid someone to spy on her. It was infuriating and hurtful.

The duchess continued. "It was naughty of you to associate with that man, but at least you were intelligent enough to not be caught. His actions have only accelerated the match. All's well that ends well."

Maddie's emotions were too big to be politely contained. She wanted to yell and cry and hit something—or someone. She stood.

Still uncertain where to go or what to do, the butler entered. "A Mrs. Courtright and a Miss Courtright, Your Grace. Are you at home to receive them?"

Maddie's ears buzzed at the announcement. It was the moment she had been dreading. Would Mrs. Courtright spew her poison? Would her aunt escort Maddie to the door with her trunk? Instead of dread, a small flicker of anticipation lit inside her. Would being cast out be so terrible?

"I don't believe I am acquainted with them," the duchess said.

"They are American." The butler's gaze darted to Maddie.

She sank back down to the settee and picked up her embroidery hoop to hide her trembles. "They are acquaintances from New York."

"In that case, show them in," the duchess said.

Mrs. Courtright entered in an ill-fitting pink dress more suited to a girl debuting in society than a middle-aged chaperone. Miss Prudence Courtright, tall and pretty, with an elegance her aunt was lacking, followed.

Inconsequential talk about the Courtrights' travels and the weather followed as tea was served. Each passing moment ratcheted up the tension across Maddie's shoulders. Her mouth pursed, Mrs. Courtright put down her teacup as if readying herself.

Miss Prudence Courtright sat forward on her chair. "We hear congratulations are in order, Miss Barnes. Everyone back home will be amazed and delighted on your engagement. Do your parents know?"

Mrs. Courtright cast a narrowed look toward her niece but made no comment.

"I have written to them, but I don't suppose the letter has made it to them yet. You are the first from back home to hear the news," Maddie said.

Having the jump on the on-dit seemed to mollify Mrs. Courtright, who lived on gossip, but Maddie would need to offer a more coveted prize in order to ensure the woman remained silent. There was no need to for the Courtrights to know Maddie and Thornbury might wed by special license.

"Of course, if you and Miss Courtright are still in London, I will be sure you are issued invitations to the wedding." Maddie sipped at her tea, ignoring the sharp look from the duchess.

Mrs. Courtright's face lit with glee as she turned to her niece. "That would be ever so exciting, wouldn't it?"

"Very exciting. Thank you." Miss Prudence Courtright rose and tilted her head in Maddie's direction. "As I recall, you are very knowledgeable about plants, Miss Barnes. Would you point out some of your favorite English flowers?"

Maddie was hesitant to leave the duchess with Mrs. Courtright, but Miss Prudence was moving toward the door and it would be churlish to refuse. "Of course. Let's take a quick turn in the garden."

As promised, Maddie named and recited information about the plants as they strolled the path. Miss Prudence stopped next to a patch of budded tulips. "That was a very neat solution."

Maddie swallowed. "What do you mean?"

Miss Prudence's eyebrows arched, and a tiny smile curved her lips. "Offering my aunt an invitation to the social event of the year. She won't want to jeopardize your union with ugly gossip from back home."

It wasn't mere gossip but the truth. No need to admit that to Miss Prudence if she wasn't aware, but Maddie feared she was being manipulated. "I am trying to escape the whispers. Do you plan on saying anything?"

Miss Prudence looked genuinely surprised. "Goodness, no.

I've managed to keep my aunt quiet this long, which was no easy feat."

"Thank you," Maddie murmured.

"Younts deserved even worse. I didn't know Kathleen well, but I heard about what happened to her." The fire in Miss Prudence's voice was heartening.

"I'm sorry we weren't acquainted better, Miss Prudence." Maddie wondered how many other young women in New York she had dismissed. While Miss Courtright might not share her interest in the natural world, they did share a similar outlook on life.

"Call me Prue." After Maddie offered up her own name for use, Prue smiled. "You have landed on your feet. Congratulations."

Too familiar feelings of dread rose up to clamp around Maddie's stomach. "I'm not sure that I haven't landed in the fire, but thank you. Is your family expecting you to make a match while you are here?"

"They expect it, but I'm finding the choices to be less than inspiring. I am not being introduced to upper echelon of the ton after all."

"You're not missing anything," Maddie said dryly.

They shared a small laugh. The silence of a burgeoning friendship was slightly uncomfortable, and Prue was the first to fill it. "I hear your brother, Duke, is traveling. Has he made his way to London yet?"

"He has not made himself known to me if he has. Are you well acquainted with him?"

Prue's composure slipped slightly and revealed blushing cheeks. "No. I doubt he even remembers I'm alive."

Her answer was less interesting than her reaction, but before Maddie could question her further, Mrs. Courtright called in a singsong voice, "Yoo-hoo, Prudence! It is time to take our leave."

Maddie touched Prue's arm. "Thank you for everything."

"If you spot a big handsome gentleman who might take an

outspoken American as wife, do let me know." Prue tossed a smile over her shoulder at Maddie.

Once the Courtrights departed, Maddie didn't rejoin the duchess on the settee. "May I call on Miss Coffey?"

"If you must. You will not have time for such friendships once you and Justin are married. Your focus must be fully on him and his ambitions." The duchess didn't even look up as she made the pronouncement.

After informing her maid of her plans, Maddie retreated to her room and fell face-first onto the bed. She was an heiress without actually possessing enough coin to save herself. Her dreams of becoming a well-respected botanist of healing plants disintegrated. She would be like all the other women who trudged willingly or unwillingly into marriage to become the property of a man. She wouldn't even be a footnote of history. Tears leaked from the corners of her eyes.

Left on her own, she might crawl under the covers and cry until her eyes were swollen shut. While Adriana might not be able to offer a solution, she could provide a shoulder to help carry the burden and sadness.

Once at the Coffey town house, Sally took herself belowstairs to the kitchens to wait. To Maddie's surprise, Adriana opened the front door before Maddie's hand was even on the knocker. Adriana's usually serene expression was troubled.

"What's amiss?" Maddie asked.

Adriana took Maddie's elbow and tugged her inside. "Mr. Northcutt is here. In our drawing room."

"What?" It had been the last thing Maddie had expected her to say. "Why?"

"He is waiting for you."

"How did he...?" Anger sizzled through her. Had he planted more than one spy at Thorn House? Who was it? Sally? Coachman John?

Maddie stalked into the drawing room. Damien stood looking out the window with his back to the door, but he whirled around on her entrance. Adriana closed the door but hovered behind Maddie.

Damien didn't appear to have slept well, and strain showed around his eyes and mouth, and yet he was still the most handsome man she had ever seen. She knew how that mouth could smile and what it felt like on her lips... and other places. A blush whooshed through her that had started as anger and was fueled by memories.

He held his hands up. "I had to see you."

She made a gesture as if presenting herself. "Here I am. Now goodbye."

"Will you please let me explain?"

"All right, tell me. Who else is doing your dirty work now Seamus has been dismissed?" She tried for the icy indifference the duchess was so good at but landed squarely in passionate anger.

"No one, I swear it."

"Then how did you know I'd come here?"

"He's been here for over an hour, Maddie, and planned to stay all afternoon, if necessary. It's lucky my stepmother and father are out." Adriana sent an exasperated look at Damien.

"I came as soon as Seamus landed on my doorstep with all his belongings," Damien said.

"You got him sacked with no reference. What is the poor man going to do now?"

"I will employ him until he finds a position that suits him. Drummond or Bellingham will be happy to provide a glowing reference. He will not return home a burden or wander the streets a pauper, I promise."

Maddie wanted to hold on to her anger, but of course Damien wouldn't use and discard Seamus for his own ends. Could the same be said of her, however? "You spied on me and orchestrated our meetings."

"I did." His admission was painful to hear.

"It was not fate but your thirst for revenge that brought us together." Her accusation was as pointed as an arrow.

"When I became aware of your existence and of your dowry, I did plan to thwart a marriage between you and Thornbury. I wanted to leave Ralston humiliated and without access to your dowry."

"Did you even care what would happen to me? How is what you planned any better than what Ralston did to your mother?"

"I—" He bit his lip and looked to his feet. "I quickly discarded the plan."

"How quickly? Before or after..." Maddie stole a glance at Adriana, but she was studying the spines of a row of books.

"Before. Long before. Please believe me, Madeline." Nothing but sincerity and what might have been desperation shone from his eyes. "I'm sorry."

She wanted to believe him. "I'm sorry too. Sorry I did not heed your warnings as to your deficiency of character."

He ran a hand down his face. "I deserve that. I suppose I thought by warning you it absolved me of any guilt."

"Do you feel guilt and regret?"

"Guilt? Yes. Regret? Not a shred. Perhaps it makes me a bastard in every sense, but I will never regret what we shared."

He spoke in the past tense. What they shared was over and done. She knew that last night, of course. What did his intentions matter? He hadn't tarnished her reputation or acquired her dowry for his own; he had merely stolen her heart and ruined her for any other man from now until eternity.

"Did you truly desire me?" Why was she torturing herself?

He took a step forward but didn't touch her. "From the moment we met in the garden, you have surprised me. Enchanted me. I took you to bed because I desired you."

"You probably say the same about any reasonably attractive woman who bats her eyelashes in your direction. I've seen the way the ladies look at you."

"How?"

"Like they would let you have your way with them in a darkened gazebo. Just like I did." The bitterness in her voice made him wince.

"Women of the ton pursue me because I offer a safe sort of danger. I am their dirty secret. None of them would ever approach me at a ball and ask me to dance. You are nothing like them."

"Our trysts were a dirty secret."

"In my twisted way, I was trying to protect you. You became more important to me than revenge." He touched the back of her hand, and cursing her weakness, she unclenched her fist for him. "Will you allow me to make a meager sort of amends?"

Her anger flared. "I don't want a parting bauble. I was not your mistress."

"No! Of course not." Horror at her assumption was in his voice. "Nothing like that. I want to show you something."

Her gaze dropped to the front of his breeches and then over to Adriana. "This is not the time or place for such a thing."

His lips twitched, and even the slightest of smiles added to his masculine beauty in a way that made her stomach roll. "You are incorrigible, Miss Barnes. What I have to show you is a short carriage ride away and mostly proper. In fact, I would also like to invite Miss Coffey."

Adriana, who had seemed entirely focused on the books, spun around. "*Mostly* proper? This has the hallmarks of recklessness."

Maddie wanted to go on one last adventure with Damien. That certainly made her reckless or foolish or both.

"You can act as a chaperone," Maddie said.

"No one is likely to see us anyway," Damien offered.

"So you are taking us somewhere private with no witnesses? What could possibly go wrong?" Adriana asked with a roll of her eyes.

"Alcott is around the corner. I'll fetch the carriage." He

stopped in the doorway. "You should bring your sketchbook, Miss Coffey."

Maddie and Adriana exchanged a puzzled look, but Adriana gathered her drawing things.

Alcott, dressed in dark tweeds and looking like a pirate, was perched on the unmarked black-lacquered carriage sitting at the curb. He touched the brim of his hat and offered Maddie a nod.

"Hello, Alcott," she said.

"Hello, miss."

Damien handed first Adriana and then Maddie into the carriage, and they started off with a jerk.

"Where are we going?" Adriana clutched her sketchbook to her chest.

"A few streets over, Miss Coffey. If you have any misgivings once we arrive, Alcott will whisk you home."

As promised, the carriage came to a stop in surprising short time. Was that disappointment Maddie felt? Had she actually longed to be abducted by Damien?

Damien pushed the carriage door open. Maddie blinked hard. They were directly in front of the Chelsea Physic Garden. Shock and excitement trembled her limbs and made her stumble on her climb out of the carriage.

Damien caught her arms. She looked up at him and then back to the forbidding gate guarding the gardens. "B-But we're not allowed. I mean, I've been turned away. I'm a woman."

"It's your dearest wish to tour the gardens, yes?"

She nodded unable to put words behind the brilliant hope and joy bursting inside her. "How?"

Damien pushed the gate open. No snobby gatekeeper was there to turn her away this time. A man dressed in woolen trousers, a white shirt rolled to his elbows, and a dark vest stood turning the brim of his cap in his hands. Tanned deep-set wrinkles around his eyes and mouth spoke of a life spent outdoors gardening. He wore leather gloves that extended up his forearms and a second pair was tucked into his vest.

"Tom, this is Miss Barnes and Miss Coffey. Miss Barnes is the botanist I was telling you about. Her specialty is medicinal plants. Tom is the head caretaker of the gardens. He knows more than most will forget about things that grow."

Tom gave them a little bow and grin, his dark eyes twinkling merrily, and doffed his hat once more. "Ach, the boy knows how to butter his bread, don't he, miss?"

"He does indeed." Her voice wavered.

Damien looked pleased with himself as well he should be. Maddie wanted to throw herself in his arms. Access to the gardens was worth more to her than the largest diamond in London. He had understood how much she longed to visit the gardens only to be denied because of her sex. He was willing to break the rules for her happiness.

This was his apology. His parting gift. After this, their paths would diverge, and if they saw one another, it would be from across a ballroom, her a duchess and him a bastard half brother to her husband. The knowledge hurt in a way that was beautiful and tragic.

Tom cleared his throat, and with effort, Maddie tore her gaze away from Damien. "Follow me, Miss Barnes, and I'll show you my garden. Put these on." Tom handed her the gloves.

Maddie spent the next two hours lost in the beauty and danger of the poison garden with Tom as her guide. While the garden might be funded by wealthy men of science, it truly belonged to Tom. He didn't know the Latin names for the plants, but he was intimately familiar with every sprig and leaf and blossom. He knew exactly what kind of soil and how much sun and water they needed to thrive.

Damien had thought to bring her paper and lead, and she made copious notes and sketches of her own. There were plants she knew well and some she had never heard of. Not only did Tom impart his knowledge but he also provided cuttings of a few of the more prolific plants that could provide relief from common ailments if harvested and processed correctly. She couldn't wait to cultivate them at Thorn House.

From the corner of her eye, she saw Damien check his pocket watch and give Tom a nod. "I'm afraid Lord Stratton will arrive soon, and we must be gone before then or Tom will get a tongue lashing."

"I certainly don't want you to get in trouble on my account, Tom. Thank you so much for the information and also the cuttings." After handing back the gloves, she held up the notes and a small leather bag thoughtfully provided by Damien, which was stuffed full of plants.

"Truly my pleasure, miss. Northcutt mentioned you had an interest in plants, but I didn't expect you to be a scholar. You know more than any dandies who wander the paths." He took her hand and pumped it. Perhaps it was inappropriate based on their stations in life, but Tom was her better in the garden.

They gathered Adriana, who was frantically sketching a giant moth perched on the leaf of an elephant ear.

"I only wish I had my paints with me to capture the subtle colors." Adriana looked from her half-finished drawing to Damien. "Thank you, Mr. Northcutt. This has been delightful. I never thought I'd see these gardens."

Alcott was waiting outside, and the three of them climbed into the carriage. As they pulled away, another carriage arrived, and Lord Stratton stepped out.

Maddie sat back with a sigh, cradling her reticule with the care and love of a mother. "I don't know how to thank you, Damien."

"You deserved to see the gardens. As did you, Miss Coffey. I am only righting an injustice."

"It was even more amazing than I imagined," Maddie said.

The carriage ride was too short, and with Adriana present, Maddie couldn't speak her thoughts and feelings freely. There was much she wanted to say, but in the end all she could do was squeeze his hand on stepping out of the carriage and murmur, "Thank you, Damien. For everything."

The carriage rattled away and took Damien—and her heart—with it. There was a finality to the moment she couldn't bear to examine.

20

Maddie went straight to the stillroom to deposit her treasure after arriving back at Thorn House. She had been gone longer than she'd intended, but she needn't have worried. No one had noticed her absence. The house was in a state of agitation.

She pulled one of the parlor maids aside. "What is going on?"

The maid's eyes were huge. "His Grace is ill, and a physician is here consulting."

Maddie took the stairs two at a time and found the duchess and Thornbury in the hallway outside the duke's rooms in discussion with a white-haired gentleman wearing half-moon spectacles and carrying a black bag.

Rather than inserting herself, she waited until the man departed and fell into step beside him as he descended the stairs. He didn't glance at her, but his lips pooched in a disapproving frown. "Can I help you, young lady?"

"I'm the duke's niece. What has happened?" she asked.

"I'm not sure if I should—"

"I have extensive experience in tending to the sick, sir. I will help." One thing she had learned was to never ask. It gave them a chance to deny her.

The physician stopped on the landing out of sight of her aunt and Thornbury and out of the hearing of the servants. "You would be willing to nurse His Grace?"

While it was true she had no warm feelings for Ralston, she would also never let him suffer if she could be of use. "Of course, but I'll need to know what has happened."

The frown turned from disapproving to worried. "The duke is suffering from a high fever and racked with a phlegmy cough. He is confused and agitated. There is little to do except keep him cool and comfortable. This evening I will bleed him, which should extract some of the poison, but only time will tell if he will recover or not. Her Grace is too upset to be of use. Can you remain at his side until I return?"

Bleeding was an ancient, primitive practice she had never seen benefit anyone. In her opinion, it was good luck that a patient survived it. "I will tend to him."

"Make him take some broth if you can."

"I'll do my best," she said already turning back to the stairs and the duke's rooms.

Her aunt's eyes were red-rimmed but dry. Thornbury was grim. Neither of them appeared eager to reenter the duke's sickroom.

"I'm sorry to hear of His Grace's illness," Maddie offered tentatively.

They ignored her. Thornbury said, "I will sit with him until the doctor returns this evening, Mother. You are overwrought."

It was a word that had never been ascribed to the duchess. "You are being foolish. We cannot risk you falling ill as well. You are the heir. My only son. I will manage."

"But Mother—"

"I will stay with him." Maddie raised her voice and her hand.

Their gazes swung to her, and she took a step back at the naked emotions visible in their faces. There was worry and anguish and frustration. As a family, they seemed cold, especially compared to her rambunctious brothers, but perhaps she had done them a disservice.

"I have experience in tending the ill. I spoke with the doctor, and he bade me to remain at the duke's side until he returns." Maddie didn't wait for their denial or permission, merely sidestepped around them and entered the duke's rooms, closing the door behind her.

Heat rolled over her like a furnace blast, making it difficult to take a full breath. The windows and draperies were closed tight. Maddie blinked to adjust her sight to the dim light.

A timid-looking maid hovered at the foot of the bed, attempting to hide behind the post. Maddie laid a gentle hand on her shoulder and guided her toward the door. "Can you bring me broth and a basin of cool water?"

The maid's relief was palpable as she made her escape down the hall. The duchess and Thornbury hadn't moved from their positions of sentinels outside the door. Maddie gave them what she hoped was a reassuring smile. "I will let you know if there is any change. Both of you should try to rest."

Mother and son retreated, but their steps were slow and aimless. She put them out of her mind and focused on the duke. The first thing she did was open the draperies and push the window open. The breeze lifted the stuffiness. She used the poker to reduce the fuel piled in the hearth to tamp down the churning heat.

The duke was restless, and when she laid the back of her hand against his forehead, she found him hot and dry. Each rattling round of coughing left him exhausted. Heartier men than the duke had succumbed to lesser sicknesses, but she had also borne witness to weaker men recovering from worse. Only time would tell.

She made a list in her head of the herbs she would need from the stillroom. A potion for his fever. A salve for his cough. His body needed rest in order to recover.

The maid returned, but before she could make another

escape, Maddie handed her a cool, damp washcloth. "Press this on his forehead and await my return."

"Yes, miss." The maid approached the duke with hesitant steps but did as Maddie bade.

Maddie couldn't blame her. A fever sickness could spread throughout a household or even a town. It could be indiscriminate in its victims. Once in the stillroom, she assembled the salve for the duke's chest and a potion for his fever.

On returning to the duke, Maddie dismissed the maid and got to work. The next few hours passed fitfully. The duke's fever would recede allowing him to rest, but then it would flare once more. Maddie forced the duke to take her medicine. In normal circumstances, she would never be strong enough. It spoke to how ill he was that Maddie could hold his hands down and force medicine down his throat.

It was after she was reapplying salve to his chest that the duke had a moment of clarity and asked in a husky voice, "Madeline?"

She laid a hand against his forehead. Still feverish, but his temperature was markedly reduced. "How are you feeling, Your Grace?"

His lips parted in a slight smile, but it was wiped away with a coughing fit. "What is wrong with me?"

"An illness has settled in your lungs." She continued to rub the salve onto his chest.

"That smells like you are preparing to roast me on a spit."

Maddie smiled but continued her work. "There is garlic and sage, along with some other helpful herbs in the salve. Your cough has lessened."

"Yes, I think it has." After Maddie finished, she tied the duke's nightshirt closed at the neck and covered him with the blanket. When she was done fussing over him, he said, "I had a dream you forced me to drink poison."

"Not a dream and not poison. Meadowsweet and *Echinacea* to help reduce your fever. It's working, I might add."

"I still feel horrible." He paused to consider and added, "But not as horrible as I did earlier."

"Your fever will flare again, but I will continue to give you medicine to make you more comfortable."

"Will I recover?" His shadowed eyes were intense, and she didn't shy away from his gaze.

"It's too soon to tell, but you're strong." She hesitated, but this might be her only chance with him in his right mind. "Your Grace, the physician is returning soon and plans to bleed you."

"And?"

"I would advise you to refuse. It is a barbaric practice that will only make you weaker. You need your strength to fight whatever has infected you."

"Pritchett is very experienced. You are a mere girl." Even as ill as he was, the duke managed to lace his words with condescension.

She stood tall over him and fixed him with a glare. "I am a woman, Your Grace, and understand more about how to heal you than your physician does."

"You sound like my old governess. She was formidable." His voice was fading, and he closed his eyes.

"Can I tell him you do not wish to be bled?" She shook his shoulder gently.

His eyes fluttered open. "Fine. Tell him I don't wish to be bled."

The duke slipped into a deep sleep interrupted by the occasional racking cough. Not long after Pritchett arrived carrying a jar of leeches. She shuddered.

"What is this?" Pritchett looked around. "The fire needs to be stoked and the draperies closed. The chill is likely to settle into his bones."

The room was not chilly in the least, but Maddie closed the draperies as a compromise. The doctor glanced at the duke, whose fever was on the rise. He muttered incoherently and kicked at the covers.

Pritchett set the jar down on the night table along with a pair of tweezers and a bleeding basin. He lifted the sheet. "What is that stinking concoction on his chest?"

"A salve of garlic and other herbs. It has calmed his cough."

Pritchett harrumphed and used a linen square to rub off as much of the salve as possible. "Primitive solution."

"And bleeding him is not primitive?"

"It's been proven over centuries to draw poison out of the body."

"Sir, the duke specifically said he did not wish to be bled."

"The duke is in no state to have an opinion."

A sense of panic welled up in her chest. In Pritchett's estimation, she was a girl with an empty head. Actually, even worse, she was a girl who believed plants could heal like the witches of old.

She needed reinforcements. As if hearing her silent plea, the duchess entered, holding a handkerchief to her mouth. "How do you find His Grace?"

"Unchanged. Bleeding is necessary," Pritchett said.

Maddie turned to her aunt. "He is not unchanged. My salve has eased his cough, and my potion lowered his fever. We had a conversation. He expressed his desire not to be bled."

"He must have been talking out of his head." The duchess waved a hand, dismissing her.

"No, he was not." Maddie firmed her voice. "He asked me if he would recover. I told him time will tell. He said the salve I rubbed on his chest smelled vile and told me I was formidable like his old governess. Then he agreed that he didn't want to be bled. At least not yet."

The duchess pinned Maddie with her gaze. "Are you sure he wasn't delirious?"

"He was not." Maddie could sense her aunt waffling and imbued as much confidence as possible into her words. "I know you consider my interest in plants silly, but trust me. Give my medicines a chance to work before resorting to bleeding."

Her aunt turned to Pritchett. "If he is no better by tomorrow morning, you can bleed him. For now, let's give Madeline's concoctions a chance to work."

Pritchett shot Maddie a glare that might have incinerated her if she wasn't long used to such treatment from men. As such, it barely left her singed. As soon as the duchess had escorted a blustering Pritchett away, Maddie returned to the duke's side to reapply her salve and administer another dose of her meadowsweet potion.

Maddie lost track of how long she had been sitting with the duke. She dozed when his fever fell and tended to him when it rose to unbearable heights. Despite her bravado in denying Pritchett his bleeding, she doubted herself. What if she was wrong in her methods and the duke died?

Guilt and worry intertwined and gave her nightmares so when the duke called her name, she thought she was dreaming.

"Madeline? Are you still here?" His voice was husky.

"Yes, Your Grace, I'm here." She rose and offered him water, which he sipped and then broth which he waved away.

"My son. Do you know him well?"

"We are to be married." It was a nonanswer because she didn't want to admit she knew nothing about Thornbury's thoughts and feelings. Except that he didn't want to marry her.

He shook his head, his usually neat and pomaded hair falling over his forehead and reminding her of Damien.

"Not Justin. Damien Northcutt. Do you know him well?" His eyes were bright. Was he out of his head?

"Yes, I know him."

"Tell me. Please."

She hesitated and then said tentatively, "As I'm sure you are aware, he's set himself up well through his winnings at the gaming tables. He's gifted with sums and makes decisions based on mathematics and not chance."

The duke made an encouraging noise, so Maddie continued.

"He was greatly affected by his mother's circumstances and death. His servants are all people who wouldn't be given a position in most households. His housekeeper has a young son. A delightful little boy who Damien dotes on. His butler has a penchant for blue ruin. His coachman is a rough character who is not afraid to tell Damien exactly what he thinks."

Damien had created a family though they had no ties of blood between them. "He is charitable, although he has hidden his good deeds under his rakish persona. He's funny and can be carefree when he's happy, which doesn't happen often enough in my reckoning. And he—"

"Will you ask him to visit me here?"

Surprise held Maddie immobile for a long moment. "Her Grace would not approve."

"No, she will not, but this is a wrong I must right before I die." The duke stared into the canopy of the bed.

Maddie rose and laid the back of her hand against the duke's forehead. His fever had receded, but it was likely to rise again. "You aren't going to die, Your Grace."

"You don't know that for certain, do you?"

She didn't. He could close his eyes, go to sleep, and never awaken. Her silence spoke volumes.

"Will you send him a note and beg an audience on my behalf?" he asked. "Please, Madeline."

He took her hand in a stronger hold than she expected considering his condition. The duke had been a cold enigma since her arrival in his household. His entreaty and intimate touch left her unsure.

The mantel clock had struck two in the morning only a few minutes earlier. "I'll send a note, but he might be abed or otherwise engaged." *Or both.* The horrible thought assailed her. What if he had taken another woman to his bed to soothe himself?

A sting of tears had her blinking rapidly. She had no right to be maudlin. She was to be married, and she and Damien had made their peace with one another that very day.

With the note sent, Maddie insisted Ralston take broth and spooned it into his mouth. Despite his grousing, his color was better after the small amount of sustenance. He dozed, and Maddie paced, waiting on Damien's response.

Damien loathed Ralston. His life had centered on revenging his mother's heartbreak and death. And yet despite the animosity, or perhaps because of it, Maddie couldn't imagine Damien passing up the chance to confront his father face-to-face. Whether Damien could admit it or not, he craved an acknowledgment by his father.

A quiet scratching sounded on the door. Finally a reply from Damien. Instead of handing her a note, the butler stepped back to present the man himself, looking like he'd risen from a deep sleep and rushed to answer the call.

"Damien," she whispered.

21

Damien swallowed. He'd drunk himself to oblivion to try to keep Madeline out of his dreams, and yet it seemed fate had other plans. Not only had his plan failed, but she was here in the flesh, and it was all he could do not to pull her into his arms.

He couldn't do anything so untoward as hug her much less kiss her senseless with the butler standing an arm's-length away and his father possibly on his deathbed. The situation must be dire for Damien to be invited to Thorn House.

"I received your note. Is he...?" Damien glanced over her shoulder.

"He's sleeping, but it's almost time to wake him for his next dose. Come in." She stepped back to admit him and closed the door in the butler's startled face.

Damien shuffled to the edge of the bed and stared down at Ralston. He was a shadow of his former self. His sallow skin was punctuated by dark circles under his eyes. His cheekbones appeared sharper than usual. His usually neat hair was untidy. An underlying rattle accompanied each rise and fall of his chest.

It was startling to see Ralston laid so low. Instead of feeling triumphant, Damien was filled with disquiet and fear. His life and decisions had been influenced by Ralston. In a way, Ralston was his north star. What would happen with him gone? What would Damien's purpose be? His thoughts were muddled from the brandy and lack of sleep.

"Should I hide the pillows?" Madeline's attempt at humor made him think there was still hope for a recovery.

"Will he live or die?" Damien tried to steady his emotions, but an embarrassing tremble in his voice betrayed him.

She took his hand, lacing their fingers. "He took some broth earlier, and my medicines seem to be easing his symptoms. But... it's too soon to know for certain."

"He truly asked to see me?"

"He wanted me to tell him about you, so I did."

He gave her hand a squeeze and cast her a wry glance. "Should I be worried about what you said?"

"I only imparted what I have observed about your character."

"Good Lord, now I'm terrified. Did you tell him I took advantage of your trust, and you should hate me for it?"

She rocked her shoulder into his arm. "I told him you have made a living based on your intelligence and that you have a generous heart even though you try your best to hide it."

He shook his head slowly. "Is that really how you see me?"

"I see what is true," she said simply.

Ralston stirred, and Damien retreated to the window to let Maddie fuss over her patient. She dosed him with a liquid and rubbed a pungent salve over his chest before plumping his pillows and tucking the coverlet around him. A cough had him doubled over, and she offered water. After several gulps, he settled back into the pillows, breathing like he'd run up the stairs. "Your medicine may help, but it tastes vile."

"The fact you are complaining about the taste means you are improving, Your Grace. I can see if the kitchen has some honey to spare if you'd like?"

"That would be a welcome improvement. Have you heard from my son?"

Maddie looked over her shoulder toward him, and Damien started to realize Ralston was talking about him and not Thornbury. He stepped forward into the soft light from the candles beside the bed. Ralston's breath caught, inciting another round of coughing.

"I'll retrieve the honey." Maddie backed toward the door but paused to look at Damien. "You'll be all right?"

"Yes," Damien whispered.

Once the door was closed, Damien sank onto the chair beside the bed.

"Did you think to use her to get to me?" Ralston asked.

Damien clutched his knees, his unease with the conversation growing. "I had the thought upon meeting her, but I quickly abandoned the notion."

"Why? You know we need her dowry. I thought your life's mission was to see me pay for my sins."

"It was. It is. Or—" With a sigh, Damien pushed his hand through hair passed on to him by Ralston. What other perfidious traits had Damien inherited? "I don't know anymore. Things have become muddled since meeting Madeline."

A coughing fit had the duke sitting higher against the pillows. Once he'd regained control, he said, "Whatever punishments you have imagined meting out against me are no less than I deserve."

Damien could finally ask the question that had burned in his heart for so long it had left a scar. "Do you regret the way you treated my mother?"

"I loved your mother." It was impossible to question the sincerity and agony in the duke's voice.

"Then why...?" Damien waved his hand about to attempt to encompass the tragedies that had befallen them.

"I looked for her. I hired a man, but he came up empty. I assumed she had left London to start anew, never guessing she was under my nose and in such peril."

Damien rocked back in the chair, his hands drawn into fists. "No. You're lying. You threw her out."

"No. I offered to set her up in a cottage near Bishop's Ferry. I could visit her. And you. I couldn't claim you, of course—I had wed Elizabeth by then—but I never meant for your mother to suffer. I loved her."

It wasn't true. It couldn't be. Could it? The story he had told himself all these years was erasing itself, but he wasn't quite ready to rewrite it.

"Why wouldn't she take your offer? Why choose squalor?" Damien wasn't sure if he was asking his father or himself.

"Despite the situation she found herself in, your mother was a God-fearing, moral woman. She attended church every Sunday and prayed for forgiveness, but we were in love."

"Yet you married another."

The duke turned his face away, the flickering candle casting deep shadows and making him appear ragged and aged. "I was expected to marry someone who matched my breeding."

"My mother was too common."

The duke swung his gaze back to Damien. "You have moved through society enough to understand its vagaries. If I had taken your mother as my wife, she would have been ostracized. My title and station would not have been enough to protect her. I would have been a laughingstock and lost influence in the House of Lords. As the child from our union, you would have been bullied and tormented. The dukedom would have suffered irreparable harm."

It sounded like a rote list of excuses the duke repeated in order to make himself feel better. "I was bullied and tormented as your bastard child anyway. Did you ever consider what you might have gained by marrying my mother? Happiness, perhaps? Contentment? Love?"

What sounded like a noise of protest morphed into a coughing fit that left the duke breathless. Maddie reentered with the honeypot. She offered the duke a sip of water and pressed a cool compress on his forehead.

"I fear this is too much," she said. "Make plans to talk another day when you are well, Your Grace."

"No. There may not be another day, and my regrets are already legion," the duke said in a raspy voice.

Maddie sent Damien a pleading look, but the conversation was the draining of an infected wound gone too long, and he could no more stop it now than the duke could. Neither would have any peace.

"My mother suffered." Damien could not keep bitterness from seeping into his voice.

"Yes." The duke plucked at the edge of the cover over his chest. "I believe she chose to work for the church and live so poorly as a means of atonement. You were innocent and never should have had to suffer so."

"My uncle found me."

"I thank whatever God your mother believed in every day for that fact."

"Did my uncle know you were looking for us?"

"I sent my man to him after it was clear your mother had disappeared and wasn't returning, but your uncle claimed to know nothing of her whereabouts."

"Even if he had, I doubt he would have shared that information with whatever man you hired." Damien shook his head. "You would have stood a better chance if you'd gone to see him yourself, fallen to your knees, and begged him to help."

Color flushed into the duke's face, a combination of embarrassment and outrage, perhaps. Or maybe it was the fever. "I would never have—"

"Exactly," Damien said shortly. "You loved her but not enough to humble yourself to marry her or ask for help finding her. Or me."

"You were not real to me then, Damien. I couldn't even be sure she was actually carrying my child."

His admission was an unexpected blow, and Damien was struck silent.

The duke continued, "Of course, as soon as your uncle brought you to my doorstep, I knew you were my blood. You were so angry at the world. At your uncle. At me."

Damien remembered the embers of hatred stoked at the sight of the man who had betrayed his mother. "I wanted to stay with my uncle."

"And what? Become a tiger in Winder's household? Mucking stables and sleeping in the mews?" The duke hit his fist against the mattress. "Your uncle wanted more for you. As did I. As did your mother or she wouldn't have made sure you could read and write and do sums."

It was the clergyman at the church who had tutored Damien in part for his mother's labor. He wasn't sure how much his mother was paid for slaving at the church, but it wasn't enough.

"Are you not grateful for the life you live? You have servants seeing to your needs instead of being a servant to some ungrateful peer like myself." The wry humor in the duke's voice was disconcertingly familiar.

"I wasn't grateful then, but I can't deny I appreciate my life now." It was a grudging admission to make. Although the duke wasn't aware, his generosity in sending Damien to school had lifted many others out of the abject poverty he had suffered in. Even imagining young Timothy living on the streets made Damien's heart crimp and go cold.

"You are the physical image of me, Damien, but you are more like your mother than I think you realize."

The mother Damien remembered had been selfless and kind even while facing hardships and sickness. "I am nothing like my mother."

The duke's shoulders lifted in a barely perceptible shrug. "Perhaps not. I can only judge you based on what I have heard of your character."

Damien glanced toward Madeline, but she was busy wringing

out a cloth to keep the duke cool and comfortable. "Did you mourn my mother's death?"

"She had been lost to me for years before her death." It was a fair answer Damien couldn't fault even though he wanted to hear how the duke had suffered. In a softer voice, the duke said, "I dreamed of her often though. I imagined her happy and smiling under blue skies and vast fields. The news your uncle brought me shattered that dream, and ever since, I have had nightmares about the poverty and squalor she endured."

Did it make him a terrible person that he took satisfaction in the haunting of the duke's dreams? He was his father's son after all.

The duke's eyes grew heavy and slow-blinking. "I don't ask for your forgiveness—that is too generous a request—but I would beg a modicum of your understanding."

Could he give the duke the absolution he sought? Damien wasn't sure he was capable of loosening the grip on the hatred he'd nurtured for so long. Madeline's hand fell on his shoulder, and she gave it a squeeze. He wanted to lean into her, wrap his arms around her waist, and breathe her in. Soon she would be as lost to him as his mother had been to the duke, and Damien would move on with his life. Yes, it would be empty and dark without Madeline, but he would survive.

"I understand better," Damien said even though it was a struggle.

The ghost of a smile crossed the duke's lips before his eyes closed and the tension left his face leaving him looking almost peaceful. A stab of panic had Damien rising and moving closer. "Is he...?"

Madeline shook her head. "No. Just sleeping."

They remained shoulder to shoulder, watching the duke take rattling breaths.

"Do you think he was telling the truth? About looking for my mother?" Damien asked softly.

"Why would he lie? And it explains why he paid for your education as soon as he found out you were alive."

"Guilt? Obligation?"

"Both, no doubt, and probably more feelings besides. It is complicated, isn't it?"

"That's one way to describe it, I suppose."

"Much like our situation," she said lightly, but the air grew thick and potent.

He grasped her hand but didn't reply. What could he say? He was as unsuitable for her as his mother had been for the duke, and anyway, she was engaged to another. His father couldn't have married his mother. Damien understood how the world worked now in ways he couldn't have fathomed as a child. His mother had been too proud to accept being a kept woman tucked away on one of the duke's estates.

She might have still been alive if she'd been less stubborn. Damien admired her moral strength even as he resented it. Growing up in a cottage at one of the duke's country estates sounded idyllic compared to his early childhood.

What would their relationship have been like if his father had visited and spent time with him? Would Damien still have nurtured a kernel of hate for his father and his father's legitimate son? Maybe. Probably.

Would a life lived out of obligation destroy Madeline's spirit? How could he watch it happen? What if he begged her to run away with him right now? He glanced at his father. His raspy breathing filled the silence. Madeline wouldn't leave him in his sickbed to be bled by physicians and given poisonous concoctions meant to heal. Moreover, Damien trusted Madeline to know what to do. The duke—his father—would recover because of Madeline and her skill.

After everything he'd learned that night, he wanted the duke to recover. Damien had more questions that only the duke could answer. Perhaps the understanding he gave the duke could one day become forgiveness. What would that look like?

Damien didn't know, but for the first time, he wanted to find out.

Before he could put any of what he was feeling into words, the duchess burst through the door. "What the devil are you doing here?"

It was the first time Damien had ever seen the woman less than perfectly coiffed. She wore a mobcap and a dressing gown of brocade unevenly belted so the white hem of her night rail showed at the floor. Her face was red but without powder or rouge. Her high color was from her fury.

He sketched a half bow that held a bit too much irony, but his feelings of goodwill didn't extend beyond his father at the moment. "Your Grace. I was summoned by your husband."

The duchess gasped and looked to the duke, but he was still asleep although less restfully.

Like a nanny who had had enough of her charges, Madeline took an arm apiece and steered the duchess and Damien out of the bedroom and into the hall. "I will not have my patient upset. He needs rest, not to referee the two of you."

The duchess pointed at Damien but directed her question to Madeline. "What is he doing here?"

"The duke asked to see him."

The duchess retreated a step and crossed her arms over her belly, holding on to her elbows in a protective gesture. "Is he dying then?"

"No. In fact, I would say he has improved somewhat and will continue to do so—" She gave them both a glare and said in a slightly raised voice, "If he is allowed to rest."

The duchess's chin worked, but Damien couldn't tell if she was on the verge of tears or giving Madeline a setdown. Neither happened. The duchess didn't look in his direction but asked, "What did he tell you?"

"We talked of regrets and understanding." Damned if he was going to recount the first significant conversation he'd ever had with his father to a woman he couldn't bring himself to like.

"If your business with Ralston has concluded, I want you to leave. Immediately."

He dropped his chin in the barest of nods and stalked to the stairs. Madeline was on his heels.

"Madeline. You need to attend to the duke." It was an order given by a duchess used to getting her way.

Madeline ignored her aunt and followed Damien to the front door. She stopped him, her hand fisted in his sleeve, her gaze searching his face. "Are you well?"

"I will be better as soon as I make the acquaintance of my brandy decanter."

Her lips thinned and she shook her head. "That will not change what you've learned this night."

"No, but it will dull the memories until I can examine them in the light of day." He covered her hand with his own. "I need time. That's all. I'll be fine."

She looked like she wanted to say more, but the duchess was at the top of the stairs. "He's coughing, Madeline."

"Go. Do what you do best. Heal him with your knowledge."

She took a step back and then another until their hands parted. "I'll send word on his progress."

He nodded, ducked out the door, and took a deep breath of the chilly night air, feeling unbalanced and lost now that the pillars of revenge and hatred had been weakened. What was he to do now? What was his purpose?

He'd never felt more unmoored and alone.

❧ 22 ❧

Maddie's reprieve was over. The duke was recovered, albeit still weak from his fortnight in bed. Unfortunately, a sense of his own mortality remained to torment the duke. Her marriage to Thornbury was to take place that very afternoon by special license.

The closer the not-so-blessed event grew, the starker the decision she had to make became. Her plan was harebrained and reckless and would leave her ostracized from society no matter how it turned out.

If things went badly, Alcott had promised to drive her to Cornwall so Maddie could throw herself at the mercy of Lady Geneva Dorn—no matter that her letters had gone unanswered. From there, she could regroup, send word to her family to beg funds, and book passage home.

Home. It was a concept she thought she understood. Her home was the white clapboard house in New York. Home was her mother and father and brothers. Home was where her heart was, and where was her heart?

It wasn't across the ocean; it was in London in the hands of a gambler.

She was the one who was taking a chance this time. Damien cared about her. At least, she was fairly certain he did. Alcott had more confidence in her plan than she did. He did not think a trip to Cornwall was in her future. Hope that he had the right of it bloomed in her heart.

Maddie slipped into the stillroom. No matter how short of time she was, she refused to leave the cuttings she made in the Chelsea Physic Garden behind. She carefully packed them in damp cloths and wrapped the glass vials where she was rooting some of the cuttings in a petticoat and added them to her small carpetbag.

Jars of salve and medicines she had mixed while at the house were lined on a shelf. Her bag was already full and heavy, and she was late. Cursing, she pulled out her extra dress, a chemise, and her night rail to make room. Those she could replace. If she could even find the plants, the medicines took days, sometimes weeks, to make. The last jar she stuffed in the bag was a sleeping draught in case Damien got tetchy.

One must be prepared when planning a kidnapping.

Cradling the bag in both arms, she made her way to the door leading from the stillroom to the garden. Alcott should be waiting with the carriage in a small alley leading to the mews of a nearby house.

The back garden gate was in sight, and her shoulders relaxed with her deep sigh of relief.

"And where might you be going?" The very ducal voice of His Grace hadn't been dimmed by his illness.

She froze midstep, not sure whether to confront him or make a run for it. If she wasn't carrying a heavy bag full of breakable jars, she could escape, but as it was, the duke was quicker and stronger than she was. Her hesitation was her downfall. The duke was close enough to grab her before she made her decision, although his hands remained on his walking stick.

She pasted on a smile. Her bag made tinkling noises as the

vials and stoppered glasses knocked against one another. His gaze dropped to the bag, his brows drawing over his eyes.

"What have you there?"

"Where?"

"The bag, Madeline," he said dryly.

"Oh here! Some cuttings and basic medicines." There, she'd told the truth. Hopefully God would reward her. She shifted the bag and her feet, putting herself out of arm's length.

"What are you doing with them?"

She slid her foot backward another few inches and fought the urge to look over her shoulder at the garden door. "Since I'm wedding Thornbury, I decided it was time to give up my interest in medicine and plants. I'm handing off my collection."

"To whom?"

"To Miss Coffey. Her father is Baron Coffey. Are you acquainted? He is an avid outdoorsman and loves horseflesh. Perhaps you should invite him to see your stables."

"You believe you can give up your love of medicinal plants and healing so readily?"

Her attempt to divert the subject had failed. "Her Grace has told me I must concentrate on learning to be a duchess and help-mate to Thornbury. And bear sons. At least one, preferably more."

"Will being a duchess make you happy?" He leaned onto his walking stick with both hands and looked to the gray sky. A rain-drop hit his cheek and trailed to his jaw. Had the duke ever cried? She couldn't imagine it.

More sprinkles fell and made the leaves dance. Knowing the plants were being nourished under the cleansing rain made her happy. She couldn't imagine not being able to watch plants grow and blossom.

"No," she whispered, not sure if he could even hear her.

He dropped his gaze back to her. His usually cold eyes flashed with emotion that seemed closer to the surface since his illness. "Are you going to my son?"

She could pretend he was referring to Thornbury, but they both knew he wasn't. It was time to put all her cards on the table. What did she have to lose except everything? "Yes. With the help of his coachman, I am going to kidnap him, abscond with him to Scotland, and marry him over the anvil. If he'll have me, that is."

The duke didn't move or change expressions for longer than was comfortable. Saying it aloud only affirmed how ridiculous her plan was.

The duke did something unexpected. He laughed. It was rusty and reluctant and made his shoulders shake. It was Damien's laugh.

"You laugh just like him," she said with a fair amount of wonder in her voice, then added with a little laugh of her own, "Or I suppose, he laughs like you."

The duke's laughter died to be replaced by a look she would call wistful on any other man. "Does he deserve you?"

"I don't know that I deserve him. He is a good man, and I love him."

"The dukedom needs your dowry and heirs."

"Thornbury and I would make one another miserable."

"Yes, you would." The duke looked thoughtful. "Your parents will withhold your dowry if you do not marry someone they approve of."

"I know, and I don't care."

"Will Damien care?"

She might not know exactly what Damien was thinking, but she was sure of this. "He would not choose money over happiness."

"Like I did."

She hadn't meant to lay the sin at the duke's feet, and now she feared he would force her back inside. Her bag was growing heavier by the minute. If she was going to make a run for it, she would have to leave it behind.

"Your Grace?" The butler's voice rang out from the house. "Do you need assistance?"

"Are you going to stop me?" Maddie's arms were already loosening in preparation to drop the bag, grab her skirts, and run. The foggy mist would help hide her.

"I will be inside in a moment," the duke called out never letting his gaze waver from Maddie.

"I wed for duty. I wasn't brave enough to follow my heart. I hope my son did not inherit that weakness. I will cancel the wedding contract to Thornbury and write to your parents and tell them you have my blessing. It might not make a difference, but perhaps they will still offer you a dowry." The duke raised his chin toward the garden gate. "Escape while you can. I wish you luck and happiness. I would ask you one boon, however."

Maddie's arms tightened on the bag, and she shuffled her feet backward. "Anything."

"Write to me. I have the feeling it will be a rollicking tale."

"I will. I promise. Thank you, Your Grace." She turned and burst through the gate with renewed purpose.

❧

DAMIEN WAS IN A BLACK MOOD. A MISTY RAIN HAD DESCENDED on the city while he'd been drinking and gambling in a not-so-respectable tavern on the edge of Clerkenwell. It had been years since he'd frequented such an establishment, and while the card play had been made more challenging by the rampant cheating by all parties involved, Damien made sure he lost. The men at the table needed the coin more than Damien did.

As dawn broke, he meandered a circuitous route back to his town house. What had he been hoping to find in his old haunts? Recognition of people or places who had populated his youth? Or had he simply been inviting someone to rob him as penance for escaping the squalor? Alas, he was unscathed if one didn't count a pounding head and sore feet.

He checked his pocket watch. The appointed time was upon him. Madeline might even now be repeating vows to Thornbury, binding her to him until death. He wanted to drop to his knees and scream to the heavens until his lungs burst.

Instead, he balled up the pain and shoved it away. He would walk the streets until exhaustion overtook him and only then would he return home to drink himself into a stupor. He would not imagine Madeline consummating her nuptials with Thornbury.

Damn and blast it. Now he was imagining it and wanted to burn his eyes out of their sockets.

A carriage slowed beside him. He spared it a mere glance but did a double-take on recognition. He stopped and looked up at Alcott. "Go home. I plan to walk for hours yet."

Alcott looked to the sky. "This rain is going to settle in. You'll get soaked and catch your death."

"I don't give a damn. Leave me be."

"Get in the carriage."

Damien ignored him and stalked on. Alcott kept the horses at a walk beside him.

"I'm not asking. I'm telling. Get in the carriage." Alcott's voice was calm but firm.

"Last I checked, I'm the one who pays your wages. Therefore, I'm the one who gets to order you about." Damien didn't slow. An alley branched from the main road thirty or so paces ahead. He would duck down it and wind himself to a seedier part of town where he could find a pub to hide in.

Alcott tutted. "I'm taking my orders from someone else today. Get in the carriage."

A very distinct click cut through the anger buzzing around Damien's head. Incredulous, he turned to face his coachman, who held a pistol aimed at Damien. "Have you gone mad?"

"Maybe."

"You wouldn't dare."

"I wouldn't take that bet."

"Who are you working for?"

"Quit being a stubborn ass and get in the carriage." Alcott was wearing an oilskin greatcoat with the collar up and a brimmed hat that sloughed off any rain.

The mist had thickened and was soaking through Damien's wool jacket. "I don't care if I catch cold, and I don't care if you shoot me. In fact, go ahead and put me out of my misery."

God, he sounded petulant, but he couldn't help it.

"Well, I care because I'd be the one nursing you back to good health." The door to the carriage swung open, and Madeline poked her head out.

Damien was stunned. So stunned he could only stammer out a disjointed series of questions. "What? Why? Here?"

"Alcott reminded me that I needn't follow the rules. Would you like to get in out of the cold?" She sat back onto the squab of his carriage.

Madeline was in his carriage. She wasn't standing in the formal drawing room of Thorn House getting married to his half brother. Damien looked at Alcott, who was giving him an honest-to-God smile.

"I've never seen you this flummoxed." Alcott's amusement was flavored with more than a shot of satisfaction. "Get in with you."

Damien pulled himself inside the carriage without lowering the steps and sat across from Madeline. Alcott signaled the horses, and they clattered along. Damien squeezed his eyes shut, counted to five, and opened them again.

Madeline was still there, sitting with her legs crossed, her elbow propped on one knee, and her chin cupped, studying him right back.

"You are really here? It's not the blue ruin causing me to hallucinate?"

"Of course I'm here. Although it was a close thing. The duke caught me sneaking through the garden with my bag."

Damien tried to shake the cobwebs out of his head. "He didn't drag you back to marry Thornbury?"

Madeline's expression turned thoughtful. "He gave me his blessing and asked me to write to him with the tale."

"The tale?" Damien felt extremely stupid.

"Oh, I should have mentioned this before you climbed in the carriage." Madeline sat back and clasped her hands together. "I'm kidnapping you. With Alcott's help, of course."

Damien rubbed his forehead. "Kidnapping me? Using my own coachman and carriage?"

"Yes, well, one must improvise when planning dastardly deeds."

"May I inquire what your dastardly plan might be?"

"We are eloping to Scotland?" The lilt in her voice betrayed her uncertainty.

"And if I refuse?" He crossed his arms over his chest.

Of course he wasn't going to. One thing had become perfectly clear over the past two days of torment. He loved Madeline. He might not deserve this boon from the fates, but he would not deny himself what he wanted most in the world.

"Then..." She drew the word out and looked out the window. "Alcott promised to see me safely delivered to Cornwall. From there, I will attempt to return to America."

"I'm thinking that won't be necessary," he murmured while shifting to sit next to her.

With a smile bright enough to banish the fog outside, she turned and wrapped her arms around his neck. "Are you certain?"

He made a show of really thinking about her question, and she punched his arm, making him laugh. "I've never been more certain of anything."

"Good." She let out a sigh, nuzzled her face into his neck, and kissed him above his collar. A shiver went through him.

"But are *you* certain? Our life may prove to be a difficult one. After this, I won't be able to float at the edges of society to make my living off overstuffed peers. We will be shunned."

"I'm not so sure about that," she said thoughtfully. "But even if we are shunned, Bellingham and Drummond will remain your friends."

"Yes, but Drummond cares less for society than I do, and Simon is more interested in politics than parties. We might find ourselves traveling through Europe. Paris is recovering and might offer a man of my talents a living."

She pushed away from him slightly with a gasp. "I've longed to travel and study the countryside. We can take the long way around. I also have talents that can earn coin, you know."

He smiled. "Yes, I know."

"Your father has offered to write to my parents with his blessing."

"What?"

"I was shocked as well. There is no guarantee my parents will still agree to honor my dowry."

"I have money saved. We won't starve anytime soon."

Her high spirits faded. "What about Costa and Alcott and Mrs. Henshaw and Timothy? We can't abandon them. None of them would ever find employment elsewhere."

"Alcott is a useful chap and will accompany us. As far as Costa and Mrs. Henshaw and Timothy... I would suggest we buy a cottage in the country. Something charming and big enough to settle in between our adventures. The country air will do Timothy good, don't you think?"

"Boys need room to roam and a cozy village would do Costa good as well. What about Everleigh?"

"I'm not sure Simon and Jessica will want us as neighbors." An image of a possible future flashed in Damien's mind. His and Madeline's children growing up alongside Simon and Jessica's. It was tempting. More than tempting. It was perfect.

"We can look elsewhere—"

"Actually, Everleigh is perfect," he said.

Damien's plans had never gone further than a few weeks in the future. Things could change in an instant—fortunes were lost on the roll of a die, hearts were betrayed, people died. But must tragedy be inevitable? Happiness wasn't promised, of course, but Madeline's bold play had upped the odds. He was not idiot enough to turn his back on the chance.

"I hope you don't come to regret your choice." He brushed the hair back from her face.

"I've never been more sure of anything. I love you, you know."

"Yes, I know." He smiled and kissed her nose before settling into the corner of the squab and stretching out his legs. It was going to be a long trip.

She punched his arm. "And?"

"And?" His raised his brows, but he was done evading his own feelings where she was concerned. She needed to hear the truth, and he needed to speak it. He cupped her face and gazed into her eyes.

"You are the most curious, brave, talented, intelligent, and beautiful woman I have ever met. How could I not adore you? I started falling in love with you the moment you ordered me up a tree to pick mistletoe berries for you, and I completed the journey when you slipped your hand into my breeches." Her blush made him chuckle. "I don't deserve you, but I will cherish you the remainder of my days."

She blinked rapidly. "That was lovely."

He kissed her, sweetly and gently on the lips.

When they broke apart, she plucked at the lapel of his jacket. "It's a long way to Scotland. It will take many hours."

"Days actually."

"How will we pass the time?" She gave him a coy look from under her lashes.

"I forget to mention the naughtiest woman I have ever met." He pulled her body against his. "Do you plan to have your way with me before we are wed, Miss Barnes?"

"A successful kidnapping should feature a fair amount of

debauchery, shouldn't it?" She hiked up her skirts and straddled him.

"Indeed, it should," Damien murmured.

And it did.

EPILOGUE

Two years later

Maddie closed the gate and locked it, slipping the key into her apron pocket. Her poison garden wasn't as deadly as some, but Timothy was a curious boy who was showing an uncommon interest in gardening since their move to Everleigh. Her plantings were medicinal with some flowers tucked in to encourage pollinators.

She had harvested enough petals, leaves, and roots of various plants to replenish her supply of fever reducers and salves for coughs and cuts and minor ailments. Most she sold through the local apothecary, but a handful of women would come to see her asking for special concoctions she could provide.

Maddie and Damien spent time on the continent as well. With letters of introduction from Bellingham and Ralston, Damien was welcomed into the elite echelon of society in the various centers of Europe. Maddie found the scientific circles to be more accepting of women than in Britain, and they would often spend two or more months away from Everleigh. Damien would gamble, Maddie would share knowledge with other botanists, and together they hosted eclectic dinner parties attended by royalty and scientists and artists.

But they always returned to their home in Everleigh. There was nothing special about the house itself. It was the people inside that made it a home. Maddie found herself craving the feeling of home now more than ever.

She rubbed her lower back and balanced the basket holding her harvest on her slightly rounded belly. If her calculations were correct, she still had at least four months to go. Jessica, only three months beyond the birth of her first child, the heir to the dukedom, had promised to come and help her through the birth. Maddie was grateful at the friendship that had grown between them.

"Let me carry that for you, my love." Damien fell into step beside her and plucked the basket out of her hands.

"Fine, but be careful. Don't touch the leaves. They might give you a rash."

He shuddered. "I learned my lesson with *Arum maculatum*."

"You remembered the Latin. Well done." She smiled but kept her gaze where she put her feet on the uneven ground. Already she felt ungainly with her fuller breasts and belly.

Damien transferred the basket to his opposite hand to offer her his arm. She took it. He was always anticipating her wants and needs.

"You should rest," he said gently.

"I will laze in bed as soon as we reach the house."

"Good, because I received a note. Ralston is arriving this evening." Damien sounded apologetic.

"What? He wasn't planning on arriving until next week."

"His work in Vienna was concluded early, and he decided to come to Everleigh before returning to London."

Ralston and Damien had mended their relationship as much as was possible considering the complications of their past. His duchess did not approve, but to Ralston's credit, he sent letters and often stopped to visit them.

After all, Maddie was expecting Ralston's first grandchild, although he or she would remain unacknowledged. Thornbury had married a fresh-faced, very rich daughter of a baron two months after their broken engagement. She was malleable and focused on being the best wife possible, although she still hadn't produced a babe. Thornbury seemed content with the marriage.

"How are your feet?" Damien asked.

"Tired."

"Would you like me to rub them for you?" Although Damien's offer sounded innocent enough, his half smile was decidedly wicked.

"Is that all you plan to rub?" she asked.

"You are incredibly naughty, Mrs. Northcutt." He tutted. "Of course, I think it best if you removed your dress so I can have full access to your... feet."

Maddie burst into laughter and grabbed Damien's hand, picking up their pace. She was suddenly eager to reach home... and their bed.

Afterward, tangled in the sheets together, Damien pressed a kiss on her temple. Fiercely he whispered, "I love you to eternity, and our child will want for nothing."

Maddie set her chin on his chest and smiled up at him. "You are the best husband and will be the best father the world has ever seen, Damien."

His breath escaped in a shudder, and his body relaxed against hers. He had needed to hear that, and she promised herself to reassure him every day, every hour, if necessary.

"How can you be so certain?" he asked.

"We promised long ago never to bluff one another. I have studied you and gathered data. You have proven the theory true by the way you treat me and take care of others. I have no doubts."

He tightened his hold on her. "I thank the universe every single day that you kidnapped me. I can't wait to tell our children the story."

They dissolved into laughter. Loving Damien Northcutt was the greatest gift of her life.

I HOPE YOU ENJOYED DAMIEN AND MADDIE AND THEIR adventures! They were a ton of fun to write. Next up is Adriana's story. It's a tale of unrequited love and a marriage of convenience. I love it so much! THE MARRIAGE EXPERIMENT is sexy and a little angsty. I can't wait for you to read it.

One-click THE MARRIAGE EXPERIMENT!

Read on for an excerpt:

Dawson lay his head back, closed his eyes, and rubbed at the bridge of his nose. A headache was brewing behind his eyes. He'd never thought to be in his current situation. A slug of emotion worked its way into his throat but he swallowed it back down. He didn't have the time or energy for grief.

After surviving the horrific suffering of Waterloo, he'd thought his life charmed. Until he'd received word of the deaths of his father and mother to illness. By the time he'd been granted leave and made his way back to England, his two older brothers had fallen ill.

The youngest of the brothers, Cyrus, had thankfully been away at school, and Dawson bade him to remain there. One of them had to survive to carry on the family name. Dawson nursed his brothers through their fevers, but it was of no use. They'd died a day apart.

Dawson fell ill two days after burying them and fully expected to join his brothers and parents in the ground before the leaves turned on the trees. Instead, he had fully recovered within two weeks.

Why had he survived when his brothers had not? The question dogged him, and he worried it like a bone in the middle of the long, lonely nights. He was not the better man. As a third son, he had chosen the military over the clergy. He had gone to war and emerged physically unscathed. The morally gray orders he'd carried out haunted him sometimes, but it had all been for the greater good. Or so he told himself.

Now he was left to manage three estates with only his wits and common sense. He had not grown up at his father's knee being taught the intricacies of estate management like his older brothers, the heir and the spare. It was daunting.

And then there was Cyrus to worry over. Tragedy had instilled an obsession to live life to the fullest for Cyrus. He had always been a happy, energetic boy, and he still was, but responsibility was a foreign concept. Cyrus had taken to drinking and carousing and running up debts at the gaming table. Bills from the tailor and boot maker had been sent straight to Dawson. Would Cyrus's Grand Tour be the making of him or spiral him further down the path of excess and ruin?

A light tap sounded on his study door. Dawson straightened and tried to look as if he had everything under control. "Come."

Hayworth, his butler, cracked the door open. "Miss Adriana Coffey is here to see you, my lord. Are you receiving?"

His heart leapt like a spooked deer, and he rose from his chair. "Yes. I will receive her."

Adriana. Now that he was the earl and she was out in society, of course, their paths had crossed. She was lovely and sparkling and he could not take his eyes off her when they were in the same room. Unfortunately, he was very aware of the tender connection between her and his brother. Cyrus and Adriana had grown up together, and a match between them had been an unspoken expectation from the time they were eight or nine.

But while Adriana was in London dancing and being courted, Cyrus was galivanting across the Continent nowhere near ready to settle down. Still, she sent a letter every week to Cyrus through him which meant her interest in his rapscallion brother had not waned with the distance.

Adriana entered with her bonnet askew and pieces of her thick chestnut hair escaping to bounce around her shoulders. Her dress... His mouth grew cottony. It was at least two seasons out of date, too tight, and entirely bewitching. Curves he hadn't been aware of were outlined on her willowy frame.

"Thank you for receiving me, Dawson." She pulled her gloves and bonnet off and commenced to pace.

She was one of the few who hadn't taken to calling him West-horpe at his ascension to the title, and just the use of his given name settled him back into his old skin. "I would never deny you. You are obviously troubled. How can I help?"

She stopped abruptly as if she had been unaware her emotions were wearing his rug out, and sank into the chair across from his desk, fiddling with the ribbon of her bonnet. He resumed his seat as well, not wanting to loom over her like a worried nursemaid.

"I have a letter for Cyrus. Can you include it in your corre-spondence with him?" She retrieved the missive from her retic-ule. The paper trembled in her outstretched hand.

"Certainly." He set the letter on the ink blotter. The paper was crumpled and the wax seal messy. He had sent around a letter Cyrus had written to her only the day before. What news had his brother shared to prompt such a quick reply? "I will see it posted immediately. Will you stay and take a cup of tea?"

Adriana crossed and then recrossed her ankles and shifted in the chair, threading the ribbons through her fingers. It was odd seeing her so discomfited. Compared to other debutantes who tended to flutter around ballrooms like drunken butterflies, Adriana had learned how to be still in order to observe the world around her. She tended to float around the edges of any social function or sit with the wallflowers not even trying to get noticed.

A master of color in her art, she eschewed the usual white gowns for a palette of jewel-toned colors that set off her dark Italian coloring and strong features. She was the most interesting and beautiful woman in any room even if the rest of the ton thought her an odd bluestocking.

"This was not intended to be a social call. I only planned to stay a moment to give you the letter." She smoothed her skirt self-consciously. "My maid is in your kitchens."

"You would be doing me a favor. I need a bracing cup and a break from rows of figures."

She hesitated, but finally nodded. Dawson rang the bell, ordered a tea tray, and studied Adriana. Obviously restless, she rose and went to peer out the window. It overlooked his modest garden. Like Dawson, she loved the outdoors and he suspected she found London as stifling as he did.

"Do you wish to discuss it?" he asked haltingly.

"Discuss what?" She turned her head, but her body remained aimed at the window as if she longed to take flight.

"Whatever was in my brother's letter that upset you so." Had he run off with an Italian opera singer? Or a French dancer? Damn his brother.

"Cyrus's letter was full of his usual amusing stories. He is enjoying himself." She gave him a tight smile. "Your garden is lovely. My friend Madeline would enjoy exploring the plantings."

"You are welcome anytime. I would be happy to give you and your friend a personal tour."

"Oh, I would never impose upon your time. You must be very busy."

"I miss getting my hands dirty." He joined her at the window in a splash of sunlight. Clouds gathered on the horizon promising a downpour by afternoon.

Sympathy crossed her features, pulling her mouth into a small frown. "It must be overwhelming to step into the role of earl when you never expected it."

A slug of grief lodged in his chest like a bullet fire from point-blank range. Six months hadn't eased the heartache. He cleared his throat, but his voice still came out rough. "So many people are counting on me. The estates keep the local townships thriving. If I make a hash of it, others will suffer through my ignorance."

She laid a hand on his arm. "You will do a fine job. Not only are you intelligent but you work hard. You won't let anyone down. Your father and brothers would be proud."

Letting his father down was his greatest fear. He'd loved Dawson, but he hadn't given as much thought or focus to him which as a child had suited him fine. He had preferred the freedom and solitude being the third born had afforded him.

"I hope you are right," he said gruffly.

Hayworth led a maid holding a tea tray into the study. Once the tray had been placed on his desk and the servants were gone, he went to pour them both a cup. He added two sugar cubes and a dash of cream to Adriana's and took his black.

She looked up from her cup with a slight smile of surprise. "You remember how I take my tea?"

He merely shrugged and took a sip of his. "Unless your tastes have changed?"

"They have not, unfortunately. I will own to having a bit of a sweet tooth." She took a sip and glanced at him through her lashes. "I seem to remember you taking yours with sugar as well. Obviously, your tastes have matured."

"Only through necessity. Sugar was impossible to come by in the army. I hated the bitterness at first, but now I can't abide it sweet."

"Did you enjoy your time in the army?" She made a sound and shook her head. "That was a silly question. I read about the horrors of Waterloo."

"It was nightmarish. So many young men dead. On both sides. Such a waste. But, it wasn't always like that. I enjoyed the comradery. It reminded me of my brothers when we were all young." He smiled into his tea, turning the cup in his hands. The countless nights spent at campfires drinking bitter tea and talking into the night melded with memories of his brothers romping through the fields and forests surrounding Westhorpe Manor.

"I envied your family when I was young. To have siblings was a dream of mine. I would pretend I had three sisters." Her smile was ghosted with loneliness.

"You've gained a brother, haven't you?"

His idle comment wiped the smile from her face and a tingle went up the back of his neck. He had honed his instincts while carrying out Wellington's orders on the Peninsula and beyond. They had proven more useful than his saber or pistol.

"Not a true brother. We didn't grow up together. It's not the same."

"Of course not. My apologies." He tried to tease out her emotions. Anger, perhaps? Was there fear as well? Dawson did not know Richard Pace-Verney well, but he would make it his business to discover what sort of man inspired such antipathy from Adriana.

An awkward silence followed. She set the cup back on the tray and rose. "I must take my leave. We are attending the Fairfield's ball this evening. Will you be making an appearance?"

"I sent my acceptance, but it depends on how much headway I make." He gestured to the stack of correspondence and the ledger on his desk.

"And here I am distracting you."

He wanted to assure her she was a welcome distraction and if she wanted to sit with him and read while he worked, he would enjoy simply looking up to see her, but the words got stuck. He had not been blessed with charm or a smooth tongue. Too many years spent in the company of men had rendered him useless with the fairer sex.

She cleared her throat and made her way to the study door. "Thank you for the tea and your assistance in sending my letter to Cyrus."

"Of course. I'll see it posted today." He wanted to offer more, but his tongue tangled like it usually did around her. Hayworth waited in the hallway to escort Adriana out.

Adriana bobbed a quick curtsy, and Dawson gave her a shallow bow in return. He hated the niceties expected of him in London and much preferred the relative freedom of the country. Did Adriana pine for the same?

Dawson watched Adriana and her maid disappear down the

street from the drawing room window. Then, he made his way back to his study and picked up the Adriana's letter to Cyrus.

His conscience barely twinged as he lit a taper to soften the wax seal. Carefully, he opened the letter and spread it out, smoothing a hand over the creases.

He noted the general messiness of her hand and the blobs of ink she'd done her best to clean. She written the letter in a rush that spoke of desperation. Next, he read. By the time he reached the end, his hands were fisted and his lip was curled back, fury battering him.

While Adriana didn't spell out exactly what was going on, the dots were easy enough to connect. As her father's only natural born child, Adriana would inherit a sizable estate and income. But the baron would feel obligated to see his step-son taken care of as well. A marriage would be convenient for everyone. Except Adriana.

How far would Pace-Verney go in order to secure her inheritance? Would he ruin her? Adriana obviously feared him. He was a big man. Dawson had witnessed what could happen to a woman at the mercy of dishonorable men. It sickened him.

And Adriana was pinning all her hopes of rescue on Cyrus. While Cyrus had many good qualities, he was still a boy and only concerned with the pleasures of the moment. His letters to Dawson had detailed the string of beds of ladies and not-quite-ladies he was leaving in his wake.

Cyrus would read Adriana's letter and might even worry for her—at least until the next hand was dealt or the next lady crooked her finger. He wouldn't drop everything to return. He had no desire to marry. He would not save her from the grinding inexorability of a match with Pace-Verney.

If Dawson had been merely an earl or a rank-and-file soldier, he would be powerless to protect her. Luckily for Adriana, he was something more. He dashed off a note, and while he waited for a reply, he made plans.

One-click THE MARRIAGE EXPERIMENT!

ALSO BY LAURA TRENTHAM

A Mysterious Masquerade, Fieldstones Adventure Book 3
A Dangerous Desire, Fieldstones Adventure Book 4
The Fieldstones Adventures Boxset

CONTEMPORARY ROMANCE
Sweet Home Alabama Novels
Slow and Steady Rush, Book 1
Caught Up in the Touch, Book 2
Melting Into You, Book 3
The Sweet Home Alabama Collection

COTTONBLOOM NOVELS
Kiss Me That Way, Book 1
Then He Kissed Me, Book 2
Till I Kissed You, Book 3

CHRISTMAS IN THE COP CAR, BOOK 4
Light Up the Night, Book 5
Nobody's Hero, Book 6

LEAVE THE NIGHT ON, BOOK 7
When the Stars Come Out, Book 8
Set the Night on Fire, Book 9

HIGHLAND, GEORGIA NOVELS
A Highlander Walks Into a Bar, Book 1
A Highlander in a Pickup, Book 2
A Highlander is Coming to Town, Book 3

. . .

Heart of a Hero Novels
The Military Wife
An Everyday Hero

I love to hear from readers! Come find me:
Laura@LauraTrentham.com
www.LauraTrentham.com
Sign up for Laura's Newsletter
Join Laura's Facebook Squad

Are you interested in receiving a FREE book?!
Join my newsletter! There will be links in your Welcome Email for TWO free books!

Sign up for Laura's Newsletter

ABOUT THE AUTHOR

I hope you enjoyed *The Courtship Calculation*! If you have a chance please leave a quick review! Although, many readers know me from my Southern-set contemporary romances, the first books I wrote were the Spies and Lovers series! I grew up reading the historical "bodice rippers" of the late eighties and early nineties along with wonderful gothic romances. Now that I have the opportunity to publish all of the Spies and Lovers series, I'm so excited! The Spies and Lovers world has expanded with the Laws of Attraction series!

I was born and raised in a small town in Northwest Tennessee. Although, I loved English and reading in high school, I was convinced an English degree equated to starvation! So, I chose the next most logical major - Chemical Engineering- and worked in a hard hat and steel toed boots for several years. Now I live in South Carolina with my husband and two children. In between school and homework and soccer practices, I love to get lost in another world, whether it's Regency England or small town Alabama.

My first two Falcon Football books received TOP PICKS from RT Book Reviews and a STARRED review from Library Journal. KISS ME THAT WAY, Cottonbloom Book 1, won the Stiletto Contest for Best Long Contemporary and finaled in the National Readers Choice Award. THEN HE KISSED ME, Cottonbloom Book 2, was named an Amazon Best Romance of 2016 and was a finalist for the National Excellence for Romance Fiction. TILL I KISSED YOU, Cottonbloom Book 3, is a finalist in the Maggie contest. LEAVE THE NIGHT ON, the latest Cottonbloom book, was named an iBooks Best Book of the Month and a Recommended Read from NPR. AN INDE-CENT INVITATION and A BRAZEN BARGAIN were both finalist for the 2014 Golden Heart® Award.

NOTE: This is a work of fiction. All of the characters, organizations, and events portrayed in this novel are either products of the author's imagination or are used fictitiously.

THE COURTSHIP CALCULATION

Copyright © 2023 by Laura Trentham

Cover by Erin Dameron-Hill

Edited by Victory Editing

eISBN: 978-1-946306-42-5

All rights reserved. No part of this book may be used or reproduced in any manner whatsoever without written permission except in the case of brief quotations embodied in critical articles or reviews.

Created with Vellum

Printed in Great Britain
by Amazon